THE INCORRIGIBLE MR. LUMLEY

THE BRIDGETHORPE BRIDES BOOK TWO

AILEEN FISH

ASPENDAWN PRESS

CHAPTER ONE

April 1810
Newmarket, Suffolk, England

The air held a hint of excitement and promise of a fresh beginning. For David Lumley, the new year began in spring. Not with the first foal in the family stable, but with the Craven Race Meeting in Newmarket, the first official meeting of the year. This was going to be a grand year for Triton, he could feel it. Fernleigh Stud would be the name on everyone's lips again.

The crowd at the racecourse was as large as David expected. He surveyed the grounds from his position near the judging station. The social Season in London had yet to begin, so the wives of the horse owners were all in attendance at the Craven. From the way they all leaned close to each other and whispered in the coffee house, they were eager to discover the latest *on-dits*. David was always astounded when he overheard how much went on in the

1

homes of the *ton* during the winter months. His life seemed thankfully dull in comparison.

He had no desire to listen to gossip, but soon he'd be unable to escape it. He'd promised to escort his sister, Hannah, in her first London Season. In preparation over the winter, Mother had dragged him to afternoon teas and the morning calls she and Hannah made to their neighbors in the village near Bridgethorpe Manor. Dull, precisely timed events where the conversations were by rote up to the moment someone let slip she'd heard *news*. No matter on whom the juicy tidbit focused. All other voices in the room silenced so the speaker's slightest inflection could be heard.

It was all too much for a man to bear.

David wound through the milling people on his way to the stables. He found his groom, Peter, in the stall with Triton, just completing his work. As the boy gathered his tools, David patted the bay's shoulder. "How is he this morning?"

"Right as always," said Peter. "He's got a bit of the devil in 'im. He'll be after showing them other horses who's king."

"Just as long as he wins. I'm counting on him."

Peter put the tools into a bag and opened another, removing the carefully folded shirt made in the colors of Fernleigh Stud, the orange body with yellow sleeves. He donned the garment and the black hat that completed the uniform.

David stepped back as the youth saddled the horse and then freed the reins from the iron ring on the side of the stall. Together they led Triton out of the stables and to the examination area. Other grooms and horses milled about in preparation for the race. David glanced at the schedule. "We're entered in the third race. You'll have him warmed up?"

"Of course, sir. He'll be ready to race 'is best, never worry."

Peter's cocky grin said his boss always worried, but David didn't reprimand the lad. Peter was the best groom and rider he'd come across, with a natural knack for understanding what a horse was thinking. He could bring more out of an animal than any of the trainers they'd paid good money to, and the animals seemed calmer around him.

"You see that he does race his best," David called out with a growl. A useless effort. There was no sense trying to sound more authoritative when Peter knew who paid his wages, and showed due respect when the situation called for it.

Assured his horse was in good hands, David crossed the grounds, nodding and calling greetings to those he recognized. His brother Adam, Viscount Knightwick, should have arrived by now. As he scanned the gathering crowd, his gaze landed on the last face he wanted to see at the Spring Meeting, or any other race event.

Northcotte.

Blast it. David's gut knotted at the sight of the man. Ducking behind a pair of gentlemen walking in the earl's direction, David darted around the corner of a building where he could eavesdrop without being noticed. He peered out into the lane. Robert Hurst, Lord Northcotte, stood with a particularly handsome young lady, and their sharp exchange reached David's ears.

The young lady folded her arms across her chest, and the tiny, pale blonde ringlets framing her face trembled with tension. "I'm going to ride him. No one will know. I've trousers in the stable, and I can wear Bruce's shirt and cap. With my hair tucked up, no one will recognize me."

Northcotte jerked her arm. "You will not consider it. Do you want to risk everything I've left? I'll find a jockey and

Patriot will be entered as planned. You may tell Bruce his services are no longer needed."

"I'll do no such thing! That boy needs the wages for his family, and it's not his fault he's ill. You cannot hire some stranger to ride Patriot. You know he'll never allow a strange man on his back. I must be the one to ride him or we may as well scratch him from the race."

"I'll hear no more of this, Joanna. Go find Mother and let me handle this."

Northcotte released her arm and strode off toward the stables. The young lady must be his sister, Lady Joanna. She stood for a moment and watched him go, then spun on her heel and stomped off in the opposite direction.

David smiled at her forceful steps in the dirt. She seemed much like Hannah. Stubborn, impulsive, and too daring by half. He chuckled and shook his head. Those qualities could make Hannah's search for a husband drag on for years. Even her beauty would not compensate for her strong character in the minds of many men. He'd have to make certain Mother didn't expect his services as chaperone to run beyond one Season.

Northcotte's sister had to be dicked in the knob to suggest she wear trousers and ride in the race. Northcotte had the right of it—he'd be disqualified, and laughed out of the Jockey Club books, if not actually banned from competing. If Hannah ever dared such a thing, David would have her sent back to Bridgethorpe Manor for the remainder of the racing season.

Shaking his head, he followed the pretty blonde in the direction of the paddock, where he found Knightwick leaning on the upper rail of the fence. Peter and Triton loped around the space, getting warmed up before the races began. The three-year-old horse's gait was long and even, covering the ground with no effort.

As he reached the fence, David slapped Knightwick on the shoulder. "I believe we have the winning horse this year."

"You've said as much these three years past," Knightwick replied with a teasing grin.

"But this year I'm right. Triton has the heart of a winner. He loves to be out front. Start him behind the other colts and he'll run that much faster to best them."

Knightwick shook his head. "His chest is narrow, he's willful and as likely to turn in the opposite direction as run the course. We never should have bred his dam. I'm rather surprised she let the Black Knight close enough to cover her."

"You're nit-picking. Triton is the horse we've been waiting for."

Neither brother completed the thought aloud...Triton was the horse they were counting on to save their stables after the death of Zephyr, their father's prize-winning stud, six years ago.

David absently tapped his fingers on the fence rail while observing the other animals circling before them. "Did the trip to London with Mother and Hannah pass uneventfully?"

"Yes. Hannah chattered the entire trip." Knightwick offered his brother a wry glance. "Rather convenient of you to leave a week early so you couldn't accompany them."

David grunted. "I promised Mother I'd arrive in Town in time for Hannah's first ball, and would attend as many assemblies as I can. But first she must be outfitted, presented in court and all that sort of feminine thing. I'm not going to miss a race meeting this spring, not when I'm so confident in Triton."

"I'll wager Mother said you're too much like Father in that."

Laughing, he agreed. "I ask you, what purpose do I have in London? Mother is there to chaperone. I've no wish to see which ladies are on the hunt. Nor do I care to be packed into the crowded assemblies filled with the stench of too many bodies and liberally applied perfumes. I'd much rather be in a stall filled with the more natural scent of *eau de cheval*."

Knightwick glanced at him from the corner of his eye. "Maybe you'll find one of those bodies belongs to a lady you wish to know better."

"Not bloody likely. You've yet to take a bride, and you're the one with the responsibilities. My only concern is this." He waved an arm at Triton. "He and Lumley's Lass will be my primary focus until the final race meeting this year."

Knightwick made a strangled noise and straightened, staring across the paddock. "What is he doing here?"

Without looking, David knew whom his brother had spotted. "I wondered the same thing. From what I overheard, it appears Northcotte has a horse entered in one of the courses today."

"Why did the Jockey Club allow him to enter?"

"What reason do they have to block him? No one charged him with anything. He can race any horse he owns, just like the rest of us."

Rubbing the back of his hand across his mouth, as if wiping away a bad taste, Knightwick said, "I don't trust him. Tell Peter to stay with Triton at all times, even sleep in the stalls. I'll go find Nick and make sure he stays with Lass."

"You can't think he'd be foolish enough to try anything after the inquiry last year."

"Someone stole Zephyr six years ago and then killed him, and two of our horses turned up sick last year. I don't know who is behind it, but we can't take any chances. We must be on our guard whether Northcotte is at a race meeting or not."

Lady Joanna Hurst stood at the empty stall where she'd left her three-year-old colt, Patriot, a short while earlier. The groom's uniform was missing along with her horse. "Robert," she spat out as if it were a curse. She tossed aside the trousers she'd stolen from her brother's room at the inn. Robert had followed through on his words and found someone to ride Patriot.

What an inopportune time for him to begin following through on anything! All her work training Patriot would be for naught if Robert prevented her from riding him in the race. She was certain she could pass herself off to the officials as a young lad. Her own mother had mistaken her for a stable boy often enough when she wore trousers to work with the horses.

Mama had barred her from entering the stables for a week after the first time she found her thus, but as Mama rarely ventured down there, she didn't see Joanna return to work the next day. To train a horse properly, one must sit astride. There was no way around it. And wearing trousers was the only way to sit correctly.

None of that mattered at the moment, however. Patriot must win today. Her horse would do anything she asked of it, except be ridden by a groom he didn't know. She searched her mind for something she could do to help her horse through the change in rider at this late hour, but came up empty.

Grateful the mud from recent rains had dried, Joanna rushed off as quickly as her boot heels would allow in the rough dirt. It was too late to convince Robert to let her ride, but perhaps talking to Patriot would calm him. Patriot always listened to her.

Unlike her brother, the horse had some sense.

As luck would have it, Robert was talking to a pair of men near the paddock. She bit back an indelicate curse she'd learned from the grooms. She had to keep her temper controlled. Schooling her features into a smile suitable for the most fashionable drawing room, she strolled up and slipped her hand around her brother's arm. She spoke in a voice rich with treacle. "There you are, brother. I've been searching for you."

The look he slanted warned her against causing a disruption. She batted her lashes in response. "I'm so excited to watch our horse compete. I couldn't sit any longer. I had to come look for him."

The other two gentlemen nodded. "The thrill of the race is undeniable," one agreed.

She didn't recognize them. They appeared to be a few years beyond her brother's thirty years. The second man, a thin, dark-haired scarecrow with white side-whiskers, peered down his hawkish nose at her and lifted an imperial brow, but said nothing.

Robert patted her fingers with enough force to ring out like a slap. "A lady doesn't belong here by the paddock. You might damage those lovely kidskin boots I bought you. Mother must be wondering where you are."

He looked across the paddock toward the grandstands. Suddenly his features went slack, and he cursed beneath his breath. Joanna followed his line of sight and spied two men who appeared to be watching their little group. She could make out their features but didn't recognize them. Turning to question Robert, she was interrupted before she had the chance to speak.

Her brother took her arm roughly and nodded to his companions. "Gentlemen, I'll look for you after the event. If you will excuse me, I must make certain my mother does not want for anything. Come along, Joanna, dear."

As if she had any choice. She took two steps for each of her brother's strides and still she was being dragged.

"Please slow down. Who were those men you were speaking with?"

"Business associates. No one you need know. You must at least make a pretense at behaving like a lady when we are in public, if you're ever to marry. I'll tell Mother you are to remain at her side, or you won't be allowed to attend any future race meetings."

Allowed to attend...the very words made her blood boil. Just a few years ago, Robert was her playmate, or so he let her believe. The distance in their ages meant they hadn't truly been close, with him away at school by the time she was old enough to remember. But when he was home, he'd taught her chess and various card games and made her feel important. He often rode the countryside with her and never once chastised her for riding astride.

Lately she felt more like an obligation, one he was searching to end. The pressure he put on her to marry was quite unbearable. And the restrictions he imposed on her time with their horses were her biggest concern. A life without horses was truly not to be borne.

"Robert, please let me catch my breath. Mama will assume I'm ill if I appear before her flushed and breathless." She tugged again on the arm he still gripped.

His hand relaxed. "I'm sorry. But I'm only looking out for your best interests."

"My best interests would be met by having Patriot win today."

"As would mine, but I'll not allow you to ride him in the race, so this is the end of that discussion. A disqualification would be worse than a loss, going forward. Now, there is Mother in the coffee house, sitting at the window. Please humor me and stay with her until I come for you both at the end of the day. Wallis will escort you two to the grandstand when it's time for Patriot's match."

Joanna bit her tongue on all the retorts that came to mind. Of course Robert would send his groom to take them to watch the race, and not be bothered to do so himself. Just more proof she was a burden and not a pleasant companion. She entered the crowded eating establishment and made her way to the small table where Mama sat with her maid. Letting go of the last of her frustrations, Joanna smiled at them. "How are the scones? Did you save me any?"

"Of course, dear girl." Her mother's sweet, round face looked pale in the morning light streaming through the window. Her blue eyes seemed as faded as the blonde hair showing beneath the edges of the black bonnet she'd continued to wear after her year of mourning had passed. "I admit, however, I was tempted to eat these last two if you hadn't arrived soon."

Mama poured tea for Joanna and handed her the cup. When they'd left the inn that morning, Joanna told her mother she would meet her shortly after checking on Patriot. Discovering Bruce was ill, followed by her muddled attempt to replace him as rider in the race, delayed her more than an hour. Mama must have requested a fresh pot of tea, as the drink was still quite warm, and it took away the chill of the morning air.

"How is your horse this morning?" Mama didn't understand Joanna's passion, but she humored it.

"He's frisky and eager to run. But his groom isn't. I fear Patriot won't perform well with another boy on his back."

"Oh, dear. And you've put so much time in his training. But this is only the first of many races. He'll have his day."

Yes, Patriot would do well in the future, but her main concern was whether Robert would continue to let her attend race meetings, or if she must wait to hear reports of his activities. She would simply expire from worry if she couldn't watch Patriot compete. She glanced at the clock on the wall, then sighed. She still had hours to wait for the racing to begin.

Joanna contemplated her mother again. The dark circles beneath her eyes were not as prominent today. "I'm very pleased you came with me to the race meeting."

"I always enjoyed the races with your father. I'm happy to chaperone you here."

Her words sounded earnest enough, and her face didn't contradict them, but given the weeks where Mother would not even join them for meals, Joanna wondered what had brought about this gay mood. She would not press the issue, however. She would simply enjoy her mother's company for as long as she had it.

CHAPTER TWO

From the grandstand at the end of the Rowley Mile course, David waited to hear the roar of the crowd telling him the horses drew near. He tried to think of anything but Northcotte, to quell the acid burning in his stomach. Lass was entered in this event, and though she'd appeared small and slight when she'd warmed up next to the other horses, David could see she was ready to compete.

He fidgeted in his seat, straining to see down the course, watching for the flash of yellow and orange. He heard the increasing sound of thunder as they grew close.

Knightwick sat silently beside him, but his arms unfolded, and he leaned forward in his seat when the noise grew louder. The runners appeared at the rise of the hill two furlongs out, and David spotted orange. Lass was gaining on Whiskey, passing his flank. "Atta girl," David called out.

She surged the next furlong on the downhill side into the Dip, getting a nose out beyond Whiskey and catching up to Fair Star. As they climbed the final furlong uphill, Lass closed in on Robin in second place. Canopus held the lead, right up to the finish.

The judge called out the winning colors for the first three places, with Lass's orange and yellow coming in third.

Knightwick grinned and clapped David on the back. "Fine run. She did us proud in her first race."

David sat back in his seat, the tension of the day finally breaking. Now he could enjoy the rest of the races, knowing the meeting wasn't going to be a total loss. "She did do well, didn't she? Peter promised me she would. She and Triton both. We'll see how the colt does."

"I wish Father were here to see this." Knightwick's voice barely reached David's ears under the crowd's excited chatter.

"I do, too. Maybe if Triton wins, it will bring Father around."

For the past five years, David and Knightwick had been attending the race meetings without their father, the Earl of Bridgethorpe. The year before that, their prize stud horse, a tall, well-muscled black called Zephyr, had been stolen from the Southampton Race Meeting, and found dead in a nearby field two weeks later. The three of them had attended the remaining races that year while waiting to hear the culprit had been caught. No one had seen anything out of the norm, or if they had, the man in question held such power and position that no one would speak up.

Over the following winter, Bridgethorpe lost the determination to continue the search. "It's no good, boys. My heart's just not strong enough."

The last time he'd seen his father, David feared he would not live to see summer. The old man sat at his desk each day, staring out the window at whatever held his gaze. It was most likely something in Father's mind, not the bleak gray weather and leafless trees beyond the glass. He'd grown thin, his pallor more pronounced, and he often had a tremor in his right hand.

Knightwick nudged David's arm, pulling his thoughts back to the racecourse. "Are you going to meet Peter at the weigh-in? Collect your winnings?"

"What? Oh, no." He shook his head and grinned. "I'm not done winning today."

He was determined to send home news of a first place before the weeklong event was through. A win was what they needed to bring their father back to life.

JOANNA GREW RESTLESS IN THE GRANDSTAND AS THE DAY passed. She longed to be with Patriot, wherever he was. In the past, she'd attended various race meetings with her family and lost herself in the market tents, rather than watching other people's horses compete. The fortuneteller was always a fun diversion, even if the grand love she predicted for Joanna had a different description for the gentleman each time she visited the woman.

Not for her were the evening balls and theatricals enjoyed by the other young women and men while in Newmarket, either. Now, all she cared about were her family's horses and how well they ran. Her mother would faint if she were aware of how much time Joanna spent at the course's stables when she claimed she was investigating the ribbon vendor's booth, or the town bookstore. Her maid, Molly, was easily bribed with a new bonnet or packet of sweets, and Joanna had a feeling the young woman took advantage of some of that time to flirt with a certain groom.

Being required to sit the entire afternoon was too much to bear. "Mama, may I find Molly and go rest until Patriot's event? I don't wish to watch every sweepstakes and race. I cannot tell the horses apart, so it's of no interest to me."

"Be still, dear girl. Your horse will run soon. We have only two sweepstakes to go before the Oatlands Stakes. If you leave now you mightn't return in time."

Joanna chewed on her lower lip, unconcerned her mother could see her. Her horse needed her; of that she was certain. How was he handling the excitement, the crowds? The knot in her stomach had been growing all day, and she would never be able to eat supper if it didn't loosen soon.

The individuals who'd left their seats in the grandstand rushed to return, so word must have come the next race was lining up at the starting post a mile down the course. Joanna watched the men file down the rows, not really seeing faces, not really interested in who they were.

Until *he* appeared.

Taller than most men, yet not quite as tall as his companion, the gentleman with wavy chestnut hair made his way toward his seat in the center of one of the lower rows. He spoke to various people he passed, his smile friendly, open. He wasn't the most handsome man she'd ever seen, but something about him made her wish they were at an assembly where she could coerce an introduction from their hostess.

Perhaps it was the way he carried himself. His bearing was almost military, shoulders back, revealing the broad chest covered in a plain woolen waistcoat and coat. Just before he sat, he laughed at something his companion said and she wished she were close enough to see if the laughter carried into his eyes. Were they fair or dark? Whatever the color, she'd wager they were quite expressive.

The man following him had to be a brother, for the two were cut from the same cloth. The second only a smidgeon taller, and perhaps that much more polished in his style. Perhaps he was titled. The difference in their bearing made her think of a son brought up to be an heir and one who was free to choose his own path. Yet this taller, polished brother didn't hold a candle to the first, in her book. If she had to choose one as a suitor, she'd pick the first.

Hearing her own thoughts, Joanna burst out in a laugh, which she quickly swallowed. A suitor was the last thing she wanted. Mama gave her a stern shake of the head and Joanna looked down the course for the horses to appear.

She must be desperately bored for the thought of suitors to enter her head. All of her mother's harping had finally sunk in. As much as Joanna hated to admit it, she must find a husband soon. But that was of no concern today.

The next two races each ended in a flurry of cheers, and Joanna sat up straighter, clenching her hands around her reticule. The Oatlands Stakes, a two-mile distance, would be run next. Patriot's race. *Please, let him do well.*

Where was Robert? She looked about the grandstand but didn't see him. She wanted to ask him what strategy he had set, and why he thought it was a good plan. As the horses came into sight at the rise, Patriot was pinned between two other runners.

What idiot was riding him? How was Patriot supposed to make his kick while buried in the pack? "Ohhhh," she moaned.

"Are you all right, dear?" Mother leaned closer and took her hand briefly.

"I'm fine, but Patriot isn't."

"Yes, he does seem to be putting on a poor show, doesn't he? Robert will not be pleased."

At the moment, Joanna didn't care whether her brother was pleased or not. It was his own fault Patriot was behind. If Robert had let her ride...

She held her breath until her throat burned, then released it in a huff. One of the horses dropped back at the base of the Dip. Patriot was free to make his move, at least, but was so far behind the front-runners, Joanna had no hope for a win.

Her heart pounded in her ears. The horses began the final climb, and the big bay began to pull away. A gray colt tried to keep up, to no avail. Patriot gained on the gray, but as they crossed the Finish Post, Patriot was still half a length behind.

"Hurrah, he placed third!" Mama clapped her hands and smiled widely.

Joanna's stomach sank. Third place. She just *knew* he would have won if only Bruce hadn't been ill, or she had been allowed to ride. Her disappointment weighed her down in her seat. There were no more races, but she had no desire to rush to see her horse like she normally would. If she saw Northcotte now, she'd probably forget her upbringing and rail into him in front of everyone. She folded her shaking hands across her lap and shut out the noise of the excited crowd, and hoped Mama wasn't eager to return to the inn.

DAVID SAT UNMOVING FOR A MOMENT, UNABLE TO BELIEVE what he'd just seen. Triton had done what no horse from Fernleigh had since Zephyr. He took the win in his first ever race. The gray colt finished half a length behind him, and Northcotte's black stallion was third.

Knightwick pulled him to his feet. "You did it!"

From the corner of his eye, David noticed Northcotte's sister and mother sitting a few rows back. The dowager countess appeared pleased with their horse's third place, but the sister's frown showed her disappointment. She met his gaze, then looked away when her mother spoke.

Someone reached for David's hand to shake it, offering congratulations, and several others slapped him on the shoulder, accepting their own losses as owners or bettors good-naturedly. David smiled, nodded, and hoped he said the right words, but something kept the excitement of accomplishment from fully engulfing him.

Perhaps it was the fact his father wasn't there to share in the joy. Everything David did with the horses, he did with love of seeing the animals develop into well-trained, beautiful and fast creatures. But some small part of him, the boy he'd been, still longed for praise from his father. Still wanted to see the man smile.

Now that the reality of the win was upon him, he had to admit to himself it would not change anything. It might have a year ago, before David's aunt and uncle had died, but nothing their horses did would ease that pain. All David could do was hope his father might at least show some interest in the stables again. Show some interest in life.

As he and Knightwick walked to the Coffee Rooms where the Jockey Club held court, David noticed a group of men standing near an open door at one end of the stables where those who didn't own property nearby sheltered their horses. "Something looks amiss."

Knightwick followed his gaze. "I wonder what is happening. Perhaps two grooms are fighting over the outcome of their race."

"If that were the case, Old Edwards would be off to one side taking bets on the winner. I don't see anyone betting."

His brother laughed. "Quite so. Let's go investigate."

The voices of the onlookers reached the pair before they got there, with words such as *ill* and *murder* being tossed about. Knightwick spoke to a man on the edge of the circle. "What's the excitement about?"

"Near as I can tell, either a horse or a rider has been killed."

"You aren't certain which?"

The man shrugged. "They haven't called for the horse doctor or the people doctor, so I can't say."

In David's mind, that just meant the victim was beyond treatment. He was about to ask if the constable had been sent for when the man pushed through the crowd and entered the stables. David strained to hear anything within the building, but the gossip in the crowd was too loud.

A short time later, two stable hands carried out a body on a board, covered by a horse blanket. Knightwick nudged David's arm. "Let's go to the Coffee Rooms. They'll know anything we need to know. We can get our winnings and take our horses home."

The Coffee Rooms were packed with people eating at the tables, and milling about talking about the day's races. Knightwick led the way and stopped to speak to an earl. "Have they mentioned who was killed in the stables?"

The earl nodded. "A groom, he was. Not a local boy. Worked for Lord Northcotte. Heard he took sick this morning and someone else rode for him. They found him dead in a stall during the Oatlands Stakes."

David met his brother's pointed gaze, but neither of them spoke. After their discussion of Northcotte's possible involvement in the death of Zephyr, and the near death of their horses last year, it seemed beyond coincidence his name should be floating about this current death. No one said murder, but the constable had just arrived. They'd have to see where the investigation went.

CHAPTER THREE

*J*oanna stormed up to the library door of their London town house, her heels beating a clipped rhythm on the polished marble floor. Waving off the footman, she threw open the door without knocking. She marched to the massive oak desk where her brother sat. "How dare you!"

Robert lifted his gaze from his papers without raising his head, peering out from beneath his heavy, fair eyebrows. "How dare I what?"

Joanna forced her hands to relax. Fighting the urge to stomp her foot, which would only prove what she assumed her brother believed of her, she threw back her shoulders and glared at his receding hairline, for he had returned to scratching out a list. "You know what. How could you?"

He set the pen in the inkwell and blotted the paper, then straightened in his chair. "Dear sister, this discourse would be completed all the sooner if you would simply tell me which action of mine has displeased you this time."

Joanna's right leg twitched again with the need to stomp,

but she remained stiff. "Mama tells me you've decided to select a husband for me."

"What would you have me do? You've shown no inclination to make the choice on your own." With his elbows resting on the edge of the desk, he steepled his fingers, raising one eyebrow in that manner he'd adopted since the death of their father two years ago. Where some young men might find the weight of an earldom sat heavily on their shoulders, Robert seemed to relish the role.

"I've only had one Season. How can you expect me to decide so soon? It's not as if we can't afford to remain in London until summer. And how was I supposed to properly entertain potential beaux last year when I had Patriot on my mind?"

Robert's lips thinned. "Does this mean he's not foremost in your thoughts this year? I should never have agreed to let you train that horse. No gentleman will want you if word gets out what you've been doing."

She refused to say it, but that was exactly her concern. She had no intention of giving up horse training once she married, which greatly narrowed her chances of finding a suitable match. Northcotte's Patriot was on the lips of most members of the Jockey Club to become the prominent three-year-old. His third-place finish at Newmarket hadn't dimmed her hopes her horse would come into his stride now that the first official race was behind him. While she had no plans of becoming a breeder of horses, or anything else for that matter, she enjoyed nurturing the spirited colts and fillies in her brother's stable.

She would only be happy if she could marry a man with a good stable. A kind, gentle sort who would allow her to continue to train horses. She didn't even care whose horses they were, her brother's or her husband's, just so long as she didn't have to put her dreams aside.

Robert would not be looking for that sort of man as he sought a husband for her, unless he hoped to have access to another man's stud. He'd look for an heir to a title, or possibly a wealthy businessman who might be interested in backing the Northcotte stable. A marriage to suit his own whims.

She must be allowed to make the choice herself. "If I promise to make a decision by the end of the Season, will you let me select my own husband?"

He leaned back in his chair and contemplated her, his expression the composed mask she recognized. At last, he nodded. "I'll continue to consider my own list of candidates, however, in case you fail to produce a satisfactory suitor. But we can put the decision off until later in the Season."

"Just promise me you won't let anyone other than Bruce ride Patriot."

His brows dropped sharply. "I'm sorry, that isn't possible. He didn't survive his illness."

"What? But he was fine that morning. Did the doctor say what it was?"

"The constable is still investigating. But I'm certain it's nothing you might catch."

That hadn't crossed her mind. Aside from feeling she'd lost a friend, she now had to worry they would find someone Patriot was comfortable with. And she wouldn't be there to help him adjust. She was stuck here in London.

After retrieving her pelisse, hat and gloves, Joanna stormed out the front door where the groom, Wallis, waited with a pair of horses. Just seeing Patriot awaiting her lifted some of her frustration. The handsome black towered over her, even though she was rather tall herself, but he was like a kitten when she sat on his back. That was another area of potential problem in finding a husband. Few men would allow their wives to ride stallions. Once she married, she'd not be able to ride him, however, since he belonged to her brother.

With Wallis following, she set out for Hyde Park. Unlike most runners, Patriot had been trained to accept both a lady's saddle and a man's. Pressing her crop against Patriot's right side as she rode, she could mimic riding astride. It was more awkward to ride that way, but it was a small price to pay to be able to ride him where others might be shocked at her riding astride.

Hopefully, Rotten Row would be empty at this early hour, with gentlemen of the *ton* likely sleeping off last night's revelry. While in London, Joanna was unable to let Patriot have his head and she feared he would lose some of the speed they worked so hard to gain. At the end of the week, Robert would take him back to Newmarket for the Second Spring Meeting. She would follow a day later, if he allowed her to attend, making faster time in a carriage than the walking pace the racehorses traveled.

A swelling in her throat threatened her breath when she considered the training of her beloved horse was most likely to end soon. She'd done all she could. She must be content to watch him from the sidelines with her brother.

The trails of Hyde Park were occupied by nannies and dog walkers, their charges doing their best to run wild. Joanna kept Patriot at a calm pace, only urging him faster when they reached Rotten Row. She allowed him to trot the length of the path before turning him. As she again approached Park Lane, she heard shouts above the thundering of hooves.

A handsome bay stallion raced past her in the opposite direction. A block behind him, a man in riding dress ran after him. Without hesitation, Joanna urged Patriot around and took chase. She clenched the pommel tightly with her bent leg and pressed her crop firmly against Patriot's side.

Holding her horse's mane, she bent as low over his neck as possible while sitting aside.

She gave Patriot his head and he lengthened his stride, slowly gaining on the other horse, whose course kept shifting around the traffic. Ahead of them, men shouted to clear the road for the runaway. Joanna waited until she was beside the stallion's head then reached for his reins while speaking to him in calming tones. Her left leg trembled with the tension of staying mounted. The other horse shied away, his eyes wide with fear.

Joanna nearly fell but caught herself in time. Patriot continued to keep pace with the bay, and she kept talking to it. Seeing a familiar street corner ahead, she guided Patriot toward the right, forcing the bay in that direction. The horses slowed slightly, and she heard Wallis' mount in the distance behind them. Somehow, she managed to make the turn onto the narrow side street, which was a dead end.

The bay slowed drastically in the crush of street peddlers, carts and shoppers. Joanna grabbed his reins, encouraging him to a walk. He whinnied and shook his head, but his ears responded to her voice. His eyes narrowed almost imperceptibly. Whatever had spooked him was now a distant memory. Patriot sidestepped beneath her, vocal in his displeasure at the other stallion's presence. "Easy, boys, easy. There's no mare here to challenge for."

She got the horses turned and met Wallis at the corner. The groom was panting as hard as his mount. "My lady! His lordship would 'ave my 'ide for lettin' you ride off like that. It's a wonder you weren't thrown."

She handed off the stallion's reins, noticing the deep crease between Wallis's brows before she put some distance between the two stallions. Some years ago, he'd told her that more than half of his grey hairs were attributable to her escapades on horseback. He no longer spoke to her that way since her come out, but the fondness he held for her shone in his eyes. "I'm sorry, Wallis, but I knew Bertie would not carry you fast enough to catch the bay. I had to ride after him before he hurt himself."

"A runaway horse is *not* sumthin' what should concern a lady. What will his lordship say? What will the Dowager Countess say?"

They turned the horses back toward Rotten Row while Wallis lectured her in his fatherly way. She bit her tongue when she wanted so badly to defend herself and her love for speed. Riding fast was not ladylike. Defending oneself to the servants was even less so, even one who overstepped his place out of concern for her well-being.

The horseless rider she'd seen earlier now trotted up on foot, obviously winded. He grinned at Wallis and reached for his horse's bridle. "My thanks, good man."

Wallis leaned forward with the reins. "It's milady you should be thanking, milord."

Something was familiar about the finely dressed man, and Wallis seemed to know him. She couldn't quite place the handsome face, but was certain she'd seen him quite recently.

He flashed her a brilliant smile. "Ah, my lady, then. I'm much in your debt. Triton wasn't of a mind to take a leisurely stroll this morning."

"Fernleigh's Triton?"

"Yes, the same. You've heard of him?"

"Heard of him? I've seen him race." She laughed, now realizing she must be speaking to Lord Bridgethorpe's son. She looked again at the large bay with no distinguishable markings. "Had I known it was him I chased, I might have let him escape. We lost to him at Newmarket."

"We? Forgive me, my lady, but while you look familiar, I cannot place you. I'm certain I'll know your husband's name, if we are competitors."

"I speak of my brother Northcotte's horse." She patted Patriot's neck and tipped her head to one side, holding back a smile. He was the man who'd beguiled her in the stands. "This is Patriot, who, I believe, just ran down your horse, Lord Knightwick."

Recognition registered on his face before he schooled his expression into a mask of politeness. "Of course. But I'm not Knightwick. You find his brother, Lumley, in your debt. You are Lady Joanna?" He inclined his head, eyeing her with a cool gaze.

She nodded, quelling a shiver, trying to determine what she'd said that made all the warmth flee from his manner. Surely, the man wasn't so competitive he couldn't hold a casual conversation over horseflesh. Perhaps it was the thought of a woman rider overtaking his winning stallion. She was suddenly grateful to have met him in passing on the street and not in a ballroom where she might have considered him an eligible match. Their families were equal in status. His father's stables bred some of the top runners until recently. Her own father had raced a few good runners before his death.

Thank the heavens she saw the real man before she fell victim to that charming smile and rakishly wavy brown hair that made her fingers itch to touch.

He bowed stiffly. "Please offer your mother my belated condolences. Your father was generous with his knowledge at the track. He's missed. I won't keep you from your outing. Again, I thank you for catching my horse. Good day."

With that, he mounted up and rode off without looking back.

Joanna watched him go. Such an odd exchange of words. She must remember to ask Robert what he knew of the man, to find some answers to this puzzlement.

CHAPTER FOUR

*D*avid willed his legs to relax, to keep from sending the wrong signal to Triton. His horse walked calmly back through Hyde Park, but David's thoughts still raced. How had he not recognized that horse?

He grunted.

He knew damned well how. He had eyes for nothing more than Lady Joanna. He'd heard her name mentioned as one of the fairer of the second-Season hopefuls on the market, but she'd been just another pretty face when he saw her at the race meeting. Now that he'd seen her up close, the fact she'd not been called an Incomparable made him wonder what the other young ladies looked like.

But her beauty was second in his thoughts, or should have been. Seeing her brought her brother to mind, and the dead groom at the Newmarket stables. David had heard there'd been no sign of injury on the body, so they were investigating the apparent illness he'd suffered that morning. The fact the groom worked for Northcotte didn't ease the concern David and Knightwick had for the safety of their own horses.

As he considered possible reasons someone would want to kill a groom, David paid little attention to where he guided Triton, and found himself in Shepherd's Market where his friend, Laurence Pierce, had rooms. Just the man he needed to see.

The portly butler led David to the library to wait for Pierce, who stumbled in with his hair freshly combed and his face still puffy from sleep, fussing with the knot of his cravat. "Good God, Lumley. Why don't you sleep half the day like normal men?"

David chuckled. "Too much time in the country. I'm up with the cows most days. You would be too, if you stayed out of Lady Kemberton's bed."

Pierce leaned back in his chair and propped his feet on the hassock, throwing an arm over his eyes. "And why would I want to do that? Why would any man forego her warm, plump pillows for a cold, hard mattress?" He sighed, a sound more tired than wistful.

"Far be it from me to suggest a man give up pleasure while he can take it." David sharpened and aimed his barb. "All too soon one might find oneself too old for that type of entertainment."

Pierce peered out from beneath the brown sleeve of his coat. "There is only a year between us, old man, so any evil you wish upon me might soon fall upon yourself."

A footman entered laden with a coffee tray, which he set on the low table between the gentlemen. Pierce poured one black cup for David, then loaded another cup with as much milk as coffee.

David took a sip of the hot brew. "What do you know of Northcotte?"

"Skinny lad, a few years ahead of us at Oxford, was he not?"

"I was hoping for more recent news, say the last four years?"

"He came into his title in '08, as I recall. But he's been the main force behind his family's stud for longer than that." Pierce's right eyebrow rose. "Is that why you're here, now? You've always suspected him, or his father, in Zephyr's death. What have you learned?"

"I haven't learned anything, but there were some odd goings on at Newmarket, and I saw his three-year-old in Town this morning." David went on to explain his meeting with Lady Joanna.

Pierce barked with laughter before David could finish. "You were rescued by the fair Lady Joanna on Rotten Row? Perhaps I should rise with the cows, if that's when the best entertainment is to be found. This will be on all the wagging tongues at Lady Henderson's ball this evening."

"I was not rescued. A cat darted out from beneath a parked cart and startled Triton, causing me to lose my seat. He got a head start whilst I was lying on my arse wondering why the stars were still out. It could have happened to anyone."

Pierce choked out his next words between guffaws. "And how lucky for you an expert horseman—er, horsewoman— was nearby. Triton might have run all the way to Newmarket without you."

"I'm delighted to have provided you with this morning's merriment. If you're quite through making sport, I've more news. The dead groom was supposed to ride the horse Lady Joanna was on in Hyde Park."

Pierce's mustache twitched. "The lady rode a stallion and overtook Triton? Really, Lumley, it's too early for these tales. Next, you'll tell me she rode astride for all the *ton* to see."

David searched his memory. "No, she sat aside. I realize

how unbelievable that is, but it's beside the point. Her horse is the point. Or the groom who was supposed to ride it."

"I'm not following. What does one have to do with the other? Lady, horse, groom? And why am I losing sleep over all of it?"

"It's too odd that it's Northcotte's groom who was killed, when he's the man I suspect was behind the other poisonings." David tapped his fingernail on his cup, then set it aside to keep his fidgeting from being obvious.

"Are you certain this groom was poisoned?"

"No, they haven't reported anything beyond finding the body, and since I was at the race meeting, I knew about that."

Pierce stretched and yawned loudly. "Perhaps it's my lack of sleep speaking, but I don't understand why the man would kill his own groom. Surely not to throw suspicion from him."

"I doubt that would be the reason. But the boy might have known too much. Or he could have accidentally ingested the poison. The times before, the horses' water buckets were tainted, so anyone drinking from them took ill to varying degrees."

"Do you intend to speak to the constable about your theories?"

"Not until I have proof," David said.

"And how do you plan to find this proof? Last I'd heard, Northcotte wasn't overtly welcoming to the Lumley clan."

David smiled and sat back in his chair. "With a little help from a new acquaintance. My mother has been pleading for me to escort Lady Hannah to whatever events strike her fancy; that is the whole purpose of my being in London at this time of year. I shall endeavor to see that my dear sister and Lady Joanna become fast friends."

He didn't care to know Northcotte's sister any better, but she might know something that could solve the mysteries plaguing him.

～

JOANNA AND MISS AMELIA CLAWSON PRANCED DOWN THE front steps of the small town house belonging to Amelia's parents, their maids following in a more subdued manner. Joanna laughed and circled in place when she reached the curb, her arms spread wide. "Isn't it a beautiful day?"

Amelia shook her head but laughed. "You act as though you've fallen in love, and we haven't yet been to our first ball."

Joanna laughed once more, then the warmth of a blush traveled over her face. She was not in love. "I did meet someone. He's too cold-natured for my liking, but he gives me hope for the other gentlemen in Town."

With a loud gasp, followed by a clap of her hand over her mouth, Amelia gaped at her with wide eyes. "Who is he? Does he have a handsome brother for me?"

Tipping her head to one side, Joanna thought for a moment as they began strolling down the street to shop for ribbon. "Why yes, he does have a very handsome brother. Do you know Lord Knightwick?"

Another gasp. "You met Knightwick?"

"No, his brother, Mr. David Lumley."

"How? Where? Why was I not there with you? You've just arrived in Town."

Joanna plucked at the button on her Spencer, straightening the front of the blue garment distractedly. Shrugging her shoulders and sighing dramatically, she spoke. "You won't ride with me, so you won't have the opportunity to meet gentlemen such as these. I was riding Patriot this morning when I had the opportunity to do a service for Mr. Lumley."

She detailed her chase, adding theatrical flourishes to her run while riding sidesaddle, and the reactions of the two stallions upon Triton being caught. In truth, she knew she could easily have been thrown if the two animals had been more upset, but she had been quite lucky.

Amelia looked suitably impressed. "You didn't! Isn't his horse a runner?"

"Just so, as is Patriot. My horse will prove himself on the courses this year, you'll see."

Patting Joanna's arm, Amelia apologized. "I didn't mean his horse is better. Or faster. Or whatever. But you shouldn't have let your groom catch him? What must people think? Surely you were seen."

"Oooh, you sound like my mother. You're exactly the daughter she wishes me to be. But I can't undo chasing the stallion, and I don't wish to undo meeting Mr. Lumley, which was my true point in mentioning the event to you."

"I forgot. If he resembles Knightwick, he's likely very handsome as you say. Was he grateful for your help, or embarrassed to be saved by a lady?"

Joanna considered the way he had ridden off so abruptly. She would not share that part of their meeting. There was no fun in that. "He seemed suitably gracious. He was well aware he might never have caught Triton on his own."

"And did he ask to call on you? Perhaps thank you again?"

"Well, no. He didn't say anything suggesting he wished to see me again." Not that she cared to speak to him after his rude departure. "It doesn't matter. The promise of what lay ahead makes me happy this morning. He's handsome and he loves horses. Those two qualities are very high on my list for an ideal husband. If there's one like him in London, there must be more. Perhaps one of them will be able to look beyond my work with horses and will think I make the perfect wife."

"It's likely we'll run into him at some assembly or other. And he now has reason to request an introduction." Amelia always saw the brighter side of a situation. "Perhaps he'll have his brother with him, and perhaps I'll be with you."

"You never told me you have an interest in Knightwick, Amelia."

Her friend looked off at the row of houses across the street. "I've no aspirations to marry an earl's heir. My grandfather was in trade, and my father is only a baron. My income isn't enough to attract a titled gentleman."

"Well then, you may marry any man you choose. Many would want a wife like you. Your hair is such a rich shade of brown, and the shape of your eyes is so striking. You're enjoyable to talk to and you carry yourself well in company. You're the perfect bride for any gentleman."

Amelia laughed. "If only the right gentleman would come along. I've had two Seasons for some man to think I'm perfect, and I stand before you an unmarried, unattached woman."

"I'm very grateful for that. Who would I talk to if you were an old, married woman already?"

They reached their intended shop and walked inside. "I need just the right shade of lavender, not too wide, to match one of my dresses," Joanna explained.

Joanna examined the goods for sale, asking for cuts of laces and ribbons for various garments, and thread to match. Once they were back on the street, her thoughts returned to Knightwick. "You don't really want a man like him, do you?"

"Who, Knightwick? Why would I not? You aren't referring to that Cambridge incident, are you?"

"No, silly. I meant that he's such a rake, of course," Joanna said.

"Why, because he keeps a demimonde? I'm certain even your brother has used the services of one."

"Amelia!" Joanna glanced about, but the people walking near them appeared not to have overheard. "His employment of a demimonde is reason enough. But there are other allegations. What about the young lady Lord Knightwick jilted?"

"I heard that was all gossip," Amelia said. "He'd not made any declarations toward her, nor paid her any particular attention. She was merely the daughter of a friend of his aunt's whom he called on once or twice out of consideration for the older ladies' friendship."

"Hmm. I suppose people do tend to make too much of many tidbits they hear. But I'm still not certain I'd care to have such a man as a husband."

"He would be your brother if you married Mr. Lumley."

Joanna shook her head with a laugh. "I never claimed I wished to marry Lumley. I only hope to find a man such as him, who would let me continue to train horses."

As they rounded the corner, they stopped abruptly to avoid collision with a man who was barreling down the walk while reading a piece of paper in his hand. He halted and nodded at them. "I beg your pardon, ladies. How rude of me. Why, Lady Joanna, it's delightful to see you again."

Joanna recognized the scarecrow who'd been with her brother at Newmarket. "I don't believe we've been introduced, sir."

He bowed. "Sir Frederick Aldwen. Your brother and I are...business associates."

She was no more comfortable in his presence there than she'd been at Newmarket. Taking Amelia's arm, she stepped around him. "I shall let my brother know we saw you. Good day."

He spun around and fell into step beside her. "Yes, it is a nice day. Very pleasant for walking. You've been shopping?"

"Yes." She tried to tread the fine line between polite and disinterested.

"I planned to call on your brother this afternoon. Perhaps,

if you aren't otherwise occupied, I could give you a ride home?"

Closing her eyes for a moment, Joanna searched for another obligation. Amelia piped up for her. "You haven't forgotten you said you'd call on my aunt with me, have you, Lady Joanna? She's so looking forward to your visit."

Joanna smiled. "Of course, I won't disappoint the dear woman. She has suffered so much of late."

"Well, perhaps another time." Sir Frederick stopped and bowed again. "Good day to you both."

As he walked away, Joanna hugged her friend, grinning widely. "Do you even have an aunt?" she whispered.

"I do, but she lives in Yorkshire. I don't believe we could visit her and be back in time for Lady Harrington's ball tonight." They both laughed and continued on their way.

Joanna was quiet for a moment, recalling their earlier topic of conversation. "What did you mean, 'that Cambridge incident,' regarding Knightwick?"

CHAPTER FIVE

*J*oanna took the offered glass of lemonade from her dance partner, desperately trying to recall his name. Mr. Digby? Rigby? No, that wasn't correct. "Thank you, Mr. Bigby."

He bowed, his puffy, pink complexion aglow in the bright ballroom. Admittedly, the crowded space was uncomfortably warm, but surely that didn't account for the way the man's pale, thin locks were plastered to his head. Even the cup he'd handed her was damp.

Seeing Mrs. Clawson seated on a chaise beside Joanna's mother, Joanna rose on her toes in search of Amelia. Her friend was so petite she was impossible to find in any crowd. Her distinctive laugh often gave her away, but she was certain to be on her best behavior at Lady Harrington's ball and refrain from such outbursts. She should've returned directly after the last set finished, so her next partner would find her.

Unable to see her friend, Joanna wondered how long she must converse with Mr. Bigby. No one had asked to stand up with her for the next few sets, so she might be trapped there until the supper dance.

Mr. Bigby cleared his throat. "Miss Smithers looks quite recovered from her recent complaint, does she not?"

The miss in question appeared quite robust, enjoying the attentions of three young beaux. "Yes, she does."

Mr. Bigby's next observation was lost when Amelia appeared on the arm of a lord whose title Joanna couldn't recall. Handing her cup to a footman passing by with a tray, Joanna exhaled a sigh of relief. "There you are, Miss Clawson."

The lord greeted Joanna before taking his leave. Joanna wished Bigby would follow suit, but the man hovered just behind her right arm. Amelia glanced his way and tilted her head in question, but Joanna couldn't say anything untoward in his presence. Instead, she asked, "Who is your next partner?"

Amelia's smile widened. "Sir Richard Tanton. I cannot believe he approached me," she added in a whisper.

Lowering her voice and speaking close to Amelia's ear, Joanna said, "The marquess' son? But I thought he had an acknowledged *tendre* for Lady Elizabeth."

"As did I. But the *on-dits* has it her father turned him down."

Joanna swallowed a gasp of surprise and looked for Mr. Bigby again. She was relieved to see he'd left her side. "The poor girl! She must be heartbroken. And you do not mind that Sir Richard had set his cap on another before you?"

Her shoulders lifted briefly, but her face didn't betray any emotion. "This is my third Season. Every eligible gentleman has most certainly considered some richer or prettier lady before me."

"Do not believe such a thing. There are new faces at the assemblies each Season, gentlemen as well as ladies. Perhaps we will both find husbands by summer." The likelihood of her own success depended on being partnered with someone other than Mr. Bigby and his perspiring palms.

Sir Richard approached just as the musicians were warming up for the next set. After acknowledging Joanna, he led Amelia toward the center of the room. Joanna glanced back at her mother, who was deep in conversation, then made a slow perusal of the large crowd.

Her gaze landed on one striking visage drifting above the sea of coifs and curls around him. *Mr. Lumley.* His brown hair was perfectly styled, his cravat elaborately tied. He spoke to someone at his side as they walked her way, but his companion wasn't visible through the crowd. Joanna's stomach quivered when he smiled down at the lady. She knew it had to be a lady because of the way his eyes laughed. He looked up, catching Joanna's stare, and his eyes brightened even more. He guided the young woman at his side around a clutch of giggling wallflowers.

Joanna refused to admit her heart dropped seeing how pretty the lady on Mr. Lumley's arm was. She cared not if he'd escorted someone to the ball or found a willing partner for whatever entertainments he had planned for the evening. The gentleman wasn't her concern. Schooling her features, she smiled politely as the couple stopped before her.

The lady spoke. "Lady Joanna, my brother, Mr. Lumley, has asked to be made known to you."

Her brother? Looking more closely, she saw a resemblance in their coloring, slender build, and the laughing glint in their eyes. She realized she'd met Lady Hannah, along with a dozen or so other young ladies, at a tea upon her arrival in London. "Mr. Lumley, Lady Hannah, how lovely to see you both again."

"I felt our meeting yesterday did not qualify as an introduction. Lady Hannah mentioned having met you at Miss Brown's tea, so I begged her assistance."

"Yes." Joanna turned to Lady Hannah. "I didn't recognize you at first. I've met so many people so quickly, I've difficulty matching names to faces. Is your mother here?"

"Yes, but she's sitting with one of her friends, so my dear brother volunteered to escort me around the room to find you. He's so good to me."

Joanna wondered what cataclysmic events must transpire for Robert to come to her aid thusly. Thankfully Mama's good spell continued, and as long as Mama enjoyed these evenings Joanna was unlikely to find herself at his mercy. Aunt Ophelia attended almost as many assemblies as Joanna, so she would step in happily if the need arose. "You're lucky to have such a kind brother."

Mr. Lumley brushed aside his sister's praise. "Lady Hannah has a partner for the next set, but I find myself in need. I'm certain your card filled first thing this evening, but I can't risk not asking. Is there a chance you're free?"

For a moment she couldn't draw a breath. He'd sought an introduction and wanted to dance with her. After riding off so abruptly when she'd caught his horse. He was the last man she would expect to see at the ball, much less dance with. But he was inordinately handsome, and his family well thought of, so it might raise her standing in the eyes of others to be seen on his arm. Not to mention, she couldn't refuse him without causing a scandal. "Yes, I'm free."

He responded with a half-smile that sent a wake of warm ripples throughout her.

Lady Hannah spoke. "My brother tells me you enjoy riding. None of my friends in London cares for it. Would you allow me to join you one day?"

"That would be delightful. I often ride alone for that very reason." In truth, other than Amelia, Joanna had only a few friends in Town, and none had been raised around horses like she had. They preferred to be seen sporting about in a curricle, or some gentleman's phaeton.

Lady Hannah's next partner arrived and began conversing with her, and Mr. Lumley moved to Joanna's side. He bent to speak near her ear. "I must thank you again for catching Triton."

Joanna smiled politely, wickedly trying to remember if he'd actually thanked her at the time. "It's really nothing more than I would have done for anyone. Any horse, for that matter."

"You must be quite the horsewoman. I don't know that I'd allow my sisters to ride Triton, or any stallion."

Her smile dropped at his words. "Oh, you restrict which horses your sisters may ride?"

He laughed. "It's not likely they would listen to my commands, if I did. I think Hannah is much like you."

He continued to watch her, and his gaze probed deep into her soul. She shivered at the familiarity he presumed. It wasn't as if he could actually know her secrets just by sight, though. She lifted her chin a small measure but didn't look away. "How so?"

"She knows her mind and refuses to be told what she thinks, what she believes, if it runs contrary to her mind." His voice was tinged with admiration. That surprised Joanna.

She tipped her head to the side in a nod. "I think she and I might become good friends, in that case." Against her will, her lips spread slightly. She didn't wish to give the impression the offer of friendship extended to Mr. Lumley, too. After their brusque meeting, she would need to know him better before deciding that.

The musicians played a few warning notes. Mr. Lumley offered his arm. "We must take our place." He led her onto the floor, coming to stand in the two lines beside Lady Hannah and her partner. Amelia was nowhere in sight.

When Joanna's gaze returned to her partner, Mr. Lumley winked. She gasped. What was he about? She hadn't taken him for the flirtatious type. He was showing himself to be everything but the snobbish prig she'd first met. Instead of responding, she pushed her single, long curl behind her shoulder and looked away. She would not play his games.

A shiver of curiosity deep inside begged her to reconsider.

As the music began, Mr. Lumley walked forward and circled her. "Do you attend many race meetings?"

"As many as I can. I'm afraid my mother expects me to stay in London for the Season, so I'll miss many of the spring meetings."

He continued to time his conversation for when they drew close. "Yes, mothers are like that. Mine has similar ideas about my time."

"Yours is eager for you to find a match? I thought that urgency was reserved for eldest sons."

Chuckling softly, he took her hand in the next set of steps. "Perhaps in some families. I have the inconvenience of having parents who married for love. My mother wants the same for all eight of her children."

Eight children. She hadn't realized his family was so large. Lady Hannah had been alone with Lady Bridgethorpe when Joanna met her, so Joanna was uncertain how many sisters she might have. Like most girls, Joanna had longed for a sister while growing up. And there were times in recent years where having someone to confide in would have been an immense pleasure. Amelia was the dearest of friends and confidants, but having to write letters when they weren't in London took away the joy of the moment when there was news to share.

Joanna and Mr. Lumley separated and strolled around the other couples. When they met again, she asked, "Are any of your brothers or sisters married?"

He shook his head, his smile becoming flirtatious once more. "My mother would tell you I'm married to the stables, but I beg to differ. The horses keep me busy, I'll admit, but I haven't felt the need to marry before Knightwick does."

Joanna heard Lady Hannah's laughter, as Mr. Lumley must have, for he nodded her way. "I believe Lady Hannah will be the first of us to find love."

Something in his voice made Joanna look up in time to see the wistful emotions passing over his face. All too soon, he was again the affable gentleman. She spent the rest of the dance trying to determine what his thoughts had been in that moment. The idea of losing a beloved sister, perhaps. She couldn't imagine he wished to be first to find love, after saying he was in no hurry to marry.

Men were such a silly sort. They knew they must marry at some point, but worked so hard at making certain it couldn't happen. There must be a kind of freedom in bachelor life that women didn't experience. She had friends who swore they preferred spinsterhood, but Joanna wondered if that was sour grapes speaking. Even with her concerns of losing the time to spend in the stables, she looked forward to having a home of her own, and children to share her days.

When their set ended, Mr. Lumley walked her back to where her mother sat. "May I get you a glass of lemonade?"

"No, thank you." She fanned herself with her silk fan. None of their friends had returned yet. Finding a topic of conversation with this man was easy, though. "Will you be racing more than one horse this year?"

"Yes, Lumley's Lass is doing well. And your brother's runners? How many is he entering?"

"Patriot is the only one he's raced so far. He doesn't tell

me his plans, however, so I don't know about future meetings."

"I realize I misspoke earlier, but I do find it unusual that he lets you…no, wait, that will get me into trouble again. I don't use my runners as pleasure horses while they are competing. I worry about injury. Your brother doesn't seem to have that concern."

Joanna laughed, knowing just how wrong that was. "When Patriot leaves London for the next meeting, I won't see him again until I return to Hampshire after the Season. I've argued in vain I trained that horse, and most of the ones he's bred in the last few years, so I ought to know how to ride without injuring him."

A faint line appeared across his brow as he looked at her. "Oh, I didn't realize you were serious when you mentioned training horses. I thought, perhaps, your brother humored you. Do you work with another trainer?"

"No, Father released the man who worked for him a year before his death. My brother and I both work with the foals, but mine seemed to be more competitive as they matured. Robert reluctantly let me continue, especially when Father died, and he had so many duties to attend."

Mr. Lumley tipped his head to one side as he continued to study her. "You must have a special touch."

Joanna smiled but had to look away. Meeting his gaze sent shivers through her. Was it simply because he allowed her to talk horses in a ballroom, something she never imagined she would do, or was there some other emotion he awakened? Before she could think longer on it, Amelia joined them, and the conversation turned to more acceptable topics. But as she danced with various partners the rest of the evening, her thoughts continually landed on Mr. Lumley.

∾

THE RIDE THROUGH HYDE PARK THE LUMLEYS AND LADY Joanna had planned for the following day was postponed due to rain, but the next day dawned clear and bright. Late that afternoon, David watched Lady Joanna descend the staircase, her pale green riding habit making her blonde hair that much brighter beneath her matching hat. She tugged on her gloves as she came down, apparently unaware of her audience. When she looked up, her step faltered, but she caught herself with a hand on the banister.

He was able to hide the reflexive jerk of his body, scrambling to catch her if she fell. He walked toward her, holding out a hand. "My lady, you will have all the other young ladies scurrying to their modistes after they glimpse your gown."

Lady Joanna shook her head. "Such a taradiddle. But they might look at your waistcoat and presume we planned our dress to match."

He glanced down, not remembering what he'd donned, and saw his green woolen waistcoat. "Imagine that. Lady Hannah wore lavender, so we three shall look like a rose garden." She took the arm he offered, and he led her outside where Hannah sat on her horse awaiting them.

Lady Joanna's groom held Patriot's bridle and had placed a mounting block for her to use. Once she was comfortably in the saddle, the three riders started down the street at a leisurely pace.

Hannah rode up on Lady Joanna's left side. "I hope you have no plans to run your horse. I could never keep up while riding sidesaddle. You must come to Bridgethorpe during the summer so we might sneak away and be scandalous horsewomen."

Lady Joanna laughed. "The other ladies I've met in Town grow faint when I mention riding astride."

"As well they should," David chimed in as he came up on

her right. "Young ladies should spend their time improving their minds, not baring their ankles on the heath."

"You seem to have forgotten how much you, Knightwick and your friend Laurence Pierce bared while swimming in the pond." Hannah's smirk promised to embarrass him in as many ways as possible.

"A lady would never mention such a thing, nor admit to having lurked in the trees when her brothers and a friend were skinny-dipping," he argued.

"I was not lurking. I was sketching the hollow tree. You all made such a racket I ran to see what was amiss. Thankfully you were all in the water by the time I arrived, or I might have shocked our art tutor with my advanced anatomy education."

David had to laugh along with Lady Joanna. Hannah was too bold by half. He decided to take control of the conversation. "Do you draw, Lady Joanna?"

"A little, but not very well. And never studies of the physical form. Although I've an entire booklet of horses from our stables."

He had to drop back when they came into traffic, but he directed them toward less busy streets so they might ride three abreast. "That sounds like a defiant daughter's excuse to spend more time with her horses."

She glanced David's way. "My mother couldn't understand how deep my passion for them ran. And my brother was certain I'd outgrow my love of riding."

"As did mine," Hannah said. "It's as if we could have no interest whatsoever in horses once we begin to wear our hair up."

David leaned forward to glare at his sister on the other side of Lady Joanna. He'd neglected to mention he wished to build a friendship with the lady, apparently. "Your demonstrated interest tended toward braiding manes and naming foals. Forgive us for not realizing they included racing contest entries."

Lady Joanna laughed. "I love all things about the stables."

"Surely not the odors," he said.

She reached down and patted Patriot's neck. "The odors are part of the package. Admittedly, I prefer the sweet smell of alfalfa and fresh straw to the earthier scents of the early morning. But you won't find me fainting dead away should I step in something whilst crossing the street."

Lady Joanna was intriguing, he had to admit. She would make an excellent wife for a man who attended race meetings as often as he did. He bit off that thought as soon as the words came to him. He wasn't looking for a wife. He was looking for the killer of his father's stallion.

The ladies chattered on with little regard to him being present. This gave him time to notice how gracefully Lady Joanna sat on her mount, as if she'd been born to the saddle. She held her neck and shoulders upright without appearing rigid. Her arms were relaxed on her lap as she held the reins. Her gown complemented her curves, without calling attention to them, although his gaze enjoyed landing there often. She was pleasant to look at, and just as enjoyable to talk to. A very dangerous combination.

As laughter broke out beside him, he wondered if Hannah had once again been poking fun in his direction. He knew better than to ask, for if she hadn't been, she surely would if prompted.

Lady Joanna peered at him from beneath the brim of her bonnet. "You're a man of few words, Mr. Lumley."

"I'm a man with four sisters. I've discovered my voice is unnecessary to keep a conversation going."

"Surely they allow you to speak now and again."

He shrugged. "Perhaps they are the reason I spend so

much time in the stables." He couldn't keep his grin from spreading.

"Lady Joanna, please say you'll go with me to the lending library tomorrow," Hannah begged. "We can compare which invitations we've each received and make certain we'll be at the same assemblies."

"That sounds delightful. And might I bring my friend Miss Clawson? You will enjoy her company, too, I'm certain of it."

"Yes, of course. I've met her and found her quite amiable."

It dawned on David his presence wasn't needed for the ladies' enjoyment. At this rate, he'd never gain an invitation inside Northcotte's home. His sister was having better success in her offer of friendship. He hoped Hannah would be invited to tea, and he would be sure to tag along.

CHAPTER SIX

*J*oanna smoothed her hands over the lace overdress of her gown, certain there were wrinkles she couldn't see in the pink silk beneath it. She glanced once more at the wall behind her, wondering how close one had to stand to be considered a wallflower, or if it was a matter of the length of time she remained in that spot. Admittedly, they'd just arrived at Mrs. Stanford's ball, and she couldn't be disappointed that every unmarried gentleman in the room, titled or not, hadn't swarmed to her side. But she wished at least one would.

"Stop fussing with your gown," Aunt Ophelia whispered from her side. "You look desperate."

"What if no one wants to dance with me? I'll look undesirable, which is much worse than desperate, you must admit."

"You're one of the most beautiful young ladies here. One of the prettiest this Season. If a gentleman doesn't ask you to dance, it's because he's afraid you'll refuse him."

Joanna smiled and tried to relax her hands. "You are very kind to fib that way. They all know they'll not be refused a dance unless my card is full. And since no one has approached me, there's no worry of that."

Her aunt suddenly gasped. "Oh, dear, not that man."

Recognizing Lord Westbourne, an older earl with a shocking reputation for scandalous parties at one of his estates, Joanna shared Aunt Ophelia's shock.

He bowed in greeting. "Lady Ophelia, I'm happy to find you here tonight."

"How do you do?"

Joanna noticed her aunt didn't perform an introduction, which was an obvious slight.

"I'm quite well, thank you." His smile didn't reach his eyes. "Would you care to take a turn about the room?"

"I'm afraid I can't leave my niece on her own."

The lord ran his gaze slowly over Joanna, then licked his lips. Joanna shivered. One side of his mouth turned upward. "Perhaps I should walk with her, instead."

Aunt Ophelia stretched taller as her back stiffened. "No, you should not. You should look elsewhere for your entertainment."

He gave a single nod of his head. "Perhaps another night. Enjoy your evening, ladies." He strolled off.

Joanna watched until he was lost in the crowd. She whispered, "Why is he here?"

"He was invited, I'm certain. Some of the matrons in London will invite all the rakes of their acquaintance in hopes their assemblies will be mentioned in the papers."

Another man approached, this one a tall, handsome man of middle years. He smiled warmly at her aunt. "Lady Ophelia, how well you look tonight."

"Sir Jasper, allow me to introduce my niece, Lady Joanna Hurst. Her mother was too ill to attend this evening, so I offered to chaperone her."

The gentleman nodded to Joanna. "It's a pleasure. I hope your mother recovers quickly."

"Thank you." She shoved aside her own wishes for the same, knowing it could be months before Mama was herself again. She'd had those spells ever since Papa died. Waves of wistfulness washed over Joanna, settling heavily in her middle. Her parents had shared such a deep love. If she could find only half as much in her own marriage, she would consider herself lucky.

The small group of people standing in front of her parted, and that rude friend of Robert's, Sir Frederick, strode toward Joanna. Her eyes widened as her stomach sank. She willed her feet to remain in place, when all she wanted was to run away. He still hadn't been formally introduced to her, so he couldn't be coming to speak to her. Surely not. And if he was, she felt clueless as to how to respond. To acknowledge his lack of propriety would be putting herself on the same level.

He tipped his head and smiled, which made his bushy side-whiskers puff out even more. "Lady Joanna, how delighted I am to see you."

"Thank you." For the life of her, she would not return the sentiment, politeness be damned. She looked around, hoping to find someone to rescue her, but aside from her aunt, no one of her acquaintance stood nearby.

"I hoped I might run into you tonight. Your brother mentioned you would be here."

Robert would do that, discuss her plans with a practical stranger. If she weren't dependent on his goodwill for a home until she married, she would speak to him the moment she returned.

"Am I early enough to claim the supper dance?" One of his untamed graying eyebrows lifted as he peered down his over-long nose.

Joanna closed her eyes and prayed for help. None of her

dances had been claimed yet. Where was Mr. Bigby when she needed him? Sweaty palms were much more appealing than the all-over squeamishness this man invoked. She drew in a breath to respond but someone else spoke.

"I'm sorry, that dance is spoken for, as is Lady Joanna's first waltz."

Snapping open her eyelids, she met the cheery hazel eyes of Mr. Lumley. She sighed with a smile of thanks. "Yes, that's correct. I'll be sitting with Mr. Lumley for supper." The courteous thing to do would be to offer one of the other open dances to Sir Frederick but couldn't bring herself to do so.

Sir Frederick's mouth thinned. "Well, I must settle for the first dance, then, and perhaps the last?"

She hadn't torn her gaze away from Mr. Lumley, and the warmth and laughter there gave her the strength to endure what she must. "Yes, they are both available."

Mr. Lumley raised his arm in invitation. "Perhaps we can stroll about the room until the musicians are ready to begin."

"That would be lovely." Placing her hand on his sleeve, she resisted the urge to hurry away from Sir Frederick, even though she must return shortly and dance with the man.

"I'm surprised to see Sir Frederick at a ball," Mr. Lumley said once they were out of earshot. "Are you well acquainted with the man?"

"Not at all. I observed him speaking to my brother at Newmarket and he has presumed a friendship that doesn't exist." She surprised herself at how much she admitted to a man she'd so recently met, but she felt safe when he was around.

"Guard yourself around him. I've heard stories I can't share, but his character is questionable, to say the least."

She laughed. "Do not fear I'm in danger of forming an attachment there. The man makes me quite uncomfortable."

"Your brother should attend these assemblies with you. I

now see why my mother insisted I come to Town for Hannah's Season." He nodded toward a notorious rakehell who conversed with their hostess. "The idea astounds me that innocent misses are expected to mingle with less-than-savory characters while maintaining their pristine repu-tations."

Joanna bit her lip at his indignation, but kept silent, fighting to keep her giggles inside.

Mr. Lumley glanced down at her from the corner of his eye, then quickly looked away. "You laugh at me. Did I just sound as priggish as I suspect?"

"You did. It was quite the elder brother in spirit. Is Lady Hannah in attendance tonight?"

"She is. And forgive me for preaching as I did. I'm truly not a coxcomb."

"I never suspected it. Lady Hannah enjoys your company too much for that to be the case."

All too soon, Mr. Lumley returned her to where Sir Fred-erick waited. That man took her hand and clamped it to his arm, holding it in place while leading her onto the dance floor where the others had begun to gather. His lack of conversation bothered Joanna even more than dull words would have. She forced herself to speak. "Have you known my brother long?"

"Northcotte and I are business acquaintances."

Which didn't really answer her question, and made her wonder all the more why he was dancing with her. "What sort of business are you in?"

The rapid darting of his eyes to the other dancers added to his mystery. "Banking. But one shouldn't discuss business at social functions."

She took that as her cue to quit trying to make polite conversation. How dare he put her in her place that way. She didn't recall ever meeting such an insufferably rude person. By the time the dance wore down, she wondered if she might manage to convince Aunt Ophelia to slip away before the final dance.

On her way back to her aunt, she spied Amelia speaking with Sir Richard. She offered thanks to Sir Frederick in dismissal, squeezed through the crowd, and hugged her friend. "I was afraid I would not find you in this crush."

Sir Richard nodded. "I had similar fears before I discovered her. There is hardly room to dance."

"Was that your brother's friend I saw you with?" Amelia asked.

"Sir Frederick, yes. Although he doesn't claim a friendship with Robert. He's such an odd sort."

"Let me offer my services," Sir Richard said, "if he becomes a nuisance."

Mr. Lumley chose that moment to reappear. "I'm pleased to know Lady Joanna and Miss Clawson have a champion."

"There's no need. Sir Frederick is awkward, yes, but not too forward," Joanna said. "But I do appreciate the concern."

Amelia and Sir Richard went off to dance, and Mr. Lumley remained with Joanna. He had a rogue wave falling over his forehead, giving him a dashing air in his dark olive wool tailcoat that brought out the color of his eyes. The matching breeches fitted his powerful thighs, which he surely gained from spending so much time on a horse. She held her head a little higher when she stood with him. She was proud to be seen with such a handsome man.

At supper, she ate lightly, not knowing how calm her stomach really was. Mr. Lumley dragged his chair close to hers and leaned in when speaking. "Will you be attending the Second Spring Race Meeting at Newmarket later this month?"

"No, my mother accepted an invitation for cards at Lady Hinderclay's home, a dinner and two balls that week. I don't know how I'll bear not seeing Patriot race."

"I'll be at Newmarket, so I won't be able to watch over you and my sister. I wish my parents had sent Hugh to chaperone instead of me, although I wouldn't have met you. I don't like the idea of you two being left to the whims of Sir Frederick and others of his ilk."

Rather than finding him pompous, she detected what she hoped was a bit of jealousy in his tone. That was too much to wish for. "We aren't attending a house party in the middle of nowhere. Your mother and mine will be present, or my aunt will. They've survived enough Seasons in their time to see us safely though a week in your absence."

He shoved the wayward lock of hair off his forehead. "I daresay Mother knows nothing of what these men are thinking."

Joanna almost choked on her punch. "She has a husband, and how many sons? I'm certain she has a general idea of what goes on in the minds of the male sex. Tell me, how do you think Triton will do in the next race? Who is his greatest competition? Aside from Patriot, of course."

That sent him off and running on what had to be his favorite topic. His horses. As he spoke, his eyes lit with an excitement that matched what she felt when she watched Patriot move. How cruel the fates would be if they presented such a perfect man for her and he wasn't seeking a wife.

Midway through their meal, Lady Hannah approached, walking beside Sir Frederick with a pleading look on her face. "David, Lady Joanna, may we join you?"

"Of course," her brother said, rising to pull out a chair for his sister.

Sir Frederick sat between the two ladies. "Lady Hannah was kind enough to save her supper dance for me."

Certain that jab was aimed her way, Joanna didn't take the bait. Instead, she offered Hannah a sympathetic smile. She found it rather surprising that Hannah didn't have her card full the moment she arrived. Mr. Lumley should have enlisted the aid of his friends to make her appear more desirable in the early assemblies of her first Season. But as beautiful as she was, her dark blonde hair piled in stylish curls, a fringe of bangs making her expressive brown eyes even more striking, she should not need help finding partners. "That was kind of her."

Mr. Lumley's brows drew together as he stabbed his fork into the dessert on his plate. "Who is your next partner?"

She mentioned a gentleman Joanna had met who was kind and somewhat handsome, whose family had large properties in the north. Lumley nodded.

Joanna set down her punch cup after taking a drink, and spoke to Hannah. "We must remember to find each other sooner in the evening, so we may share the latest *on-dits*."

"I don't see what you ladies find to talk about all evening long." Sir Frederick placed his napkin over the remaining food on his plate.

"There is always more news to share," Joanna replied.

"I didn't realize young ladies were interested in politics and business."

Offering a small smile to Lady Hannah, Joanna refrained from rolling her eyes. This man couldn't be any duller. "You'd be surprised at what we find to talk about when we get together." Which men to avoid at all costs was high on that list.

Mr. Lumley laughed softly. "With four sisters I can honestly say young ladies are never at a loss for conversation. As to its veracity I can't speak, but it's often most entertaining to listen to."

Sir Frederick snorted. "They should be schooled in topics

which would display their intelligence, so they might converse with their husbands when they return home in the evening."

Lady Hannah's eyebrows rose almost as high as Joanna's.

Shaking his head, Mr. Lumley said, "I'm not certain most gentlemen care to bring their business home with them."

Did that mean he would not wish to discuss his horses with his wife? Perhaps he was not the ideal husband for her after all.

Sir Frederick looked down his nose at Mr. Lumley. "That might be the case for those with family money and estates, but we who are more involved in earning our livings appreciate a wife who is knowledgeable in more practical matters."

"So you will expect your wife to be employed?" Mr. Lumley sounded as astounded as Joanna felt.

"Of course not. She must understand enough about finance to speak intelligently with my guests when I entertain. Lady Joanna will need to be schooled on what I do, once our betrothal is announced."

She choked on her punch and set the cup down with a clatter. Coughing into her napkin, she pleaded to Lady Hannah with her eyes.

Mr. Lumley patted her back. "Betrothal? The lady has not mentioned any impending engagement."

She lifted her hand to wave him away and drew in a breath to quiet her spasms. Her voice came out strangled. "I wasn't aware of any. Sir Frederick must have misspoken."

If possible, the man's affect became even haughtier. "It hasn't been announced, but I didn't misspeak."

Panic tightened her throat, making it harder to force words out. Robert had given her until the end of the Season to find a match. He couldn't have already considered anyone's offer. And surely, he'd never consider Sir Frederick.

"I'm certain you're mistaken, sir. I've not agreed to any engagement."

"As you're not yet one-and-twenty, the decision isn't yours to make. Lord Northcotte will have the final say on whom you will marry."

Heat rose up her body as her anger grew. Her hands shook until she clenched them in her lap. She couldn't meet Mr. Lumley's gaze, so she focused on Lady Hannah as she forced a smile. "The Season has just begun. It's much too soon to be making decisions such as that. Lady Hannah, do you find it as warm in here as I? Would you care to walk in the garden with me?"

Mr. Lumley jumped to his feet and helped her rise. "I shall escort you two. The cool night air will do us all well."

Without waiting for her friends, and without acknowledging Sir Frederick, Joanna fled to the hallway.

Mr. Lumley caught up with her a few steps later. "Could it be possible Sir Frederick speaks the truth?" He led her toward the ballroom, where they could go out into the garden.

"It can't be. Northcotte promised me a full Season to find a husband." She drew in a short breath, a tight band of fear keeping her from breathing deeper. The food she'd eaten churned in her stomach, and the thought of dancing again made her ill, no matter who partnered her.

"Why would your brother agree to a marriage you don't want?"

She didn't answer until they walked into the garden and stood in the light from a torch away from the other partiers. "I don't know."

Her took her gloved hand in his and patted it gently. "I'm sorry. It's presumptuous of me to ask such a personal question. Think of me as the brother of your friend, if you'd like to talk about it."

If only she could pour out her thoughts to him. But she'd just met him, and she still had some confusion about the way he'd reacted when she'd rescued Triton. Add the mortification knowing he'd witnessed Sir Frederick's declaration, and her words just would not come. "Thank you, but I would rather not discuss it."

"I understand." He glanced up as footsteps approached.

Lady Hannah stormed up to them. "David, how could you leave me with that man? I was forced to beg him to help me find Mama, or he'd have escorted me out here."

"I apologize, my thoughts were only for Lady Joanna at that moment. But you seem to have handled it well."

She folded her arms and shifted her weight on one hip. "Some chaperone you are."

"What could he have done to you in the crowded dining room? Save your histrionics. Help me cheer your friend, now."

Lady Hannah turned to Joanna. "How thoughtless of me. My plight was nothing compared to what he did to you. Do you think anyone heard?"

"I hope not. I won't marry that man, and having scandal attached to my name would prevent me from marrying anyone else."

ON THE CARRIAGE RIDE HOME, JOANNA WATCHED OUT THE window as the houses passed by. She'd danced most of the dances, met one very nice gentleman, yet all she could think about was Mr. Lumley's lips. Smiling. Quirking to one side when he considered what was said. Full and firm, they made her wonder what they'd feel like pressed against hers.

Aunt Ophelia shifted on the opposite bench and pulled

her shawl up over her shoulders. "Did you have a lovely time, my dear?"

"Quite so. And you, Aunt? Sir Jasper was most attentive."

"He's a charming man. I feel like I'm in my first Season when he's around. I knew him then, you know."

"Did you have a *tendre* for him, then? Yet you married Uncle Peter."

Aunt Ophelia tucked a curl back into place beneath her feathered turban. "My father held out for a title. A mere knight wasn't good enough for his daughter."

Joanna couldn't stop her giggle. "Uncle Peter was only a viscount, not much above a knight."

"And a very good man. I didn't regret the marriage, even though we never had children. He took good care of me."

"He was a kind man, and a wonderful uncle. Mother and I've missed him. However, I'm pleased to hear you're renewing an old attachment."

"Attachment…that is for young ladies. I find I'm rekindling something much warmer this time around. I believe you will be seeing Sir Jasper often while you're in Town."

"And after I return home, perhaps? When you come for Christmas?"

"Perhaps. If I am to be blessed a second time."

Twice blessed. Joanna would be pleased to experience that fortune a single time, but worried Robert would find a way to hinder it, somehow. He was not the same person he'd been before Father died, and she no longer knew what to expect from one moment to the next.

Father, do you see what you've done to us? Mother spent days on end in the sitting room adjoining her bedchamber, staring out the window with no expression on her face. The servants brought her meals to her and reported she never spoke. When Joanna would visit her room, Mother said little beyond, "That's nice, dear," or "I'm well, thank you." *Nice* and *well* were not words Joanna would use to describe the woman's condition.

If that was what deep love did to one, perhaps Joanna should agree to an arranged marriage like Aunt Ophelia and Uncle Peter's. Looking again at the stately houses passing by, she wondered at the families who lived there. The larger the house, the greater the likelihood of an arranged marriage, or at least one involving something other than a love match in its beginning. She didn't hold out hope for a duke or a marquess for herself, and had little interest in a home in Mayfair. As long as she had horses and children, she could be happy with any man.

Any man who'd allow her to spend time in the stables, that is.

The image of Sir Frederick appeared before her in the glass, and she jerked away, watching it fade. He could be high on the list her brother might use from which to choose her husband. She couldn't bear a life beside him, even if he had the finest stables in all of England. Even if he owned the Godolphin Arabian himself. Well, that horse had been dead so long she was being silly. But even the potential chance to train a horse of his bloodlines, while being a dream she'd never have the chance to attain, couldn't tempt her into a marriage to Sir Frederick.

Joanna shivered and drew her shawl over her shoulders at the very thought.

The memory of another man she'd seen that evening came to mind. "Do you know Lord Westbourne well?"

"He's an acquaintance of long duration, but not a friend."

"Is he...well, does he wish to know you better?"

Aunt Ophelia yawned behind her hand. "It would appear he does. Pay him no mind, but do not feel you must accept any invitation from him, should you see him again. If he approaches you at all, come find me or your mother. He's not to be trusted. And he's not offering marriage."

"I understand." Lord Westbourne was even lower than Sir Frederick. The Season had just begun, and she's already met two men to avoid at all costs. And only one man of promise, yet he didn't seem to be hunting for a wife. If only she could convince Mr. Lumley otherwise.

CHAPTER SEVEN

*D*avid felt his horse dancing beneath him once they left London, the animal eager to run on the open road. The most difficult part of riding Triton to each race was the need to go the entire distance at a walk. Not only was there a risk of injury, but letting him run would leave him much too tired to race by the time they reached Newmarket, and defeat the entire purpose of the trip. He'd have to leave Triton behind when he returned to London this time, so his trainer could work with the horse and take him on to the next course at the close of the Second Spring Race Meeting.

He made a mental note to speak with the constable about the death of the young groom at the First Spring Meeting. By now, there should be some answers as to cause and possible suspects. He'd have to keep his eyes open and be alert to any suspicious activity. He'd remind Peter that Triton and Lass were not to be left alone at any time during the next week.

But what would prevent a man from tampering with the food or water at Fernleigh? The family stables were on the outskirts of Newmarket. If someone wanted to harm their animals, it was an easy ride to Fernleigh to do so.

He couldn't become irrationally suspicious or he'd spend every waking moment in fear. His family didn't seem to be the target in this last death, so he needed to calm down. Be on alert, of course, but not in a panic.

His thoughts wandered, and as they'd done often of late, they landed on the fair Lady Joanna. A few times in the past week, he'd had a nagging urge to speak to Northcotte about his sister. Not to suggest a match for the two of them, of course, but to discourage him from considering Sir Frederick as a potential husband for Lady Joanna. The very idea made bile rise in his gut. The image of the man's hands on her porcelain skin—no, he couldn't let the thought remain in his head.

If it did, he might feel tempted to consider asking for her himself. And he wasn't in a position to discuss marriage to anyone. In a few years, perhaps.

Lady Joanna would be married by then. Since he wasn't in love with her, that was no concern of his. He would likely forget her as soon as he found what he needed to know about Northcotte. He'd forget how her blue eyes darkened when they met his gaze, how her laughter made him smile no matter how irritable he felt. How his heart jumped when he spotted her across a crowded assembly.

Grimacing, he flexed his heels in the stirrups to keep from urging Triton to a fast pace. This wasn't a good time to be alone with his thoughts. If he were not careful, he'd fancy himself falling for Lady Joanna, which was completely at odds with his suspicion her father was behind Zephyr's death.

～

JOANNA TROTTED ON HORSEBACK BESIDE LADY HANNAH AND Amelia, with Wallis following. The afternoon sun beat down on the path through Hyde Park, making her Merino cloth riding habit much too warm. The crowd prevented them from traveling as fast as she'd prefer, but the slower pace made conversation easier. Besides, the mare she sat upon would never reach the speeds Patriot ran. For the near future, her stallion would be travelling from one race meeting to the next, so she must get used to this calm, proper pace.

She turned to Lady Hannah. "This might not be the place to discuss it, but how is your father faring? I hear such tales at the races, I hardly know what to believe."

"He's in good health, but low spirits, especially since the loss of his brother and sister-in-law," Lady Hannah said.

"I recall he became ill after his horse was killed some years past."

Lady Hannah's voice held a mixture of pride and sorrow. "Not just any horse. Zephyr was his prize stud, the foundation horse for Fernleigh Stud. He was quite the runner."

Joanna frowned. "That is what I never understood. Why would someone poison a perfectly sound horse?"

Lady Hannah responded. "My brothers believe someone was envious of his wins. All I know is my father lost his joy for life when Zephyr died. We've won some races since, but it doesn't bring back the excitement for him. He hasn't been to a race meeting in years."

Joanna realized they had that in common, a parent who'd slipped into melancholia with no apparent way to recover. Her new friend would understand the dark cloud constantly hovering in the background of one's daily thoughts. And the need to escape the gloom and sorrow. She and Lady Hannah would be friends for a long time, she was certain.

"Tell me, what do you think of my brother?" Lady Hannah asked.

"Mr. David Lumley? He is rather handsome, I suppose."

"*Rather handsome.* Do you think I don't see how you study him when he's not looking?"

Joanna laughed. "All right then, he is quite handsome. And witty. Quite pleasant to be around."

"I wish you and he would form an attraction so we might be sisters. We'd have such fun together."

"Now there is a reason for marrying I hadn't considered. I shall add it to my list of qualities. The gentleman I marry must have amiable sisters."

Lady Hannah joined in her laughter. "And you, Amelia, shall marry Knightwick."

"I've seen him and agree most adamantly. I would have Knightwick in a moment, if he'd have me."

"There is also Hugh, who is two-and-twenty, and Sam will turn twenty in a few weeks," Lady Hannah continued. "You see, you may have your choice of brothers."

Amelia waved away the notion. "I've met Hugh, I'm afraid, and I can't claim any strong feelings toward him. Of the two, I much prefer Lord Knightwick. Besides, I would be called Lady Knightwick then. It suits me much better than Mrs. Lumley."

Joanna could barely maintain her false indignation as she spoke, tipping her face away from her friends. "Aha, Mrs. Lumley is fine for me but you're above such a designation. I see how it stands between us now."

"Oh, never. You deserve better than a viscount, as you are an earl's daughter." Amelia burst out in laughter again. "Who am I fooling? I could never aspire to marry a viscount, especially one who will one day be an earl. I've no wish to."

Joanna sighed. "I agree. I care not if my husband is a mister or a duke. Just so long as he loves me."

"That's a relief," Lady Hannah said. "You can marry my brother after all."

Joanna didn't push the argument that Mr. Lumley had expressed no interest in her. She let the conversation take its natural course and move on to the new pattern Amelia had seen at the modiste's shop.

She'd all but forgotten the discussion of Lady Hannah's brothers by the time the three ladies went shopping with Aunt Ophelia the next afternoon. As they rode in her aunt's carriage, Amelia was aglow from having danced twice the previous night with her hopeful beau, Sir Richard.

"He dances so divinely," Amelia said with a sigh.

"You do make a handsome couple." Aunt Ophelia's smile seemed to say she remembered the emotions of a first love.

"He asked if I would be attending Lady Foxley's Venetian breakfast at Vauxhall on Saturday. Will you all be there? I would be so nervous without you beside me."

Joanna looked to her aunt for confirmation. "I believe we accepted that invitation. I've never been to a Venetian breakfast. I'm not certain what to expect."

"It's merely a picnic," Amelia explained. "In a beautiful setting of course."

Aunt Ophelia nodded. "Some years, Lady Foxley has required Grecian dress, which is silly given the location of Venice, but Grecian was the thing that year. There will be music, food, drink, and all of the walkways to explore."

The carriage stopped in front of the modiste's shop and the footman opened the door. As Joanna followed Aunt Ophelia down the step, a familiar, and unwanted voice, rang out. "Lady Joanna. What luck. Are you shopping this afternoon?"

"Yes, as you see, Sir Frederick." She motioned toward the shop door. Hearing her aunt clear her throat softly at her side, Joanna introduced him. "Sir Frederick is an acquaintance of Lord Northcotte's."

His smile appeared forced. "Charmed. Lady Joanna, while your friends shop, would you care to walk with me?"

Joanna's brows drew together. The man was shockingly rude. "I'm engaged this afternoon, as you see. If you'll excuse us, we have an appointment."

"Then I shall call on you later."

"I'll not be home, sir. Please don't trouble yourself. Another day, perhaps." She looked to her aunt for aid.

"It was pleasant meeting you, Sir Frederick. Good day," Aunt Ophelia said, then motioned for the girls to follow her indoors.

Amelia leaned close to Joanna's ear once they were inside. "How insufferable. Does he call on you often?"

"I'm not home during the day to find out. He does leave his card on occasion, or will have Robert pass along his greeting. He's made reference to us becoming betrothed. I shudder at the thought of it."

Aunt Ophelia patted her arm. "I can speak to your mother. Perhaps she has some influence over Robert. You should not have to marry against your wishes. Now ladies, let us forget about the man and look at the new patterns."

THE EVENING AFTER DAVID RETURNED FROM THE FINAL RACE of the Second Spring Meeting, he went to White's in search of Pierce. The man was so predictable, David didn't bother stopping by his friend's rooms first. As expected, he found Pierce in the middle of a card game with a large pile of winnings in front of him. "You appear to be enjoying a grand evening."

"Lumley. What brings you to Town?"

David stood to one side, watching the deal and bets placed. "I'm in between excuses to stay away. I must escort Hannah for the next few weeks. Knightwick will accompany the horses to the race meetings."

"How did Triton do?"

"A second and a third place. He's close to winning, I'm certain. I believe I'll go get a drink."

Pierce nodded. "This game is growing dull. I'll join you when this hand is done."

David found a pair of comfortable chairs away from the noise and set his whisky on the table between them as he sat. Pierce followed shortly after, his own drink in hand. "Did you find what you were looking for in Newmarket?"

"Not exactly. The constable has no names to investigate. I'm still certain Northcotte is the culprit, however."

Pierce took a swallow from his glass as he glanced about. "You believe he killed his own groom?"

"I think it happened by mistake. I think the target was Peter, my groom. The boy killed was of the same size and coloring as Peter. Northcotte might have thought losing my groom would make me scratch from the race, maybe the entire event. This feud goes back years, with our fathers. The elder Northcotte had a stallion that had beaten all comers in challenge after challenge. Short lengths, longer ones, it didn't matter. The horse could run. My father challenged him repeatedly. His horses would come close—one would have won if not for throwing a shoe, but he couldn't beat North-cotte's stallion.

"Eventually, my father bred Zephyr. By this time, North-cotte was racing a colt out of the first horse. The colt and Zephyr were born the same year, so they went head-to-head in all of the meetings. Zephyr won each time. Northcotte couldn't bear it, sold his colt, started buying and selling mares and stallions in an effort to produce the perfect horse."

"He became obsessed, it would appear," Pierce commented.

"Yes, bordering on madness. Before any of his foals were old enough to race, Zephyr died. The next year, Northcotte's stables were back on top again."

"That is quite a coincidence. But you can't let it become an obsession. You'll be as bad as Northcotte's father. Move on. You have Triton, who will win plenty in his prime, and will sire enough for you to have your pick and sell the rest. Not to mention the stud fees he will bring in."

David leaned back, crossing one leg over his knee. "The money isn't the point. Fernleigh produces sound horseflesh known for temperament and easy gait. But the pride of owning winning horses is immeasurable. As is the loss Father feels over Zephyr. I want to bring back his joy for life."

"Just don't let the desperation of that thought lead you to do something foolish."

"How foolish can I be when Mother is dragging me around to afternoon teas and crowded ballrooms?"

Pierce's lips twitched as if he fought a smile. "Have you seen Northcotte's sister recently?"

"Lady Joanna? No, not since I've been back. Hannah told me they would be attending the same assembly tonight."

"I'm surprised you're here and not there."

David motioned to a footman to bring him another whisky. "I pleaded weariness from my travels. Mother was quite sympathetic."

"That's not what I meant. You seem to be spending quite a lot of time with the young lady, during the day as well as socially." Pierce leaned back, raising one thin black brow.

"You know why. I hope to gain information on her brother."

"I can see where it might take weeks and weeks to build

up the nerve to ask if her brother is a vengeful horse-murderer." His sarcasm was tangible. "Is there a guideline on how long an acquaintance must be in place before steering conversation in that direction?"

"Very well, it's not something I would ask her directly. But Lady Joanna might accidentally let slip something I can use to prove my case."

"These are the excuses of a man treading dangerously close to the parson's noose."

David's bark of laughter made a few heads turn. "I'm not in danger of that. She's pretty enough, and has an excellent seat—"

"Don't let her hear you discussing that part of her anatomy." Pierce grinned and winked.

"I'm not familiar enough with her person to discuss it with you or anyone else." A realization struck him. "Good God, do you suppose men are discussing Hannah's anatomy? They'd better not do so in my hearing, or they'll be trying to speak around my fist."

Pierce cleared his throat. "I'd advise you to stay out of the clubs, then, until Hannah is married."

"The devil you say. Who is it? Who has dared speak of her that way?"

"The list of who haven't is shorter. Your sister is a Diamond, haven't you noticed? If I were—"

"Don't say it," David growled. "Not if you value our friendship."

Chuckling, Pierce shook his head. "She will be married one day, you know. Some man will have all of her treasures to himself. Hmm, I might be willing to consider sampling her myself."

David launched himself at his friend. Pierce's chair toppled, sending both of them sprawling. David's elbow connected with the table in the fall, shooting sparks of pain up his arm. Rolling off his friend, David jumped to his feet, shaking his hand. "Bollocks, that hurt."

Pierce climbed to his feet and rubbed the back of his head. He righted the chair, waving off an approaching footman. "What were you thinking, man?"

"I didn't think. I reacted. Don't talk about Hannah in that manner. And don't *ever* consider making her your own. I know you too well to allow it."

"I won't, don't worry. I've never seen you like this. You're like the dog guarding the sheep."

"That's what it feels like. No man will get past me to hurt my sister. Any of my sisters."

Pierce slanted him a look that said he'd gone mad. "I don't doubt it."

David sucked on the tenderest of his knuckles, then motioned to the hallway. "Shall we play some billiards?"

"Might as well. We've clearly exhausted all safe topics of conversation." After gulping the last of his drink, Pierce followed him out of the room.

CHAPTER EIGHT

*U*pon entering the dining room at breakfast, Joanna was startled to see her brother in his spot at the end of the table. "You're here rather late. You aren't needed in the House of Lords this morning?"

He rattled the newspaper in his hands. "I must tend to some business."

Since he went back to reading, she nibbled at her toast in the silence she was accustomed to. Mama drank her chocolate in bed most mornings, allowing Joanna to enjoy the stillness before callers began their rounds or she left on her own errands. Some mornings, however, the weight of the quiet made her wish to escape their home.

"How is Mother?"

Joanna jumped at her brother's voice. "Much the same. Well enough to not require the doctor, but not well enough to receive callers."

He grunted in response. Recalling the conversation she'd had with Sir Frederick at Mrs. Stanford's ball, she decided to question Robert now, when neither of them was overstressed. "I've met an acquaintance of yours on several occasions of late. Sir Frederick Aldwen. He makes me rather uncomfortable as he presumes an introduction when none has taken place."

Her brother lowered the newspaper and took a sip of his coffee. "Sir Frederick, you say? I'm, uh, rather surprised. I wasn't aware he attended the type of assemblies you've been invited to."

"Not only has he been to the balls, but he has accosted me on the street and suggested I walk with him. He's quite uncivilized."

Pursing his lips, he ran his thumb over the corners of the folded paper. "He is rather, isn't he? I've only spoken to him regarding business matters, but I can see where he'd be awkward in some situations." His brows drew together, deepening the crease between them.

"I'm at wits end about how to deal with him. Why, at Mrs. Stanford's ball, he had the nerve to imply there was a betrothal between us."

His gaze snapped up to meet hers. "He did? Did anyone hear him say this?"

"Hopefully, no one outside those at our table heard. Mr. Lumley and his sister Lady Hannah were the others present. The tables were close together, but conversation was so lively throughout the room, I doubt anyone was listening."

"I suppose that's in our favor. But why were you sitting with Mr. Lumley? How are you acquainted with him?"

Her lips pulled tight, and she sighed. Mr. Lumley was the least of her problems. Why was Robert focusing on that man? She didn't really hope that Mr. Lumley might offer for her, but he was certainly the best of the prospects she'd seen to date. If the gentleman did ask for her hand, she would not turn him down, and her brother had better get over whatever irritation he had toward the man. "He's escorting his sister when he's in Town. Lady Bridgethorpe and Mama are old friends, and I met Lady Hannah while making calls with Mama shortly after we arrived in London."

Robert said nothing. She chewed her lip for a moment, deciding now was as good a time as any to learn where she stood. "Is it really necessary I find a husband before the end of the Season? I could join Aunt Ophelia in Bath for the summer. I know she'd enjoy the company."

"We cannot afford a trip to Bath."

"How much of an expense could it be? She has a home there, and if I travel with her, it will cost nothing but my meals on the trip, and a room at the inn on the way. I won't need additional clothes after what I bought these past months. There are many families I might meet in Bath who do not come to London."

"It cannot be considered. Do not belabor this, Joanna."

"I don't understand the sudden need to be rid of me. Didn't Father set aside a dowry for me? That money will be there whether I marry now or ten years from now."

Robert looked away and reached for his coffee. He held the cup in front of his face a moment before taking a sip. "Why postpone choosing a suitable husband? There's nothing holding you back, is there? It makes no sense to wait, when the number of titles available to you will be the same, no matter the year."

Her eyes widened. He really believed she had no other consideration than the titles of the gentlemen she met. "What if no man offers for me?"

Fussing with his paper, Robert cleared his throat. "As I've said, I'll find you a husband if you do not." His thumb strummed the papers more rapidly.

He acted so strangely of late. Meeting with odd sorts like Sir Frederick, and avoiding others she thought much more likely to be counted among his friends. She remembered that afternoon at Newmarket when Robert had been surprised to see the men she now knew were Mr. Lumley and Knightwick, and again she wondered at the apparent bad feelings between them. But Robert no longer discussed his actions with her. No longer discussed much of anything with her.

She missed the days when they'd been close. While the duties he'd assumed upon their father's death had distanced him, Robert hadn't lived at home in Hurst Court Farm since she was twelve. Before then, he'd spent most of his time in the stables, as did she. They rode for hours together. He was the one who taught her to jump the hedgerows and kept that news from their mother, who would have spent a week in her room suffering from vapors had she known.

Robert had shown her the litter of bunnies nestled under the feed room floor, and gave her a fluffy, grey-striped kitten from a litter in the hayloft. He'd sent ribbons home from the shops near Oxford while classes were in session. And when he visited, he'd complimented the hideous creations she'd fashioned when adding them to her bonnets.

She sighed and took a bite of her cold, dry toast, chewing the tasteless morsel. Mama had been happy then, and Father won often enough at race meetings to keep a grin on his face. What had happened to them? Robert grew up. Father grew sullen, and then—

The toast caught in her throat, making her cough. She would not think of it now. "I'm going riding with Lady Hannah later." She rose from her chair, wondering why she bothered to inform Robert of her schedule. He never seemed to notice her presence or absence.

His face was hidden behind his newspaper once more. "Very well. Enjoy yourself."

DAVID RODE SILENTLY DOWN THE LONDON STREET BEHIND HIS sister and Lady Joanna, with her groom following behind. The young ladies gabbed and giggled over something he couldn't hear. He doubted he missed anything other than which gentleman had said what unpardonably tactless or shocking tidbit at the most recent ball. Lord, save him from such nattering.

He was in ill humor and had been since Triton's most recent defeat to Patriot. He didn't hold Lady Joanna responsible for the loss, in spite of how she claimed to have trained the horse. Surely, her brother only humored her when it came to such a fine creature. What could she really know about training a horse to race? Her mother never would have allowed her to spend her days in the paddock, instead of practicing her stitches and musical scales.

Hannah looked over her shoulder at him. "What do you think, David? Should not a young lady be allowed to choose her own husband?"

He puffed his cheeks full of air as it escaped his lips. There was a dangerous topic. He skirted a direct answer. "Of which lady do we speak? Surely Knightwick isn't threatening to marry you to the vicar, again."

Lady Joanna's laughter bubbled back to him. "What's this? Your brother believes you'd be happy with a man of the church?"

"No, he knows precisely how miserable I would be. That is why he threatens me. The vicar at Bridgethorpe is sixty if he's a day, and rumor has it, he's been engaged three times and the young ladies all broke it off before the day came. They say one eloped with the stable boy to escape her fate."

David shook his head. "Have you no standards, Hannah? You gossip about the vicar, of all people."

"I'm only relaying what I've heard to elucidate my objection to marrying him."

"Knightwick never meant for you to do so, and you know it. He'd never choose a husband for any of you girls. Besides, as long as Father lives, *he* will agree to the match, or not." His brother might be acting as head of the family, but neither he nor David was in any rush for him to be the head in actuality. "What brought this up? Lady Joanna, is your brother insisting on a certain man for you?" He blamed the sudden racing of his heart on his exasperation with his sister.

"No. Not as yet."

That sounded ominous. "You're still young. Isn't this your first Season? He can't expect you to make a choice in a matter of weeks."

She shrugged. "This is my second Season. But many ladies are betrothed that quickly. Lady Henrietta Galbraith has had three offers for her hand, already."

He guided his horse to ride beside the ladies, where the road permitted. "She has three thousand pounds, I believe. Wealthy young ladies don't always have the chance to marry for love, when some man's estate is failing and he finds her marriage portion attractive. Those beaux tend to act quickly. You two are lucky to be in the middle of the crowd, neither too rich nor ugly."

They both gasped, and he laughed. Hannah was an easy target for his barbs. He pretended to defend himself. "Which has you more outraged, that you don't have the largest dowries of the Season, or that I believe you to be among the prettiest ladies of any Season?"

He caught a hint of pink brightening Lady Joanna's cheek before she turned to look ahead. She was a good sport, someone he would not mind spending more time with. Perhaps Hannah would invite her to visit after they returned to Bridgethorpe. Lady Joanna would get on well with all his sisters.

Hannah snorted, reminding him how young she was. "Do

not let his falderal impress you. My brother thinks himself charming and humorous."

Lady Joanna met his eye, grinning at his wink. "I'm not likely to fall under his spell. I have a brother of my own, remember. You and I are less likely to make an unhappy match, I think, knowing their sex as we do."

The ladies grew quiet for a change, and David saw his chance to gain some information. "Oh, by the way, congratulations on Patriot's recent wins."

Her grin brightened her entire face. "Thank you, I'm very proud of him."

"Are you familiar with his lines? I might want to use him…ah, for future, ah…"

"Mr. Lumley, I've spent enough time in the stable to not blush at most of the words used there. Although, it appears you are not as comfortable with them."

He tugged at his cravat, knowing the warmth he felt had to be visible on his face. "Yes, well. I'm not in the habit of speaking of horses with ladies. I haven't heard that topic recommended for the ballroom."

"Which is partly why I often find balls so dull," she countered.

He tipped his head and studied her. Did she flirt with him? That would help his purpose. Yet the thought brought a heaviness to his chest. He wanted her interested, but not so much she'd be heartbroken when he had what he needed. Watching her ride beside him, her face alight with laughter at something Hannah had said, he knew he needed to solve the poisoning cases quickly.

Joanna sat in Lady Ellsworthy's parlor on a pleasant afternoon a few days later and looked once more at the cards in her hand. Her partner, Mr. Lumley, had her on edge and she found it very difficult to focus on the play. She lay down what she thought was the right card, then looked to Lady Hannah to make her move.

Mr. Lumley drummed his fingers on the table. "I believe I shall remove to the refreshment table whilst she attempts to make a decision." Yet he made no move to rise.

Lady Hannah rolled her eyes. "Perhaps if I were trying to find a card to please you, dear brother, I would take that long. But as I'm partnered with Mr. Whitmore, I can simply play the best card in my hand." She made her move.

Mr. Lumley promptly flipped down his own card and the play went on. He lifted his gaze to meet Joanna's and offered her a smile she recognized as genuine.

That was a good word for the man. *Genuine.* He had no airs about him, which was refreshing. She couldn't understand why men acted one way at a race meeting or in the stables, and altogether differently in a formal assembly. Of course, one polished one's manners to a certain degree at any formal event, but one's essential temperament should never change.

Some gentlemen, she'd discovered, had a different manner based on how lofty their hostess was, as if the wives of barons and bankers didn't deserve the same respect as did the wives of earls. One such man sat at a nearby table as the partner of Aunt Ophelia. His fawning comments often overpowered the conversation at Joanna's table.

"That is the perfect card you chose, Lady Ophelia," he said.

Joanna wrinkled her nose at Lady Hannah, who hid her grin behind her fingers. Mr. Lumley caught their exchange and shook his head, speaking *sotto-voce.* "Is he a friend of the family?"

"I've never met the man," Joanna confessed.

Mr. Lumley looked at the next table again, but said nothing.

Lady Hannah leaned close, whispering, "Ask me when we take a turn about the gardens later."

Her brother nodded. "I believe I'll be ready for fresh air when this hand is through. What say you, Whitmore?"

Whitmore nodded. "That would be wise, to walk before it becomes too chilly."

"Excellent, now we may finish this hand?" Mr. Lumley asked with a grumble, looking at his sister.

"The play just came my way. Do not blame me for holding you up. Honestly, David, I do not know why you come to play cards. There is no prize for the first table finished." She took her turn.

Mr. Lumley slapped down another card. "I must suggest such a variation to Mother the next time we invite our friends to play. It should liven up the evening."

"Are you suggesting you find our company dull?" Lady Hannah pierced him with her glare.

"No such thing. Whitmore and I've the good luck of being partnered with the prettiest ladies in attendance, and your wit's no less sparkling."

Joanna giggled softly and looked to see if their hostess could hear their discourse. Lady Ellsworthy wasn't known for her wit and might not appreciate the banter. "Come now, you two, you must get along, even if it pains you to be civil toward one another."

"I shall speak to you, Lady Joanna, and ignore my brother. That will keep the peace. Have you been to the King's Opera House yet? I saw a performance last week that was most enjoyable."

"No, I haven't been. Northcotte mentioned escorting me one evening, but he's been so very busy of late." Some nights, the light still burned in his study when she returned home from an assembly, but the door was always closed so she never entered.

"You should have him join you one evening when we'll be attending the same ball. He could keep David company while we enjoy ourselves." Lady Hannah looked from Joanna to her brother.

Joanna noticed Mr. Lumley's brows draw together briefly before she responded. "I'm afraid he's not much for dancing."

"Neither is David. It would be perfect."

Mr. Lumley cleared his throat. "I'm capable of choosing my own friends, minx. And I'm certain Northcotte would prefer to keep an eye on his sister, should he attend, much as I do."

Lady Hannah lifted one card in her hand, then another, as if indecisive. "You say such things, but how much trouble can we get into in a crowded ballroom with half the *ton* observing?"

"You'd be surprised," he grumbled.

Joanna coughed away the laughter that bubbled up inside her. Was Mr. Lumley thinking of his own exploits, or some scandal of past years? He didn't seem the type to take advantage of an innocent, but a good many less-than-innocent ladies frequented these balls. Imagining him with a light-skirt caused a band to form around her middle. She played her turn without taking the time to be certain it was the best move. Mr. Lumley's frown told her it probably wasn't.

Thankfully, the game ended soon, and she and Lady Hannah rose. The two gentlemen followed. Mr. Lumley came around the small table and offered his elbow. "Shall we tour the garden? I understand Lady Ellsworthy has some excellent statuary."

"Yes, that sounds pleasant." With her gloved hand on his arm, Joanna followed Lady Hannah and Mr. Whitmore out the French doors.

As they wandered past the marble benches and ornate fountain, a lovely arbor covered in lavender blooms came into view. Mr. Lumley inhaled deeply, then said, "Jasmine."

"I believe it's wisteria," Joanna replied.

"Wisteria in a perfume? Do you have it made especially for you?"

She realized then what he'd referred to. "Oh, I thought you meant the arbor. Yes, my perfume is jasmine." The heat that warmed her cheeks was silly. His taking notice of little things meant nothing. He'd done nothing to indicate his interest, other than dance with her on a regular basis and go riding with her and Lady Hannah several times. Should she make her interest more plain?

Walking next to him felt so natural. Their strides matched, and he was very attentive to where she stepped, to avoid ruining her white kid slippers. The warmth of him beside her offered an unusual comfort, similar to when she hugged Patriot. She smiled at that thought. What would he think if he knew she compared him to her horse?

Joanna chewed her lip. Mr. Lumley was fully aware of why she was in London, and that her brother had given her an ultimatum. She had to interpret the fact that he'd not pushed to deepen their acquaintance as his not wanting to do so. She needed to take a good look at the rest of the gentlemen at these assemblies and do what was needed to find a suitable husband. Before her brother found one for her.

"You're quiet."

She started, and offered him a small smile. "I'm sorry. I get lost in my thoughts sometimes."

"Where did they take you on such a pleasant afternoon?"

What should she say? She couldn't blurt out her fears about finding a husband. "Just reflecting on my time in London."

"Ah, yes, the high point of a young lady's year. Has it been everything you wished for? You've only been here a few weeks, but if your schedule has been anything like Hannah's, I imagine you've been busy every minute."

"It does seem that way. I suppose it's better than having no invitations at all, but I miss having a lazy afternoon to sit under a tree and read."

"You should schedule time for that, then. Hannah doesn't read much, but perhaps one of your other friends would enjoy taking a book to the park."

She had to press closer to him to avoid getting her gown caught on a rose bush. His arm came around her shoulders, whether to steady her or him, she wasn't certain. Her skin heated from the contact, which ended too soon for her liking. When he stood that close, she could smell his soap, and the sweetness of punch on his breath. If he kissed her, would he taste as sweet? She couldn't resist looking at his lips and licking her own.

He groaned, or cleared his throat, and shifted slightly to put some distance between them. Obviously, he wasn't as affected by her nearness as she was. She sighed and quickened her pace to catch up to Lady Hannah.

DAVID LET JOANNA HURRY AHEAD AND TOOK A MOMENT TO compose himself. When she'd licked her lips, his muscles had tightened in need. He tugged at his cravat and shut out the image of her tongue pressed against that pale pink skin. Kissing her wasn't part of the plan, no matter how tempting she was.

And she tempted him mercilessly. He could no longer convince himself his interest in her was purely to discover what connection Northcotte had to the poisonings. By now, he couldn't recall why he'd ever thought she would know anything. Or why befriending her would help him find the answers he sought.

He was such a fool. Yet he'd had nothing to compare their friendship to. His relations with willing widows were all aboveboard, both parties understanding sex was the only connection between them. He had no female friends, other than those young ladies he knew through his sisters or were family connections. Plainly, he had no real understanding what spending time with Lady Joanna would do to him.

He liked her. Enjoyed her laughter and discovering what she was thinking. He was genuinely concerned that she could be forced to marry Sir Frederick.

He shook his head. He wasn't supposed to develop feelings for her. His scheme did not involve falling for her. And he hadn't really considered what would happen to her when he walked away after learning what he needed to know.

This was a bad scheme all around. As David lengthened his stride and closed the distance between him and the other three, he decided he needed to find a resolution that would be kind to Lady Joanna. Before she was hurt.

CHAPTER NINE

*P*acing the fading Turkish carpet in her chamber, Joanna wrung her hands and contemplated the evening ahead. Molly clutched a strand of pearls to her chest, her eyes pleading. Joanna shook her head. "I won't wear any jewels. It's bad enough Robert has forced me to attend this evening. Sir Frederick! Molly, have you seen the man? I'm not shallow enough to complain over his looks. If I could believe his manner was lacking due to ignorance, I should not belittle him. He's so arrogant, yet completely unaware of how a gentleman behaves."

"Yes, my lady, so you've said. But please, his lordship insists I make certain you look your best whenever you go out."

"And you have done your best, Molly. Should he complain, I'd inform my brother you're not to blame if he finds anything about me lacking. I truly doubt he'll notice, though. He will have Lady Barbara on his arm. He'll not see me."

Molly set down the pearls and picked up several hairpins.

"Will you allow me to at least secure your curls? I couldn't bear it if your coiffure fell before you returned home."

Joanna paused, her arms folded in front of her, her gaze fixed on the mirror. Molly was proud of her station, and Joanna's appearance reflected on her servant. No matter how badly she wished to appear plain and undesirable, it wasn't fair of her to injure Molly's reputation in the process. "Do what you must. But please, don't do it too well."

A knock sounded on the door. Molly opened it and Joanna saw one of the younger footmen standing in the hallway. He cleared his throat. "His lordship wishes to know if you're ready. Sir Frederick has arrived, and the gentlemen are waiting in the study."

"Thank you, Thomson. Please inform his lordship I shall be down presently."

He nodded and scurried away, showing his youth in his speed and lack of decorum. Molly closed the door and returned to Joanna, pushing a few more pins into the bun. "There, that should hold."

Joanna offered a smile she didn't feel. "Thank you. You may go now, get some rest before I need you to help me undress later."

"Yes, my lady."

Joanna's hand hesitated over the perfume bottles. Her favorite bergamot-laden scent calmed her immensely. She would prefer to wear it but didn't wish Sir Frederick to think she'd worn anything to please him. The heavier French fragrance would never do. For a moment, she wished she could run to the stables, rub her hand in some horse sweat and apply it liberally, but the moment passed quickly. Robert would not find the humor in the action.

Skipping any sort of fragrance, she rose, picked up her pelisse and went to face her doom. An entire evening listening to Sir Frederick speak on whatever he deemed suitable conversation. Remembering their exchange on the dance floor that one evening, she suddenly feared he would say nothing the entire night. People would talk about her strange escort who ignored her.

She found her brother and Sir Frederick sharing a drink. They both rose and bowed when she entered.

Robert smiled. "There you are. I was growing concerned."

"I am ready, as you see. How do you do, Sir Frederick?"

"I'm well. Shall we be off? I understand the traffic will be quite heavy."

Apparently, he didn't frequent The King's Theatre, if his only knowledge of the traffic was secondhand. Steeling her nerves, she took his arm and walked with him to the carriage waiting outside. Thankfully, they were taking her brother's carriage and picking up Lady Barbara on the way. At no time would she be alone with Sir Frederick and subjected to whatever whims he might have for after the opera. Lady Barbara was always pleasant company, and Joanna looked forward to that part of the evening.

Once they entered the opera house and found Sir Frederick's box, or the one he'd borrowed the use of for the evening, Joanna made certain Lady Barbara sat beside her. "Have you heard Puccita's work?" Joanna asked.

"No, but I understand it's very moving."

"This will be my first time, also," Joanna said.

Sir Frederick leaned their way. "I was under the impression Mozart's operas are much better. When performed in English, however."

"How interesting." Joanna unfurled her fan, giving it a nervous flutter.

"It's an obvious thought," he continued. "What's the point of them singing in a language one doesn't understand?"

Joanna's eyes widened. She caught Lady Barbara's equally

astonished gaze. "Sometimes the emotion of the words comes through, regardless of the language."

"Most who suggest they understand the Italian operas are pretentious fools." Sir Frederick's nose rose with his haughtiness.

She couldn't bring herself to respond. She only wished Robert had heard. She turned back to Lady Barbara. "Were you at Lady Faraday's musicale last week?"

The petite brunette shook her head. "I had other plans."

Robert added, "We attended a reading. It was quite interesting, or so I thought."

"Yes," Lady Barbara added. "The gentleman speaker had only recently returned from the Colonies. He'd spent six years among the natives there, learning their customs. They are quite civilized, I was surprised to learn."

Sir Frederick grunted. "I've seen paintings of the men. I can't call face paint and breechcloths 'civilized.'"

"Just a few years back, half of London wore face paint with their powdered wigs," Joanna said, trying to keep the hiss of disdain from her voice. She would not lower herself to his level.

"That is quite a different matter," he argued. "We were fully clothed, besides."

Luckily, the curtain opened as the orchestra began to play. The first act was a ballet, the fluid moves beautiful to observe. The box in which they sat was situated to the rear of the theatre, in the fifth level, just below the gallery. From there, most of the audience was visible. Joanna wasn't surprised to discover most of the attendees spent more time watching the other occupants of the boxes than the performance. More of the *ton* would be interested in who sat with whom, when inquiring about an evening at the Theatre, than how the dancers appeared.

From the corner of her eye, Joanna saw her brother lean

close to Lady Barbara and whisper something that made them both smile. For the first time, it struck Joanna her brother might be looking for a wife. He'd never said as much, but he likely would not until he'd spoken with the lady's father. Lady Barbara would make a nice enough sister. Robert seemed much more at ease this evening. The line between his brows was barely visible, and he smiled often. Perhaps, if Joanna were lucky, Robert finding his own match might take some of the pressure off her. He might allow her another Season, or at least the trip to Bath with their aunt.

Sir Frederick blew his nose into his handkerchief, then shoved the cloth into his pocket. He stared at the stage, not acknowledging Joanna's presence, if he was at all aware of her. No whispered comments from him, no shared secrets. Why did he even bother to ask her to attend, if he had no interest in getting to know her? Would he be as cold and... well, tightly bound, with his wife?

She couldn't imagine sitting at the supper table with him every evening, much less sharing closer quarters. Robert couldn't think she and Sir Frederick suited in any way. She searched for a reason her brother would insist she consider the man, but none came to mind.

There could be no reason she would ever consider marrying him. The very idea made her stomach churn.

To cheer herself up, she tried to imagine life with Mr. Lumley. Laughter in the morning room over coffee. Discussions on which foals looked the most promising. Afternoons spent riding in the paddocks. Evenings...she fluttered her fan to combat the sudden warmth of the box where she sat, and remembered where she was. The first act hadn't ended, so her woolgathering most likely hadn't been noticed by the others.

Lady Barbara leaned toward Robert as his head lowered. Joanna sighed. She wished she could find someone with whom she could share tête-à-têtes. The more time she spent in London, it seemed, the lonelier she felt.

~

DESCENDING THE STAIRS EARLY THE NEXT MORNING, JOANNA hoped to find Robert still at home. He was in the dining room hidden behind the newspaper. Joanna poured herself some chocolate from the pot at her place and took a sip. "When do you leave for the Goodwood Race Meeting?"

"At the end of the week."

"I wish to come with you. I miss how we used to attend the meetings together as a family."

She heard his sigh, but he didn't lower the paper. "Now isn't the time to be leaving Town. Perhaps you could join me at the July meeting in Newmarket."

"That is two months away. I don't know how I'll survive an entire Season without seeing Patriot race. I wish to speak to Bruce about Patriot and be certain he's still handling him correctly."

Now the newspaper lowered. Robert looked down his nose at her. "When did you develop this melodramatic affectation? You have missed many race meetings since Father died."

"Not by choice. And not since Patriot became old enough to race." Joanna took another drink to break eye contact. She was no longer comfortable letting him see what was important to her. No longer certain he wished her to have what she wanted.

"No matter. And Bruce is no longer Patriot's groom. He died."

Her throat clamped shut. "What? How? When?"

"At the First Spring Race Meeting. Apparently, whatever made him too ill to race killed him."

"That can't be." Joanna's eyes welled, but she blinked away the tears and drew in a breath. "He was exceptionally good with Patriot."

"His new groom has him performing well. He's won several races, as you know."

"Who did you put with him? Patriot is very particular about whom he works with."

"A new man. Wilfred Winkler."

She tried to picture the man but drew a blank. "I don't know him."

"As I said, he's new. But I'm quite satisfied with him." Robert took a drink of his coffee. "Once you have settled on a husband, I'll allow you to leave London, if you prefer. Or, I can settle it for you this very day, and you may come with me to Goodwood."

Her stomach plummeted. His abrupt manner didn't bode well. "Someone has offered for me? Why haven't you said anything?"

After patting his lips with his napkin, Robert met her gaze. "I still have hopes you will present an agreeable gentleman to me, so I may tell this other suitor to look else-where for a wife."

She gritted her teeth. It couldn't be the one she feared, but why else would her brother continue to allow this man to see her? "Who is it?"

"You must suspect. It's Sir Frederick."

Her skin grew warm and damp. An unpleasant rumbling churned the chocolate in her stomach. "Why did you say nothing when I told you he'd spoken as if we were already betrothed? You led me to think he was merely being fanciful. But if he's asked for permission to approach me and you did not tell him to be gone, he must assume your consent."

Robert's lips pressed tightly together. "There is more to it than that, but I'm not in a position to discuss it with you."

"If not you, then who? You are my guardian."

"Yes, which means I am looking out for your best interests. It does not imply I must inform you of all the dealings I undertake as Earl of Northcotte."

She sat back in her chair. He made no sense. "We are discussing my marriage, not the running of the estate."

"The lives of all of us, Mother, you, myself, are connected to the estate in a multitude of ways. In my case, it will continue until my death. For you and Mother, it could alternately end by marriage."

Joanna shook her head, not understanding. "You don't expect Mama to marry again, when she rarely leaves her room since Father died. Even attending the First Spring Meeting was too much for her to bear, and she's been in her room since we returned. She will never recover from the loss of her beloved husband."

"It hurts me to see her thus. I would never force her to leave our home, or to marry, but I do believe she would be happier with companionship. If she met a widower with no need of an heir, they might console each other in their remaining years."

Their aunt came to mind, with her desire to remarry, and Joanna could see his suggestion came from a place of love. She also wished their mother would be happy again.

Still, he'd said their lives were connected to the estate. That meant financially, she was sure. Were they in financial straits? No one had ever said anything. They hadn't made any changes to their lifestyle in the years after Father died.

But how would marrying her off quickly save any money? Her pin money was a negligible amount. That hadn't bothered her because she had no need for new bonnets, laces or reticules. Before they came to London, she was quite happy to wear last year's dress to assemblies in the local village. No one there looked down on her for being dressed in anything less than the height of fashion.

Mama had most likely been pleased when Joanna wore something other than her riding costume and boots.

No matter how Joanna looked at it, she could see no way her marriage would improve her brother's financial situation. And she couldn't think of another reason for Robert's urgency. She didn't care enough to consider the matter further, for all she wanted at the moment was to be with Patriot. She drew in a deep breath and let it out slowly. "If I promise to make a choice soon, may I go to Goodwood?"

"Joanna, my decision had been made."

Those were Father's words, and they brooked no discussion. She folded her arms across her chest and wrinkled her nose, grateful Robert had the paper in front of him. She wished she were young enough to get away with sticking her tongue out at him. He treated her like a child, so at times like this she wanted to act like one.

THIS ENTIRE GAME OF FINDING A HUSBAND WAS TOO DULL TO keep her interest. She told Amelia so when they trotted on horseback together down Rotten Row that afternoon. "I was so excited to come to Town, but all the gilt of my expectations has tarnished. I thought I would have suitors. I dreamed men would be lined up to fill my dance card and come calling in the afternoon to find out where I would be that evening."

"But they have been," Amelia replied. "Perhaps not droves of gentlemen, but more than one or two. Mama says the wars have taken away too many young men. In her day, there were many more eligible men in the Marriage Mart. Now, it seems they are all older widowers looking for mothers for their children. What of Mr. Lumley? Has he not revealed his intentions?"

"He has not. And he will be gone for the next sennight at a race meeting. I can only assume he has no intentions beyond entertaining himself while his sister shops the marriage mart."

"I don't believe that for a minute. I've seen the way he looks at you."

"Well, unless his looks are very suggestive and he does them in front of Northcotte, I've no hope of marrying him." She reined her mare to a walk when they approached other riders. "I want to go back to my life before London."

"Leave Town, you mean? Where would you go? Anyone who is worth notice is here during the Season."

Except Mr. Lumley, when his horses were entered in a race, Joanna thought. "Patriot is racing at Goodwood next week. I miss him and would enjoy watching him run again. I hate not seeing him win. It's not the same, reading it in the papers."

Amelia's laughter rang out. "You would leave all these marriageable young men for a horse?"

"There are men worth marrying at the race meetings, too. And I've a common interest with those gentlemen, outside of the desire for a family."

Her friend turned to look at her. "Oh, I understand, now. Your Mr. Lumley will be at Goodwood."

"He isn't my Mr. Lumley, didn't I just explain that? And yes, he will be there. He mentioned that his brother, Hugh, would be attending some of the assemblies with Lady Hannah in his absence."

"Oh, that one. Why does Knightwick never attend? I would love to dance with him. I hear he moves divinely. When you marry Mr. Lumley, will you put in a good word for me with Knightwick?" Amelia's laughter was contagious, and altogether too loud for polite society. Joanna loved it.

"I shall be sure to do so. But first, I must capture Mr. Lumley's heart. If only I could slip away without Northcotte noticing."

"Won't your brother be at Goodwood? You'd be seen. You need another scheme."

Joanna shrugged, a gesture Mama hated. "Another dream, you mean. Another gentleman's heart to steal, and soon."

"The Season isn't half gone yet, you have time."

"No, I haven't." She glanced about to make sure no one was within hearing distance before continuing. "Northcotte is getting anxious for me to marry. Sir Frederick has spoken to him about marrying me, but my brother put him off."

Amelia groaned. "It can't be true. No one's family could ever support a match with that man. What does he have to offer that might tempt Northcotte?"

"I don't know. A horse, perhaps? That would make sense. Northcotte mentioned some financial concerns. A winning racer would bring in needed funds."

"Your brother would trade you for a horse?"

Joanna ducked her head. "I don't wish to believe it. He loves me. He's a good brother. But he's changed so much since he inherited, I no longer feel I know him completely."

CHAPTER TEN

*D*avid sat in his room in the inn near the Duke of Richmond's estate where the Goodwood Race Meetings were held. The heavy fog outside kept the small space in darkness, which didn't help David's mood. He was on edge and blamed it on the upcoming race. "I hope this clears before the meeting begins. We can't have any horses going off course, and how will the judge be able to tell who won?"

His brother, Knightwick, shook his head, looking at David as if he were quite mad. "They won't hold the race until they can do so fairly."

"I'm not so sure. It seems the fates have it in for Triton. What if the judge can't see the jockey?"

"I don't think the orange and yellow Peter will be wearing can be missed, even in a fog."

David rose and stretched. "I hate waiting for the meetings to begin."

"You're more restless than Triton when he's in his stall. I swear, he can smell the pending competition."

"He knows the routine. Strange paddocks, strange stalls, familiar horses nearby. It all adds up to being allowed to run."

"Now, if he could run a bit faster and win some of the more important races, I'd be quite pleased with him."

Turning to confront his brother, David said, "You aren't pleased with his performance? He's the best runner we've had since Zephyr."

Knightwick lifted his hands, palms out. "I'm not displeased, but more wins would be preferable. He needs wins to increase his value as a stud."

"He'll have the wins. He loves to run, loves to compete. He just has the bad luck of always coming up against Northcotte's Patriot."

"Perhaps you should run Triton in the northern meetings."

Pacing back to the window, David pushed the heavy, wheat-colored damask curtain aside. "I've the impression wherever I run Triton, Northcotte will have his horse there. He's determined to destroy us."

"Are you certain that's his aim? The rivalry was between our fathers. His is now dead, and ours never attends a meeting." Knightwick absently polished the toe of his boot with his handkerchief.

"I think he's carrying on where his father left off. Who else would have tried to poison our horses last year? No one had anything to gain from it."

"I'm not certain we can blame Zephyr's death on Northcotte. I thought you were searching for proof, not trying to bring down the earl."

David slumped into the empty chair. "That was my first intention. However, the longer I've searched without finding evidence I know exists, the more I see I might never prove the Hursts were behind the killing. But if I can keep Northcotte from profiting from it, keep Patriot from winning, I can get revenge for Father."

Knightwick rested his elbows on his knees, pressing his thumbs and forefingers together as he sat quietly. "Do you hear yourself? What's this talk of revenge? Has Father ever asked you to seek it?"

"Well, no. Not in so many words. But look at him. Look at how broken he has become. He's an empty shell of a man wandering through his waking hours, enjoying nothing."

"And you think seeing Northcotte fail will restore him?"

David leaned back, throwing his weight on one elbow on the arm of the chair. "I hadn't thought of it that way. I believed having a winning runner again would give him joy."

"I don't believe he's capable of feeling joy any longer. He speaks to me of starting my nursery, but not with the excitement I expect to see in his eyes at the mention of grandchildren. He seems to be putting his affairs in order. I think his health is failing, not his mind."

"Well, can you expect any less after Aunt and Uncle Lumley died last year? He must be intensely aware of his own mortality."

"As the earl, he's always been aware of the need to continue our line. Why should he suddenly feel as though it's in danger of dying off? I'm only weeks past my thirtieth birthday. And there are three of you in the family to inherit, should I fail to produce an heir. Not to mention all the cousins we have."

David smiled. "That would never do, letting the earldom fall to me, or Hugh, or Sam. You will need to step up at some point and marry, you know."

Straightening in his seat, Knightwick pushed his hair off his forehead. "At some point, perhaps. But I've little time to think of it now, with keeping all of father's properties running. Cousin Stephen will be moving into Hambleton

Cottage after his wedding next month, did I tell you? He will act as Father's steward there."

"That is good news. He knows farming, but working the land his father left him must be difficult with his injuries. Perhaps he will learn to delegate as a steward. But now that I think on it, I thought he was moving to Yorkshire to be near his mills?"

"Jane couldn't tolerate the climate. Hambleton is only a few hours ride from her parents' home. She will be able to visit often."

"That will make Hannah happy. She was quite upset over losing her friend."

"You don't suppose Hannah will take the location of a man's property into consideration when she gets a marriage offer, do you? I highly doubt it will matter where he lives, if she's in love."

David jumped to his feet, unable to sit still. "Don't mention her marrying. I'm still not certain I care for the thought of some man pawing at her."

Knightwick laughed. "You must make an excellent chaperone for her, then. Mother must be quite at ease knowing you're attending the same assemblies. Have you considered doubling your efforts and finding a wife while you're there? Now that you've seen the available ladies, I mean."

"I've too much on my mind to think about ladies."

"That's not what Hannah writes."

David paused in mid-step. "What has she said?"

"She mentioned one miss in particular. Lady Joanna Hurst, I believe. She said you've been spending a lot of time with her."

Grimacing, David muttered, "I suppose she neglected to tell you she was present each time I saw Lady Joanna? And that I was acting as chaperone for our sister."

"I suppose she did say something of the sort. But she

remarked you seemed to find the lady's company quite enjoyable."

"She's a very pleasant conversationalist. And since she's Northcotte's sister, you can get any notion of a friendship out of your mind. I've been questioning her about her brother's stable."

"Of course. I should have guessed, knowing how much time a lady of marriageable age spends discussing stud servicing and foaling. Not to mention nefarious plots to poison the best runners in England," Knightwick said with a smirk.

"If you thought otherwise, you haven't met this lady. She claims Northcotte lets her train his runners."

Knightwick's grin spread. "And I let Patience and Madeleine take the reins of the gig sometimes on the road by the house. But it doesn't mean I'd ask their opinion when it came to choosing horseflesh."

David raised an eyebrow. Knightwick had no idea just how knowledgeable Lady Joanna was about horses. But any words David said in her favor would be taken as a sign of affection for her, and he couldn't admit to having such feelings. "The truth is, I've had a change of heart regarding using her for information. She's a very sweet girl, much like Hannah. I'd kill any man who toyed with her affections as I've been doing. I need to find a way to end this. It's quite ironic, actually. If I were searching for a wife, I can see where a lady with her passion for runners would be the perfect choice."

Knightwick nodded. "Hannah has said as much herself. Maybe you should give up this obsession of yours for revenge, and get to know Lady Joanna better. You might not find another woman as suitable later on."

Shaking his head, David returned to the window to stare at the fog. The grudge between himself and Northcotte was too large. Even if he allowed his feelings for Lady Joanna to blossom, their relationship would be fraught with tension between the men. She deserved happiness. "It would never work between us. If she found out why I sought her out, she'd never forgive me. What worries me is that her brother apparently wants to marry her off to Sir Frederick Aldwen."

"The money lender? There's only one reason anyone would ever consider that bounder for a husband. Northcotte must be in deep straits."

David shoved his hair off his forehead. "I cringe at the thought of that man touching her."

"You have become attached, whether you'll admit it or not. So, what will you do about it? Beyond dropping your scheme to bring her brother down."

"If he's in debt to Sir Frederick, he doesn't need my help in bringing him down. But marry her? I don't think I'm ready for such a step." He was not. The fear of her ending up with Sir Frederick probably made his feelings seem stronger than what they were.

Well, that and the obvious reaction his body had to her. But lust and fear did not make for a happy marriage.

ONCE THE FOG BURNED OFF, CARRIAGES AND RIDERS GATHERED at the Goodwood racecourse, a straight length of six furlongs measured off on the Duke of Richmond's estate. Excitement bristled in the air as people discussed which horses were favored to win, and what the odds were on the long shots. David sat upon the broad back of Nemo, the retired runner he used during racing season, when Triton had to be kept in condition or was at a race. Nemo had adjusted to the fact he no longer raced, but at times, he still grew skittish as if he recognized the activity around him.

Knightwick sat on his horse next to David at the end of the course, where the majority of the crowd was. There were no stands, so viewers sat in their carriages or on horseback, while some sat on Trundle, the Iron Age hill fort that rose above the Downs.

David rose in the stirrups to look down the course. "What's keeping them?"

"Perhaps they had trouble getting the horses lined up to start," Knightwick suggested.

As he waited, David noticed a familiar face across the lane. He motioned to his brother. "Is that Tom Edwards?"

Knightwick waved at the man in question. "It is. I haven't seen him since last year at this meeting." Edwards returned the greeting.

David glanced back down the road, looking for the racers. "I'd like to speak to Edwards after this race. He's been at most of the race meetings I've over the years. He might have heard something about the poisonings."

Raising an eyebrow, Knightwick asked, "You aren't leaving it to the constable to solve?"

"Whoever killed Zephyr has gotten away with it. I can't sit by and do nothing."

A roar broke out down the course. A short time later, the lead three horses came into view. David strained to see around the carriage parked next to them. The lead horse was large and brown. Patriot. Triton was half a length back. "Come on, boy," David encouraged softly.

"Run, come on," Knightwick called out.

Triton closed on Patriot. A neck behind, then his nose reached Patriot's ear. He continued to surge. At the line, Triton's head was fully out front. The judge called Fernleigh's colors as the winner. David threw his hat up in the air. "Yes! He did it!"

He and his brother clapped each other on the back.

"Good run," Knightwick said, his voice thick with pride. "Father will be pleased."

Yes, they had more good news for their father. David accepted the congratulations of the people around him, then told his brother he'd return shortly. He led Nemo across the lane in search of Edwards and found him not far from where he'd watched the race, now in the shade of a large horse-chestnut tree.

As David approached, Edwards called out, "Congratulations, Lumley. That's a fine runner you have this year."

"Thank you. We're quite pleased with Triton. He's nowhere near where Zephyr was as a three-year-old, but he's good."

"There aren't many like Zephyr," Edwards agreed. "How's Bridgethorpe faring? I never see him at the race meetings."

"No, he hasn't felt up to attending." David held back the full details, not comfortable sharing them with just anyone.

"And what of his nephew, the Lumley boy who bought his colors?"

"Stephen was injured and came home from the war last year, just after his parents died."

Edwards nodded, stroking his chin. "I'd forgotten about that, your family's loss. Poor lad. I don't believe I've met him, but the wife knew his mum. Has Stephen healed now?"

"As much as possible. You may tell Mrs. Edwards he's marrying soon and making a new life for himself."

"She'll be glad to hear it."

David steered the conversation in the direction he'd come to discuss. "Did you hear about the groom who died at the First Spring meeting?"

"I did. My wife worried I brought home some horrible illness when she heard."

"Did they decide his death was natural?"

Edwards' mouth pursed to one side, and he scratched behind his ear. "Can't say if I've heard what he died of."

"I was more concerned he might have been poisoned. Someone either wanted him dead, or he accidentally drank what was meant for one of the horses."

"You think someone is killing our runners? I know they decided the water was tainted at Chester last year, but they never came out and said who they thought the target was."

"Two of our horses were sickened, along with three others. And Zephyr was poisoned years ago. I think the target is pretty obvious."

Edwards frowned. "I hate to think someone out there is killing perfectly sound horseflesh. What are you planning to do about it?"

David shrugged. "There isn't much I can do unless they solve that groom's murder. In the meantime, I'm asking around to see if anyone has heard anything."

"I'll keep an ear open and let you know if I do."

"I appreciate it." The sound of a horn rang out in the distance calling the next entrants to the starting post. David nodded to the older man. "Please give your wife our best. I know my mother would send it."

"And you carry the same back to her, and tell Bridgethorpe his old chum misses him at the meetings. Good luck with Triton, he's a good sound runner."

David urged Nemo across the lane to fill in Knightwick on what he'd learned. When his brother returned home after the races, he could inform their father they were going to hunt down Zephyr's killer one way or another. And with any luck, Father would find some joy in his life again.

If asked later about the ride to London after the Goodwood race, David wasn't certain he could have described the weather, the road, or anyone he and Knightwick might have passed along the way. His head was in the clouds with Triton's win. He glanced at his brother, whose face also gleamed with pleasure. "I must school my features before I see Mother, or she'll think I'm in prime form to be introduced to the daughters of her friends."

"She hasn't already done so? How have you avoided that?"

"I'm not quite certain. She seems more concerned with making certain Hannah meets the right men."

"Or perhaps she thinks you've already met the right young lady."

David frowned. "There you go again. I've already stated my feelings toward her."

"You gave me all the reasons why you and Lady Joanna would not suit, but not once did you deny your attraction."

Opening his mouth to do just that, David found the words stuck in his craw. He coughed. "How could I not be attracted? She's lovely, vivacious. Do you know, at the First Spring Meeting she tried to convince Northcotte to let her ride Patriot when her groom took ill?"

Knightwick chuckled. "She sounds like Hannah. That could prove quite a handful as a wife. I think I'd prefer someone more refined."

"A hothouse lily, you mean? You don't think that would grow dull?" "With all the ups and downs of running an estate, quiet, tedious evenings would be refreshing."

He supposed he could understand the sentiment, but the excitement coursing through him at the moment kept him from finding it appealing. "I enjoy the challenges that arise at Fernleigh. I realize one stud property doesn't compare to all of Father's lands. But I think having a wife who is always agreeable would get dull."

"Be careful what you ask for…"

"Just to be clear, I'm not looking for a harpy." David wiped at the sweat trickling down his hairline.

"What are you looking for?"

"I haven't given it a whole lot of thought. Mother mentioned a horsewoman such as Lady Joanna would suit me well."

"You had this discussion with Mother? What were you thinking?" Knightwick cast him a shocked glance.

"She brought it up. I think she was trying to discern my intentions."

"She opened the door and you walked through. You realize once you crossed that threshold you can't go back. In Mother's eyes, you are seeking a wife now."

David grimaced. "But I'm not. I've no need for one. You aren't married yet."

"That has no bearing on your life. It's an excuse. Why are you waiting?"

There was a good question. Why wasn't he considering marriage, now that he'd met a lady who would fit so perfectly into his life? The quick and easy answer arose: the conflict between his family and hers. But was that enough to keep them apart?

They weren't the Montagues and Capulets. Their fathers had never come to blows or exchanged cross words in the years David had attended race meetings with Father. At most, harsh glares punctuated their lack of conversation.

Only one thing potentially stood between him and Lady Joanna. "What if Northcotte refuses to give his blessing?"

"Then you must decide whether to sneak off to Gretna Green or walk away from her." Knightwick shifted in his saddle, stretching his legs. "But once more you're avoiding the only question that matters. Do you love the lady? Do you want nothing more from life than her eternal happiness?"

"Northcotte is apparently considering letting her marry Sir Frederick. I would not wish that on any young lady. She would be miserable. Perhaps I should make an offer to keep her from that fate."

"Avoiding…"

"She's very good with foals. I would appreciate her opinion on some breeding decisions."

"Still avoiding."

"Very well! I admit it, I enjoy being with her. I look forward to seeing her smile when she first sees me. I find myself thinking of ways to make her laugh. But is that love, or am I simply encouraging her to stroke my ego?"

"It's certainly a good start. I'm obviously the wrong person to tell you what love feels like. You're the only one who can say if your feelings are enough to make you certain you can't live without her."

Live without Lady Joanna. Sit back and let her marry Sir Frederick and bear him children. Wait until the mood struck David to start a nursery and choose the first available debutant in London. Is that what he wanted?

A bitter taste filled David's mouth at the idea of Sir Frederick touching her, having control over her. Realizing much of what he felt was a protective instinct, he knew he couldn't walk away from Lady Joanna. However, he did have feelings for her, to whatever degree, and she would make him a good wife. If he didn't love her now, he would in time. Of that, he was certain.

Now he needed to convince her—and her brother—he was the perfect husband for her.

CHAPTER ELEVEN

*J*oanna stood beside Aunt Ophelia in yet another glamorous ballroom, this one decorated in Greek fashion with fake columns and large stone urns spaced out along the walls. Enormous ferns, small citrus trees, and palms planted in the urns broke up the harsh white decor. Although the guests weren't required to wear masks, they all wore Grecian gowns and togas. Joanna had laurel leaves pinned among the braids wrapped around her head. Her gown, only one side of which came over her shoulder, was a ridiculous garment. The braided gold cord that nipped in the flowing gown at her waist was the only thing keeping her from looking as if she wore a burlap sack. Or a fine linen one. Her sandals, with their ribbons wrapped up her ankles, were a bit of a treat, however. They felt almost as if she were barefoot in public, quite scandalous, and one she found she liked. It would not do to wear such shoes around the horses, though.

Amelia and Lady Hannah were dressed in a similar fashion. The two young ladies joined her in observing the growing crowd before the dancing began. Rising on her toes to look over the shoulders around them, Amelia asked, "Has anyone seen Sir Richard?"

"I haven't." Joanna was more concerned about another man's presence. Lady Hannah hadn't mentioned which of her brothers had accompanied her, but it was quite possible Mr. David Lumley had returned from Goodwood by now.

As Joanna thought this, another brother, Hugh appeared and bowed to them. "Ladies, you all look well. Who has room for me on their dance cards?"

He was a kind young man, Joanna admitted, but still had a bit of youthful padding to his face, and fair-colored side-whiskers sparse enough to make one wonder if he were required to shave more than once a week. He was a bit ungraceful on the dance floor, but always made her laugh at his wit. "I've some dances open. Which do you prefer?"

Hugh reserved a dance from each of them and moved on to find other partners. Joanna resigned herself to another ball without Mr. Lumley and prayed Sir Frederick wasn't in attendance. That would make a bad evening worse by tenfold. Or more.

Joanna laughed at something Amelia said, then she heard a familiar chuckle behind her. She turned, suddenly warm and trembling, holding back the excited grin his voice always brought. "Mr. Lumley, I see you've returned safely from the race meeting. Congratulations on your win."

He bowed over her hand. "Thank you. Patriot gave us a good run for our money. It's grand to finally beat your horse."

Her lips trembled with restraint as she tilted her head to one side. "No modesty in the win? I see you're more the type to gloat." She bit the inside of her cheek, trying hard to maintain a stern affect.

"The next time Triton bests Patriot, you can be assured

I'll be all that is polite. But for the moment, yes, I'm going to gloat and take in all the glory I can."

"Yes, because we, as owners, are due all the glory of the work our horses put in."

His eyes lit with laughter. "Just so. I've taken every step alongside that animal as he learned to run fast. I must say I'm quite done in."

"Perhaps you should enter yourself at the next race meeting. I'm sure your pedigree would stand alongside those of the horses."

He folded his arms over his chest. "All right, I admit I'm still a bit giddy with the win. You must know what I'm feeling. Or has all the excitement disappeared due to the number of wins Patriot has earned?"

She understood exactly what he described. "It's not the number of wins that dulls the pleasure, it's being unable to be there to see him win."

His smile faded slightly. "Ah, yes, I hadn't considered that. From what you've told me, Northcotte feels your presence is required in London. Well, there are only a few more meetings before the Season ends, and perhaps then you'll be able to attend at your leisure."

Only a few more race meetings also meant only a few more weeks to find a suitable husband or be forced to marry Sir Frederick. This seemed the perfect opportunity for Mr. Lumley to hint that he considered himself among her prospective choices, yet he said nothing.

She sighed and looked over the crowded room once more. The fates were unfair to her, to be sure. Why taunt her with such a specimen and not let him be available for the taking? It only served to make the rest of the choices that much less palatable.

"Is the supper dance still available?" Mr. Lumley asked.

"Yes, it's free."

"Lovely. It shall be mine, then." He bent to speak around her to the other ladies. "And what of you both? Did you save me a dance?"

"I've several open as yet," Amelia answered.

Lady Hannah wrinkled her nose. "Must I fill my card with my brother's names? I'm not so ugly as to need the assistance of family to not appear a wallflower."

Mr. Lumley shook his head. "If you prefer not to dance with the most handsome gentleman in attendance, which is your choice. It will allow me another hand in the card room."

Joanna and Amelia laughed at his conceit, which Joanna knew to be false. As tempted as she was to put him in his place and offer to release him from their dance so he might spend the entire evening at cards, she was too selfish. She wanted to spend every possible moment with him, just to have the memories to carry her through whatever life had in store for her.

It was the wrong thing to do. She should put that time into getting to know other gentlemen. Into letting other gentlemen see what a desirable companion she was. But she had no heart left for the hunt, having seen what she couldn't have. She was grateful when her first partner stole her away from her friends and led her off to dance.

DAVID CLASPED HIS HANDS TOGETHER BEHIND HIS BACK AND willed his body to stop trembling. He wasn't prone to nerves, so he convinced himself, almost, the quaking inside him was due to excitement. Having given himself permission to let his feelings be known to Lady Joanna, he couldn't wait to get started.

He had no idea where to begin. He couldn't just blurt out some poetic words. He needed to demonstrate his interest in a more marked fashion than he'd been doing all along. His interest early on was forced, but if he made too large a turn-around, it might encourage her to reflect on the reason for the differences.

When Lady Joanna moved to the dance floor on the arm of her dance partner, and the other ladies followed suit with theirs, David found himself wandering to where his mother stood with her friends. "Good evening," he said.

"Why, David, I didn't expect to see you here. I thought you were at Goodwood."

"I returned this afternoon. I didn't think to inform Hugh he would not be needed here this evening."

She laughed. "Hugh quite enjoys dancing and mingling. He'd have come, regardless." She looked about the dance floor. "Is your lady friend here?"

"My what? Mother, if I had a lady friend, I would not bring her to an affair where you might be present."

Her brows rose. "You're certainly distracted this evening, if you think I'd ask about that sort of woman, no matter where we were. Now, I know your horse won twice at Good-wood, so that can't be what's occupying your thoughts. Which leaves me one other cause. Who is she? Which one of these fair misses has turned your head?" Mother raised her quizzing glass as she studied the crowded room.

"There is no one occupying my thoughts," he lied. He wanted to be certain Lady Joanna returned his affections before letting his family know of their attachment.

"Hannah has spent a lot of time with Northcotte's sister, and I understand you ride with them often."

He grew warm under her scrutiny but would not play her game. "I escort Hannah often when she rides in Town."

"Bridgethorpe told me in his recent letter he'd heard Lady Joanna had quite the interest in racers. She seems to be rather talented in nurturing the young colts."

David wasn't sure which surprised him more, that his father still kept current on what the other breeders were up to, or that Lady Joanna's skills with a horse were that well known. "She has mentioned wishing she were at a race meeting rather than the ballroom."

His mother's eyes narrowed. "From what I've heard of the lady, she would be quite an asset at Fernleigh Stud."

Her plot was blatantly obvious. David licked his lips to keep from grinning. "Are you suggesting I hire her? I believe Knightwick is the one you should speak to regarding that. I only attend to the training of the horses and grooms."

She laughed at his nonsense. "Mind you, you'll never be too old for me to take you by the ear and haul you from the room to give you a good scolding. You know perfectly well what I meant."

Sobering, he nodded, then spoke so only she might hear, couching his words carefully so as not to encourage his mother's matchmaking. "She will make an excellent wife, I'm certain. I hadn't planned to take such a step just yet, and she's in need of a husband soon. There is also the lack of friendship between our fathers over the years. Her brother likely continues the ill will toward our family."

Mother's brows drew together. "Hannah has spoken kindly of the young man, from the few times she has met him. I'm not certain he feels as strongly about Bridgethorpe as you think."

He couldn't remember a time when he and Northcotte had been civil to each other, but then, they'd kept such a distance between them, there was no contact. "Why this sudden interest in my taking a wife? I thought this was Hannah's Season. Besides, Knightwick is the heir. He's the one you should nag."

"I never nag. I only suggest when I believe I know what's best for you." Her eyes softened when he caught her gaze. "I should not mind having that one for a daughter. I feel she'd be as good for you as she would for Fernleigh. But I won't say anything more on the matter."

"Your point is taken. But I fear a match between us might not come to pass."

Those sorry words echoed in his mind while he watched Lady Joanna dance with her various partners. *I fear a match between us might not come to pass.*

It was true. A month ago, he had no interest in her other than to gather evidence against her brother. He still hadn't given up the conviction either her brother or father had been behind the poisonings, and he needed to be able to face her with a clear conscience. She deserved that much. It would require all the gumption he possessed to walk away from finding Zephyr's killer. He would do it, though, for Lady Joanna.

At last, his turn came to dance with her. When she smiled up at him as he offered his arm, her face was alight with such joy it stole his breath. He saw the other dancers taking their places. "Ah, a cotillion. I do hope I don't embarrass you."

"You're a competent dancer," she assured him. "Is this more false modesty?"

"I? Be false in anything?" He pressed his right hand to his chest. "You wound me, madam. Let us see how complimentary you are when we are through."

The steps were intricate and bouncy, and he spent all his concentration on getting the moves correct. But when Lady Joanna glided away from him, he couldn't help but stare. Her gown teased him with hints of the shape of her hips and tiny waist. The pale curves exposed by the low neckline begged to be kissed. Did she apply perfume there, in that warm crevice, to increase its potency?

He bit his tongue to stop the thoughts and willed the

tightness in his muscles to relax before he ravished her on the dance floor.

Lady Joanna returned to his side. "Is something amiss?"

"No, no. I was merely lost in your beauty."

"And that caused such a look of pain on your face?" Her laugh was a lilting musical scale. "I never know what to expect from you."

"I'm pleased you're never bored in my company."

"Never bored, that it quite true. I think we have too much in common for that."

He considered that. Beyond their love of horses, what did they share? They were both children of earls, and preferred life in the country. She didn't speak much of her brother, but when she did, her words held the love David felt for his siblings. They were well suited in those aspects. "As long as I can be assured you're not laughing at me, I'll continue to do what I can to encourage it."

They parted again in the dance. When she returned, she offered him a flirty smile. "I fear I cannot guarantee not to laugh at you if the circumstance calls for it. My governess never quite succeeded in conquering my inappropriate giggles."

He nodded once. "I'm duly warned. And I'll do my best to avoid you when my sister is present, as she is sure to encourage such outbursts." Hannah was always with him when he saw Lady Joanna, he realized. He needed to call upon her by himself so he could deepen their acquaintance. The difficulty was doing so without his family jumping to a conclusion he might not achieve.

THREE NIGHTS LATER, JOANNA AGAIN FOUND HERSELF standing on the outskirts of an assembly, watching her friends being gracious and exuberant in a quadrille. Amelia and Hannah both had their cards filled early on, while Joanna's had a few noticeable blank spaces. She was uncertain whether the gossips had her already matched with Mr. Lumley, so the other gentlemen avoided her, or worse, she'd been labeled an undesirable through her acquaintance with Sir Frederick.

Perhaps they all knew of her love for horses, and her wish to continue to train after she married. Not many gentlemen would allow that of their wives. If that were the case, Robert would have to let her attend race meetings and skip the balls and card parties. A wife who loved races as much as her husband would be a boon to the men in that circle, surely. Her search for a husband could be accomplished with ease.

Joanna leaned to one side to hear her aunt's conversation with Lady Bracklehurst, when Sir Frederick approached. He took her hand without waiting for her to offer it and bowed. He smiled and his furry cheeks puffed out. "I hope you saved a dance for me."

She said a quick prayer for rescue as Mr. Lumley had done in the past. No one came. "I've the next dance free." She wasn't about to admit to having two open after the supper dance, too. Thank heavens Hugh had asked for that one.

"How delightful. Would the last dance be available, too?"

"No, I'm afraid not." If she didn't have a partner for the final dance of the evening before the music started, she would ask Aunt Ophelia if they might leave early. Either way, she would never give that honor to Sir Frederick.

"Perhaps you would care to take a turn about the room while we wait?"

She looked to her aunt for assistance, but the woman was occupied with Sir Jasper and failed to notice. "All right." She placed her hand on Sir Frederick's sleeve and wished she might become invisible to the others in attendance.

"I had an audience with Northcotte this afternoon," Sir Frederick said.

"How lovely." And how little she cared what he did.

"He agreed to let me pay court to you."

Her left foot caught on the heel of her right, and she would have tumbled to the floor if Sir Frederick hadn't caught her by the arm. When she regained her balance, she uttered, "He said nothing to me on the matter."

"Perhaps he wasn't aware I was attending the same assembly as you this evening. I didn't know myself until I saw you with your aunt."

Robert had said she would have until the end of the Season before he would choose for her. How could he ever believe this man suited her? "How lucky for you to see me amongst all these people."

"I've a knack for finding you in a crowd. Once we are betrothed, I won't have to search, for you will always be on my arm."

"Sir, you are presumptuous. I'm certain Northcotte didn't agree to a betrothal without hearing my feelings on the matter." She prayed that were true.

"I've all confidence he'll find my offer agreeable when the time comes. This matter of paying court is a courtesy to you. He thought you should be allowed to enjoy your full Season."

"If you wish for me to become fond of you, you are going about it wrong. I enjoy neither my Season nor your company when you speak of such things. It's quite intolerable."

The large room seemed suddenly small, the other guests crowding her, stealing her air. She needed to escape to the garden, but not on the arm of Sir Frederick. Her two friends were still dancing, and her aunt engaged with Sir Jasper. Joanna was trapped. "I would like a glass of punch before our dance. If you'll escort me back to my aunt, I shall wait upon you there."

She was unable to confide her dread to anyone until three dances later, when she and Amelia awaited their partners for the supper dance. She whispered her plight. "I fear my brother has accepted an offer from Sir Frederick. Northcotte agreed to let him court me."

Amelia gasped. "Are you certain he agreed to it? I would not be surprised if that man was not fully truthful."

"He seemed too assured to lie about something I could easily check out. And he knows I would do just that."

"How will you escape him?"

Hugh arrived at that moment. "Is something amiss?"

Amelia blurted out, "Lady Joanna's brother is allowing Sir Frederick Aldwen to court her."

Joanna grasped her friend's hand. "Please, keep your voice down. If it's true, I want to keep it from the gossips as long as possible. This could ruin my chances with any other gentlemen."

Hugh shook his head. "This can't be true. I thought you and my brother had an understanding."

Looking around them to see who might overhear, Joanna whispered, "You're mistaken. I've no understanding with any gentleman." She wondered how he had come to this conclusion. Had his brother said something to make him think so?

"We can't let you marry that man," Amelia said with a shudder. "We must think of something."

Joanna frowned. "What can we do? Hire a man to pretend to court me? And what happens when he doesn't make an offer? Sir Frederick will be free to make one, or if he already has, my brother will accept it."

"What if we invited you to so many outings, you had no time for Sir Frederick?" Hugh offered. "My sister and Miss Clawson could easily fill your afternoons, and your aunt could make certain you had no evenings free."

"We should find a place to eat our supper and worry

about this later, in a more private setting," Joanna said. "I appreciate your concern, both of you. Amelia, when Sir Richard finds you, come sit with us, and we can talk about our plans for the next week. Please, don't speak of this to anyone."

Joanna took Hugh's arm, and they followed the crowd to the refreshment area. It was too bad he was so very young. She would not be averse to marrying a kind-hearted young man such as him, if she didn't already have such strong feelings for his brother. If only she could find a way to convince David Lumley to propose. That would be the best solution she could imagine.

CHAPTER TWELVE

Sitting in the soft glow from the coals in the fireplace of Robert's study, Joanna listened for the sound of his carriage below. The moment she'd arrived home from the ball, she'd sent word to her maid not to wait for her to come to her chamber. She had no idea how late her brother might be, but she was determined to speak to him before sleep softened her anger. His actions, if true, were intolerable.

The sight of a brandy decanter in one corner tempted her. The burn of the drink would replace the burn of her emotions, but she didn't care for the taste. A glass of port would be nice, but she would not bother the servants to ask. Instead, she let herself stew while deciding precisely how to get her point across.

As it were, her words were simple when she met him in the small entry of the town house. "Do you hate me as much as this?"

Robert's sigh carried the weight of his guardianship. "What have I done now?" He removed his hat, coat, and gloves, handed them to the butler, Starley, and dismissed the man. He then strode to his study as if secure in the knowledge she would follow. Or in hopes she would not.

But she did. Her hands shook with the effort of refraining from pounding on something. "I thought we had discussed this already, yet just this evening, Sir Frederick informed me we are betrothed. How could you do this to me? I thought you wanted my happiness."

He motioned for her to sit in a chair, but she wrung her hands and paced instead. She couldn't sit when the rest of her life lay in stock and chains.

After pouring a brandy, Robert sat behind his desk. "Nothing has changed since the last time we spoke."

"Then I'm not engaged to him?"

"Nothing has been drawn up and agreed to, and will not be, for as long as I can put it off."

Her jaw slackened, but she kept her mouth closed. A lump formed in her throat, the pain making it difficult to swallow. "I am to marry Sir Frederick."

"No, I just said you are not. He has made an offer, but I haven't accepted it, nor have we talked settlement terms. When that time comes—*if* that time comes, I'll bring my solicitor into the discussion to assure you're properly taken care of." His voice was so calm, his tone level, she wondered if he realized how important this was.

"I cannot marry that man." Her voice cracked. "I do not love him. I cannot even tolerate his company. Father would not have wished me to marry this man."

Robert sighed and rested his elbows on his desk after shoving aside a stack of opened correspondence. He kneaded his temples in silence. Finally, he sat back in his chair, his gaze landing on the papers. "Father wished for many things that didn't come to pass. You're correct, however; he would not want you to be unhappy. My situation is a difficult one, Joanna. I'm not in a position to promise you something I cannot give you. I can only say this…if you do not wish to marry the man, find yourself a husband. Soon."

"It's not as easy as that. I cannot place an advertisement in the papers suggesting all suitable, eligible men apply here."

"That would make the task easier."

She gasped. "It isn't done! You're not being helpful."

"I've never sought a husband, so I don't claim to know the specifics. And I don't wish to learn them now. Believe me when I say Father left a large amount of work for me to resolve. I will get it done, one way or another, and with as little pain to you and Mother as possible. Your only job is to find a husband and marry him. You will do this, I know, because you have always done what is expected of you."

"But—"

He raised a hand. "Perhaps Aunt Ophelia would be better to advise you in this. I can send a note to Sir Frederick and ask him not to speak of any of our dealings until we are ready to read the banns, but that is all. You simply must work harder at finding a husband."

He reached for his brandy, a signal their discussion was at an end. She sat there, watching him sip his drink and avoid her gaze, not certain if she should be frustrated by or in awe of the way he turned her anger back on her. She slowly rose. "Thank you for speaking with me. I shall call on our aunt tomorrow."

She was halfway up the first flight of stairs before the tears hit. Afraid the night footman was lurking nearby, she drew in a deep breath to hold them at bay. Only when she was safe in her room did she curl up on her bed and let the painful, wracking tears fall freely.

Find a husband. Soon. But how?

AUNT OPHELIA LOOKED RESTED AND CONTENT POURING TEA for herself and Joanna in her parlor. Joanna felt the complete opposite. She'd barely slept, feeling time slipping away and taking her chance of a happy future with it.

"I'm surprised you came calling this early, Joanna. Did we have plans I'd forgotten?"

"No, Aunt. I was eager to speak with you and took a chance you'd be up and receiving callers already."

"You know I'll receive you, no matter the hour. Now, what brings you here? Something must be amiss. Is it your mother?"

Joanna shook her head. "No, mother is unchanged. It's Robert. Or something he said."

Aunt Ophelia took a sip of her tea and set down the cup. "Oh?"

"He insists I find a husband. Soon."

"I thought that was the purpose of your Season. How does this cause you distress?"

"He's made some sort of agreement with Sir Frederick Aldwen that I am to marry him."

"Without asking your opinion on the matter? That doesn't sound like Robert. Perhaps you misunderstood?"

"No. He said my only alternative is to find a man who'll agree to marry me before Robert and Sir Frederick have the settlement drawn up."

"Oh, dear. Does your mother have anything to say on this?"

"I haven't said anything to her. How can I? She isn't there anymore, if you understand my meaning. She'd tell me she's certain Robert knows what's best, then go back to staring out the window. I don't know what to do, Aunt. I don't know what to do." Joanna's breaths grew shaky. "I cannot marry that man."

"What of the man you've gone riding with several times?

Mr. Lumley. He has escorted you about at many assemblies, it must mean he's fond of you. A few of my lady friends have mentioned his obvious attentions. Has he said anything to suggest he had feelings for you?"

"No. He doesn't speak of feelings beyond those he has for his horses."

"Well then, I say he's perfect for you. Now you must make him aware of this fact."

Joanna raised her hands. "But how, short of throwing myself at his feet and completely destroying my reputation?"

"If he falls for you after a show like that, he's not the man you need. No, we need honey to catch this fly. We must work quickly. I shall arrange a card party, small of course, almost last minute. Next week. I'll check my calendar. We'll invite your friends, and the sons of a few of my friends who are of the right age but not yet seeking a wife. Their attentions should show your Mr. Lumley you are desirable. Although how he hasn't noticed already is beyond me."

She continued, barely pausing to draw a breath. "A new dress is in order, not too formal or too casual. A pale green would suit you and flatter your hair color. Some elaborate braiding around the neckline to draw his attention to your better features—"

"Aunt Ophelia! You said throwing myself at him wasn't the way to win his heart."

"Correct, but displaying yourself in a favorable manner simply lets him realize how strongly he feels about you. Why do you think young ladies are asked to perform on the piano or harp, or sing for a group of people? If you don't place yourself in an advantageous light, how is a gentleman supposed to see you?"

"But I don't play an instrument, and you've heard me sing."

Aunt Ophelia tapped a finger on her chin. "Hmm, there is

that. In Mr. Lumley's case, he'd probably prefer a woman whose talents involved a horse, but I refuse to bring any large animals into my parlor."

"He's seen me ride quite often. In fact, when we met, I had ridden down his runaway stallion." Joanna smiled at the memory.

"And he didn't propose on the spot?"

"No. Now that I think on it, once he realized who I was, he became curt and rode off. I never expected the man to speak to me again."

Pursing her lips, Aunt Ophelia said, "And you're certain this is the man you wish to marry?"

"He has been quite pleasant company since then, sometimes even flirtatious." Butterflies fluttered in Joanna's stomach, thinking of the nicer things he'd said. "I believe he might have been embarrassed at being rescued by a lady. I enjoy his company, and truth be told, I feel he's the only man of my acquaintance who might allow me to continue working with the foals. I cannot imagine my life without my horses."

Her aunt's face softened. "This need of yours to nurture young horses might fade once you have children of your own. I'm not altogether sure you should base the rest of your life on a hobby you might outgrow in a few years."

"But it's not a hobby, it's my whole life." Joanna's heart raced at the very idea she might outgrow the horses. "Would you advise Robert not to consider his fiancée's feelings toward racing?"

"Of course not. He's older and has the responsibility of keeping the family stable going. Or, if he chooses, he may sell it off." Aunt Ophelia leaned gracefully forward and topped off Joanna's tea. "I'll not say, as you expected, that he's a man so he doesn't need to consider her opinion. If Robert wishes for a happy marriage, he should look for a woman who enjoys spending time in a similar fashion, or one who prefers some time alone while he's away."

"I thank you for that. I wish father had left me a few horses that I may take with me when I marry."

"Perhaps Robert will allow you to take your mare with you."

"I would rather have Patriot." Joanna quickly held up a hand to stem the admonishment she expected. "Yes, I'm aware he's the future of Northcotte Stud and is probably not available at any price. This is what upsets me most. No matter whom I marry, the horses I train will never be my own."

∾

AFTER LEAVING HER AUNT'S TOWN HOUSE, JOANNA AND HER maid went to Amelia's home by hack. She greeted her friend with an excited smile. "I bear an invitation to play cards with us Thursday week. Do say you'll come."

"I must check with Mama, but I believe we're available. Is this being held on your behalf?" Amelia sat opposite Joanna in the morning room, where the sun had already moved past the windows.

"It is. If all goes as we hope, Mr. Lumley will be attending."

Amelia raised her dark brown brows. "Do you think he's close to making his feelings known?"

"To be honest, I'm not even certain he has any feelings toward me. Yes, he singles me out to sit with at supper, and always dances twice when I'm available, but he hasn't escorted me to any activities. Nor has he called on me."

"What about all the times you've gone riding?"

"When we ride, I visit more with Lady Hannah than Mr. Lumley. He's really nothing more than her chaperone."

"He could send a groom to ride with her, if he didn't wish to be in your company. Don't be so hard upon yourself. I'm certain he has a high opinion of you."

Joanna tugged off her gloves while she let her friend's words sink in. Could it be true? Did Mr. Lumley have an affection for her? He certainly hid it well. Yet he was the only man she'd met with whom she could imagine spending the rest of her life. "Well, we must wait to see if he attends the card party. Then we can discover how strong his feelings are."

"Who has your aunt invited? I'm afraid to hope Sir Richard might be there."

"He wasn't on her initial list, but I can ask her. She might not know him well enough to extend the invitation."

"It's no concern. I shall enjoy the afternoon in spite of his absence."

"We sent off invitations to the Lumley brothers and sister, including Knightwick if he's in Town. Perhaps you'll be partnered with him."

"I won't get my hopes up. I doubt he's in London."

"There will be ample young men to partner us all, you can be sure of it. Some of my aunt's friends' sons have been invited. And I begged her to be sure none of the young ladies are prettier than we are," she added with a giggle.

Amelia joined in her laughter. "Nor richer, nor more talented…"

"In our case, that would prove a very narrow list of ladies, indeed. It would be a very dull afternoon."

"Not with our wit, and Lady Hannah's. We shall have everyone quite entertained."

"I hope you're correct. And now you must tell me what I've missed with Sir Richard. I haven't seen either of you at the assemblies I've attended recently."

"He took me to the opera one night, and we had ices at

Gunter's. He has invited me to ride in his curricle this afternoon."

"How exciting. It sounds as if he might be close to speaking to your father. Has he hinted as much?"

"No, nothing as formal as that. He continues to ask what invitations I've for the week, though, and shows up at many of those events."

"Is he very romantic?"

"I suppose. He has sent posies to me a few mornings after we've danced together at a ball. And he always pays me compliments."

"Mr. Lumley flatters me often but hasn't sent flowers. Sir Frederick sent some one time."

Amelia shuddered. "I can't imagine that one has a romantic side. I should hate to see it, if he did."

Joanna drew in a breath and let it out slowly. "He has spoken to Northcotte about marrying me."

Amelia gasped. "He didn't. Your brother turned him down, of course."

"Not directly, no. I don't know what sort of pull the man has over Northcotte, but my brother left the discussion open until a later time."

"How could he? Did you tell him you would refuse an offer from Sir Frederick?"

"I don't have a choice in the matter. I must marry by the end of the Season, or at least have a betrothal finalized by then. He won't say why it has to be now. He says it's best for the estate. I can't be spending enough to be a hardship on him, when I only take what he's allowed me. I even offered to go live with my aunt, if I haven't found a husband by the end of June."

"You may stay with us for the summer. Mama has mentioned returning for the Little Season if Sir Richard hasn't offered for me. I'm certain you could stay with us in

Town then. You would not need an entirely new wardrobe, just a warmer pelisse."

"I appreciate your offer, but I know Northcotte won't allow it. Aunt Ophelia has suggested I force Mr. Lumley to realize he desires me for a wife, and thus he'll ask for my hand. That is why we're having the card party."

"Well, this shall be enjoyable to watch. What will you do?"

Lifting her shoulders, Joanna said, "I've no clue. I shall be vivacious and intelligent, and speak of nothing but horses, I suppose. Whatever it takes to turn his head."

CHAPTER THIRTEEN

*T*hat evening, David paused a moment at the top of the grand staircase that swept into the Duke of Kemberling's ballroom. He'd insisted to Mother, Hannah, and Hugh they should arrive early, but apparently, all of London had done the same. He would never find Lady Joanna in this crowd, and if he did, her card would be full.

Hugh nudged his arm from behind and spoke into his ear. "Are you afraid of the marriage-minded mamas below?"

"No, of course not. They won't hound me until Knightwick marries."

Grinning, Hugh replied, "Then I shall be free for many years, if they leave me alone until you're leg-shackled."

David nodded, his lips clamping together. Although a small portion of his mind had opened to the thought of marrying Joanna, the rest of his body turned cold at the very idea. He wanted a family someday, but was nowhere near ready to take time away from Fernleigh. A family deserved that time.

Hugh took a step down as newcomers pushed their way

around the brothers. "Do you see Miss Clawson? I hope I'm not too late to ask for the supper dance."

"No, but she's likely with Lady Joanna. Shall we hunt together?"

"We'll divide the territory. I'll circle to the left, you go right."

David began to descend. "And how shall I notify you when I find them? The old banshee cry?"

"That would be effective, would not it?" Hugh laughed. "But it would not earn us the gratitude of Her Grace."

"Quite so. How about we say whoever finds them first requests the supper dance of Lady Joanna and Miss Clawson for the two of us? That way, we'll both be set."

"Perfect plan. Happy hunting." Hugh wound his way through the mob at the foot of the stairs while David worked his way to the right, following the wall.

His height had the benefit of allowing him to see over most of the crowd, although some of the matrons' turbans with their gaily-dyed plumage made him feel he was hunting grouse in the brush. He doubted they'd appreciate him pushing the offending feathers aside so he could see better. Worse, Mrs. Brighthouse broke into laughter while he stood behind her, and when the feather on her hat brushed his nose, he nearly sneezed.

He was partway down the short end wall and approaching the French doors when he caught a whiff of Lady Joanna's perfume. She was nearby. Laughter rang out, sounding very much like Miss Clawson. He pushed his way toward the sound and found what he sought.

He smiled to the small group of Lady Joanna's friends, and his lips spread wider when he saw her. "There you are. I'd begun to fear you were hiding from me."

"No, never you, Mr. Lumley. We are always happy to see a friend." Lady Joanna's eyes were warm and welcoming.

His chest tightened, and all the air left the room. What was wrong with him? "I'm glad to hear it. I promised Hugh I would secure the supper dance with Miss Clawson for him, and would be honored to escort you, if that one is unclaimed as yet."

A grimace flitted across Miss Clawson's face but wasn't there long enough for him to be certain. "As it happens, I do have that dance open," she said.

"As do I," added Lady Joanna.

"Excellent. My sister is here, somewhere. If I may, I'll suggest she join us if she doesn't have an escort."

"That would be lovely. How is Lady Hannah? I haven't seen her these past few days."

"She is well. I never see her anything less than at her best."

Lady Joanna's slender brows rose imperially. "How rude of her. I won't invite her to any house parties if that is the case. My looks are most frightful in the morning when I wake."

David swallowed at the image her words brought to mind. He saw no flirtatious gleam in her eye, so he assumed she had no clue how her words could be taken. And he wasn't about to inform her. "If she has her way, she'll be married soon and too busy with her new life to attend house parties in the country."

He saw Hannah approach just as he finished the sentence. She greeted everyone in the circle, then asked, "Who's having a house party?"

Lady Joanna chuckled. "No one. We were speaking hypothetically. Your gown is exquisite. Is that design from Paris?"

David watched Lady Joanna in awe. She gracefully swept the conversation downstream with no lingering trace of it. She would be a badger in the House of Lords. The old codgers would not know what hit them.

Music began to play, and a pair of young men appeared and led Miss Clawson and Lady Joanna into the center of the room. Hannah was left behind with David and Sir Richard, who'd just joined them. Before David could offer to stand up Hannah in the dance, Sir Richard spoke. "It appears we are both in need of a partner. Will you do me the honor?" He held out his hand.

Hannah smiled, her relief barely hidden. "It would be a pleasure."

Hugh finally found David after the first song in the set finished. "I saw Miss Clawson dancing already. Did you reach her in time?"

"Yes, we'll be their escorts."

"Ah, good. Glad to hear it." Hugh patted his unruly hair back into place.

"What held you up?"

"Mother insisted on introducing me to a matron with six daughters, five of whom are out. Can you imagine? Five girls, all of whom had the misfortune to inherit their mother's bulbous nose and weak chin. And I'll be dancing with three of them."

Inwardly, David cringed. "You didn't mention my name in their hearing, did you?"

"No. Mother said she was certain you'd gone off to play cards, so don't make a show of dancing all evening."

"Thank heavens for that. I don't plan to dance with anyone other than Lady Joanna, but will stand up with Hannah and Miss Clawson, should they lack partners."

Hugh's eyes narrowed as he watched the dancers move in their direction. "Is that Sir Richard with Hannah?"

"Yes."

"Blast it. I was afraid he'd be here."

"Problem?" David asked.

"He's always in the way at these assemblies. He spends most of the night beside Miss Clawson. The only time I can speak freely with her is when we dance."

"Is he a friend of her family?"

Hugh frowned. "I don't know, but he appears to be claiming her as his own."

David studied his brother's face, the lowered brows and downturned lips. "And you wish to have that right yourself?"

Hugh shook his head as if awakening. "What? No. I've no wish to marry yet."

Folding his arms across his chest, David bit back a smile. "You can't have it both ways. The lady is looking for a husband. Either declare yourself and ask her to wait until you grow up or walk away and leave her to a man who's ready now."

"What do you mean grow up? I don't see you in any rush to meet the parson."

"There's no rule that you can't marry before us. Mother would be thrilled to hear one of her sons was settling down."

Hugh grimaced and continued to watch Miss Clawson float about the floor.

When Lady Joanna returned and her dance partner went off in search of some punch, David resumed his position at her side. She looked into his eyes as if she wished to read his thoughts, then said, "You weren't able to find a partner? There are plenty of young ladies wanting to dance, if you look about."

"I hadn't noticed. I was watching only one lady."

Her eyes widened. "I see, and is she dancing this set without you?"

He moved a step closer, lowering his voice. "I've the pleasure of speaking with her for a short time, at least."

She smiled and glanced down. "Very short. I've a partner for the next set."

"But I've your company when most men will be envious, in between dances. That is enough for me."

She nibbled on her lower lip. A sudden urge struck him to taste the damp pink flesh there. David cleared his throat and broke eye contact with her. He listened to her chat with the young man who brought her a glass of punch, wondering why, when he finally decided to spend time with her, she had an unending stream of dance partners.

At supper, he finally had her alone. Alone, with Hugh and Miss Clawson, Sir Richard and Hannah all crowded around the end of one table. He turned to Lady Joanna. "What do you—?"

"Lady Joanna, did you see the dress Miss Smithers is wearing? Pink. Not a pale pink, or pink sprigged. Bold as you please pink. And the ruffles. Have you ever seen that many ruffles?" Hannah stopped to draw her breath.

"'That many' is correct," Miss Clawson agreed. "I counted nine at the hem, and three at the neckline."

David looked at the other men, and both appeared to be quite interested in the food on their plates. He took a bite of something that swam in a white sauce. It tasted pleasant enough but was not worthy of a worshiping gaze. "Lady Jo—"

His sister and Miss Clawson chattered away, overpowering the sound of his voice. The only way he would be heard over them and the rest of the guests would be to yell, which wasn't conducive to a private conversation. He had nothing to say that couldn't be heard by others, but he sought the intimacy of words shared just between the two of them.

Lady Joanna patted her lips with the white linen napkin and offered him a smile. "This meal is delicious, isn't it?"

"Quite," he called back, even though she sat beside him. "I've heard their chef was trained in France." He hadn't heard any such thing, but gossips said anyone who was anyone wanted a French chef.

She lifted a brow and took a nibble of her food.

They continued in this manner until they all had set down their forks and napkins. David leaned and spoke in Lady Joanna's ear. "Shall we escape to the garden?"

She nodded. As he rose, so did the other men, and the six of them paired up and wound through the tables to the French doors leading outside. Oil lanterns hung in the trees, lighting the paths through the manicured beds of colorful flowers. David walked slowly, keeping a casual attitude about him. "This is much nicer. The cool air. The quiet, even with the voices of our friends so close."

"It's quite pleasant. The light in the trees gives them such a mystical appearance. One might believe in fairies and magic."

Seeing the light dance off the loose curls at her neck made him feel the magic. He longed to touch one, to see if her hair was as soft as it looked.

"Are you in Town long, or will you be leaving for another race meeting soon?"

Did she want him to stay in Town? His breaths grew shallow. A breeze sent a whisper of her perfume to him, and for a moment, he couldn't breathe. He paused in the shadow between two trees, turning to face her. "I...I'm not certain what my plans are."

"Did you receive the invitation to my aunt's card party on Thursday? She invited your family."

"Then I'm certain we shall all be there." If Mother had mentioned it, he hadn't paid attention. He'd get the details in the morning.

"I'm glad." Her lips trembled, drawing his gaze to them. He stepped closer, tempted. He bent his head, glancing at her eyes to judge her permission. She looked...hopeful. Leaning closer, he inhaled her citrusy scent and brought his lips closer to hers—

Lady Joanna shrieked and batted her hand in front of her face. "Get it away!"

David jumped back. "What?"

"That...creature."

A large moth dove past. David swatted at it, waving like a Bedlamite until he finally knocked it away. Laughter rang out down the path.

"Is that a new dance from France, brother? You must teach me so I may impress the young ladies, too."

"Very funny, Hugh," David growled back.

Lady Joanna giggled. "I'm sorry. I'm rather frightened of insects. I know it's silly for one who spends as much time as I do outdoors, but there it is. I'm a ninny."

"No apology necessary. Perhaps we should join our friends." David offered his arm, and they walked toward the others. As they passed through another shadow, he scowled. He should be grateful to that insect for saving him from doing something foolish, but he was not.

THURSDAY AFTERNOON, JOANNA ROSE TO MEET THE LUMLEYS when they entered Aunt Ophelia's drawing room. "I'm very glad you all could come."

Mr. Lumley introduced his mother to Joanna and Aunt Ophelia. Lady Bridgethorpe acknowledged them both, then spoke to Joanna. "I'm happy for the chance to get to know you better. My daughter speaks of you so often I feel as though we're close friends already. You and your aunt must call on us when you're free."

"That would be lovely, my lady. As soon as the others have arrived, we'll pick our partners for cards. Perhaps you'd care to sit while we wait?" Joanna led the woman to an upholstered chair set to one side of the room.

Lady Hannah followed, taking Joanna's hand and pulling her to one side. "Tell me what gentlemen will be here. Whom shall I have as a partner?"

"There are a few I've not met, but they are friends of Aunt Ophelia's. I'm sure one will suit you, for at least an afternoon."

"I hope that is true. I grow tired of spending so much time with my brothers. I'm glad we are friends. I miss my sisters terribly."

"Oh look, Miss Clawson is here. Let's hear how her night at Vauxhall went." Joanna led Lady Hannah to join their friend. Mrs. Clawson sat with the other matrons who were already deep in conversation.

After everyone had arrived, Aunt Ophelia walked to the center of the room and clapped her hands. "It's time to find your partners for whist and take your seats."

Much scurrying and laughter followed as the younger people paired up. Joanna searched for Mr. Lumley, when Lord Henry Vickers stepped in front of her. "Have you a partner, Lady Joanna?"

"Why, no, I do not."

"Wonderful! I'm an excellent player, never fear."

Losing at cards wasn't a large concern for her. Missing the chance to flirt with Mr. Lumley was. She searched the table to see if he'd found a partner and found him watching her, a bit of disappointment showing on his features. She smiled and motioned to an empty table. He nodded.

Joanna turned back to Lord Henry. "Shall we sit here?"

He followed her to the table and held her chair. Mr. Lumley walked up a moment later with the very plain daughter of Aunt Ophelia's friend. Joanna realized the girl was his second choice, but it made her heart swell to see him coming to the aid of a girl who wasn't likely to be anyone's first choice. Joanna smiled at the girl. "Miss Culpepper, I'm glad we'll have this time to visit."

"Thank you," she said and awkwardly sat to Joanna's right.

This put Mr. Lumley to Joanna's left. All too soon, Joanna discovered what a distraction he was. If he'd been her partner, sitting across the table from her, she still might have smelled his cologne, the deeply musky scent, and would have seen every smirk and lift of the brow as he signaled his intent to play a certain card. That would have made concentration difficult enough.

As it was, she had to keep her hands close to her, clutching her cards tightly on the small table when the desire struck to touch his sleeve as she talked to him. She made certain to speak more often to Lord Henry, since he was her partner.

After the game had finished at each table, they rotated partners, but another young man paired with her before Mr. Lumley could. When this happened yet again on the third game, Joanna sent a silent plea to her aunt.

"Shall we take refreshments now?" Aunt Ophelia asked when that game finished. She rang for the footmen to serve them, waving a hand at Joanna to find Mr. Lumley.

He found her first. "I'd hoped to be partnered with you at least once." He offered his arm and led her to walk about the room.

"So had I, but it was not to be, was it?"

At the back of the room sat a box of wooden alphabet blocks on table only large enough for two players. They would not be alone in the room full of people, but they'd be able to talk unnoticed by the others. She motioned toward the table. "Shall we sit here? It's not cards, but we could play a game while the others refresh themselves."

"Splendid idea." Mr. Lumley held her chair while she sat, then took the seat opposite. The table was quite small, the setting pleasantly cozy.

Joanna opened the box and took out the small blocks. "Who shall go first?"

"Allow me." He picked out three letters and set them on the table before her.

"You make it too easy on me." She quickly put them in order, spelling *joy*. "Now my turn."

Mr. Lumley easily spelled *patriot* from her letters. The words bounced back and forth. *Affection. Kindred. Court. Knight.*

They went back and forth in this manner for a bit. "Let's make it more difficult." He set four letters out, one above the other, which indicated she was to determine the words each letter began.

Y

S

M

H

Picking up more alphabet cubes, Joanna made *you* from the first letter, and *me* from the third. She then spelled *send*, but was stuck on the last word. Mr. Lumley reached out and changed *me* to *my*. She ran words through her mind beginning with H, and after tossing aside *horse*, she spelled *heart*.

But that meant *send* was incorrect. She took away the letters she'd placed there, and finally, perplexed, she looked into Mr. Lumley's expressive eyes. He smiled, then one at a time, he slid letters in place beside the S. T. O. L. E.

You stole my heart.

Joanna's heart fluttered in her breast. Her eyes jumped back to meet his. Did he mean it? His smile wavered slightly, then he gave a nod. Joanna smiled back, then quickly swept aside the blocks before someone else could read them.

Aunt Ophelia stood in the center of the room and called out, "Shall we play another game? Loo, this time."

Everyone began shuffling toward the tables. This game didn't require partners, so all they needed to do was find a table together and they could converse all they wanted without appearing rude. They couldn't speak intimately, but Joanna didn't care. Enough had been said already.

CHAPTER FOURTEEN

The reading room at the club was as quiet as a tomb, and equally dark and chilly. David scanned the papers for news of the race meetings around the country, taking mental note of which horses won and identifying Triton's main competition, paying attention to the meetings where Patriot wasn't entered. By entering those meetings, Triton could build his reputation as planned, thus increasing his attraction as a stud horse.

David looked around the room and wondered why so many young men were there. Were they taking refuge from the Marriage Mart, too? He'd taken the coward's way out, slipping away before his family sat down to a light dinner. If he'd joined them in the dining room, Mother would have questioned him about their afternoon at Lady Ophelia's. She'd been dying to get to know the infamous Lady Joanna, about whom he'd said little, but his siblings had said so much. His mother had certainly seen his quiet chat with Lady Joanna when they played with the alphabet cubes, and undoubtedly had many questions. She couldn't have half as many as he had.

What had he been thinking? He wasn't thinking, that was the entire problem. *You stole my heart.* It was true, he couldn't deny it, but apparently she'd stolen his sensibility, too.

"I haven't seen you in here lately," Pierce motioned toward the billiard room. "Come. Let's see if there's a table free."

David followed him and took a cue stick from the rack. His distraction would make him an easy mark for Pierce, but at least the game would distract him from himself.

"Have Lady Jersey and her ilk finally seen through you and ousted you for the cad you are?"

"Quite humorous. That explains why I never see you in an assembly room, much less a stately home." David lined up his shot for the opening break.

"You'd be surprised to hear some of the stately homes I've been in recently. I just avoid the larger, more public gatherings."

"And that is why the papers are filled with innuendo about *a certain Mr. P- and his current inamorata.*"

Pierce's chest puffed out a bit. "Do they write about me? I've heard Lady Willowbrook is quite popular with the gossips but hadn't realized I'd been recognized."

David laughed. "You make it sound as though you move about *incognito*. Quite full of yourself, aren't you?"

"Well, we can't speak about me all night. What really brings you here?"

Unsure how much to let on, David drew in a breath, but let it out again instead of speaking. Pierce was his closest friend and never one to judge, but David's feelings were so new, he wanted to keep them to himself just a few more moments.

Pierce noticed the hesitation. "Now I'm intrigued. Lady Bridgethorpe would not have commanded you to choose a wife just yet. And had Lady Hannah requested you stay away, you would have become her second shadow."

David nodded, walking around the table contemplating his next shot.

"Which leaves…a lady you are avoiding?"

David said nothing.

"Aha. Some sweet young kitten is trying to hook her claws in your cloak, or her mama has looked at your income and decided it will do."

A scowl narrowed David's vision and the cue ball missed its mark. He barked at Pierce. "Nothing of the kind. She is kindness and all that is good."

"I was right. The kitten has got her claws in you."

"I didn't even see it coming." As he said it, he knew it was a lie. "Well, I sensed something creeping up on me, but I was certain I was stronger than my traitorous emotions. I've no wish to marry, yet."

Pierce set both feet on the floor and leaned his elbows on his knees. "Is it serious, then?"

"How do you determine serious from fickle? Other than through the passage of time. The lady doesn't have the option of time."

"Northcotte's sister."

"The very one."

"You believe you could make a happy life together after the conflict between your fathers?"

"She seems unaware of any trouble, or she's given me no indication of any ill will toward my family." David leaned on his cue stick. "I doubt her father would have discussed his horses and any decision-making about them with her, or in her hearing."

"Isn't she the one who spends much of her time in the stables?"

"Yes. But there's a difference between humoring the

hobbies of one's daughters and taking them into the family business."

"All right. I'll grant you that. But does she know you wanted to have her brother charged with the death of Zephyr?"

Bending to determine the best angle for the next move, he considered Pierce's question. "I don't know that I would have gone that far with the investigation. It was more likely their father who conceived of the poisoning, and he can't be charged since he's dead."

"He was dead when your horses took ill last year."

A sickly warmth crept over David's skin, and his stomach knotted. "I know. I'm looking for reasons to believe I'm wrong about the entire series of events. That someone else was responsible."

"Have you heard anything more about the groom who died?"

"Knightwick said they thought he might have eaten something rotten. There will be no more investigation unless a witness comes forward."

"I don't care what ill blood there was between your fathers, I don't see Northcotte killing his own man."

David tapped a finger on the edge of the table. "I agree. There is really no reason to pursue this any further."

Pierce's brows dropped and his gaze pinned David in place. "I think you have better reasons than that to quit this obsession."

"I know. I can't have both. I can't have Northcotte the villain and Lady Joanna as my bride."

Pierce said nothing. David resolved to close the book on this. He needed to discuss it with Knightwick, but his heart told him what was the wiser choice. However, letting go of six years of anger and frustration would not happen overnight.

He'd have to convince his father and Knightwick to let it go, also. Knightwick might do so easily, but he had no idea what Father would say. Would he be willing to accept the daughter of his rival into the family? Bridgethorpe was a very loving man and had always taken good care of the people on his estates. He was a generous landlord, well thought of by all. When David and Knightwick paid calls on their father's behalf, the older tenants always sent a good word home.

Now that he thought on it, his father had never spoken a harsh word about the former Earl of Northcotte. David and Knightwick came to understand the dispute between the two men by the way they glared at one another at a race meeting. By the tightness in Bridgethorpe's voice when he spoke the other man's name.

He hated to admit it, but there was always a gleam in his father's eye when his horse bested Northcotte's. The rivalry ran deep.

Stephen and Jane's wedding was coming up. When David returned home, he'd speak to his father and brother. Until he did, he couldn't let anyone else know of his feelings toward Lady Joanna. On the chance Father would not allow the match, David didn't want anyone thinking he'd rejected her.

LATE SATURDAY AFTERNOON, JOANNA SAT ON A BENCH NEAR Round Pond in Kensington Park with Amelia. Aunt Ophelia and Mrs. Clawson sat across the narrow path, chatting quietly.

Joanna retied the ribbon on her bonnet. "I hope you don't mind coming here today and not Hyde Park. I've no desire to be seen. Especially by any men."

"You've had enough of Town, then, I take it?" Amelia asked.

"Of Town, of flirting, of being on my best behavior. Of smiling when my toes are trod upon. Really, this seems such a horrid way to find a husband. I wish it were more like choosing a sound horse."

"Lady Joanna!" Amelia laughed. "What would you do, run your hand over his limbs? Pry open his lips to inspect his teeth?"

She tilted her head and looked into the distance. "I'm as likely to discern what kind of husband he'd make as he would by hearing me sing. This is all extremely one-sided. Our mothers spend hours investigating who plans to start a nursery soon, and what his income is, then they throw us in the paths of those men and hope we pass muster."

"You do make it sound like a horse auction. Don't you believe in love?"

Joanna sighed. "Of course I do. I've dreamed of it for many years. Dreamed of having a London Season. This is my second one. Neither has equaled what I'd imagined."

"I disagree. I think this will be the best time of our lives. Once we marry, will we be invited to many parties? Will our husbands agree to come to Town so we might see an opera or a play?"

Joanna leaned close and whispered, "Maybe we'll be so in love with our husbands, we'll have no desire to go anywhere. Can you imagine a life like that?" She laughed softly.

Amelia chuckled and glanced across the path at her mother. She whispered back, "My mother says they were that way, didn't want to visit with family or have guests over. They were quite happy with each other's company."

"I hope both of us end up that happy."

"I think I could be with Sir Richard. What about you and Mr. Lumley?"

Joanna watched a pair of swans gliding on the pond beyond their chaperones and tried to mimic their calmness, hoping to quell the quavering in her heart. "I'm afraid to think about him. I wish he'd speak to Northcotte already, or give me a sign he intends to. I fear he won't act in time and I would rather die than marry Sir Frederick."

"Don't speak that way! Never tempt fate with statements such as that. My cousin always said she'd rather die than do whatever was her current peeve. She died at twenty, a week before her wedding day."

Joanna searched Amelia's expression for sign she was joking, but her friend looked quite serious. "You don't truly believe the two are connected, do you? That she brought about her early death?"

"I don't know what to believe. But I refuse to tempt fate."

"I don't believe in fate. In some cases, perhaps, when one's parents have planned one's life since birth, it might be called fate. But you and I would not be here, in Town, searching for husbands if that were true for us." If such a perfect man existed for her, he would have appeared by now, since her time was running out. She'd hoped Mr. Lumley was that man, but his failure to make his intentions known left her to think he was not.

"But what if our fate is to meet a certain gentleman? Perhaps it was fate that brought Sir Richard to Town this Season and not the next one, or the previous one." Amelia's creased brow showed how much she wanted to believe this.

"And fate led Lady Elizabeth's father to turn down Sir Richard's offer, so he might be free to pursue you?"

Amelia's mouth twisted. "When you put it that way is seems rather cruel. But when he speaks to me, I feel as if he was created just for me."

"I know what you mean. Mr. Lumley does appear to be the best man for me. Of course, any man who is as passionate as I am about horses might do just as well." She thought about some of the men whom she'd met at races in recent years. In not one case had her stomach quaked with the sight of the man, nor had they brought a flush to her skin with a flattering remark. As much as she might insist it were true, there wasn't another man who made her feel quite as alive as Mr. Lumley.

Sometime later, Aunt Ophelia rose and called to the girls. As they returned to Bayswater Road to look for their carriage, a curricle pulled up. Sir Frederick took off his hat and called out, "Lady Joanna, what a surprise."

"I doubt that," she muttered to Amelia.

He motioned to the seat beside him. "Would you care to take a ride with me?"

"As you can see, sir, I'm with friends. It would be rude to leave them."

"That is a disappointment. I just acquired this pair of horses and knew you'd appreciate how well they move together."

Her aunt and Mrs. Clawson walked up beside them. Aunt Ophelia said, "Perhaps another time. We are expected somewhere shortly and have no time for delays."

His brows drew together, and his smile wavered. "Perhaps I'll see you this evening. Which assembly will you attend? I could reserve my dances now."

"Lady Joanna has a private engagement this evening, sir. If you'll excuse us, we'll be on our way. Come, girls, we don't wish to be late." Aunt Ophelia nudged the two girls to move along, and she and Mrs. Clawson followed directly behind them.

Sir Frederick drove away without further fuss, much to Joanna's relief. "That man," she said as soon as he was gone.

"You cannot marry him," Amelia said.

"No, you cannot." Aunt Ophelia spoke as though she'd never allow it. "There's no concern of that happening, is there?"

"As I told you, Aunt, he and Northcotte have some sort of agreement."

"Sir Jasper has heard some talk about him. Something to do with money lending," Aunt Ophelia added.

Joanna considered that. "Northcotte can't have borrowed money from him. We are not in difficult finances. Although, he did say we couldn't afford for me to spend the summer in Bath. I first saw Sir Frederick in Newmarket, so I assumed they were buying or selling horses."

"How are you coming with encouraging Mr. Lumley? You two were quite cozy at my card party."

Speaking over her shoulder, Joanna replied, "I believe he cares for me, but how do I draw him into an understanding?"

Mrs. Clawson's soft voice barely reached Joanna with all the noise of the street. "With some men, you must make your affections quite plain."

Aunt Ophelia patted Joanna's shoulder. "I agree. We won't go so far as to be bold or brazen, but obviously we haven't been plain enough." She took Joanna's arm. "And in the meantime, I shall speak to Northcotte. That young man needs reminding exactly what his duties as a guardian entail."

They walked briskly to where the carriage waited, and after dropping off the Clawsons, went straight to Joanna's town house. Scurrying at her aunt's heels, Joanna asked Starley if her brother was at home.

"He's in his study, my lady."

"Thank you."

Aunt Ophelia entered the room without knocking. Northcotte jumped to his feet. "Aunt, Joanna, I didn't know you had returned. Shall I ring for tea?"

"Not for me, thank you, Robert. I won't be staying. I've some concerns about one of the gentlemen who has made his interests in your sister quite plain."

He smiled, his features softening as if relieved. "Splendid. Does he wish to meet with me?"

"He already has," Joanna said. "Sir Frederick."

Robert's reaction surprised her. He took a step back and went pale. He quickly recovered after grabbing the back of his chair. "Is there a problem with the man?"

Aunt Ophelia shook her head. "How can you ask that? Can you truly say you're considering him as suitable for your sister?"

"Aunt Ophelia, I know you understand how complicated the matter of betrothals can be. There are many areas to consider."

Joanna studied him, trying to see beyond the vague responses he gave.

Their aunt continued. "You cannot have seen the man in a social situation. He's awkward. No, that's too kind. He's a social half-wit. Honestly, Robert. He cannot have any social connections that would benefit either of you, and you certainly don't need business connections. You must tell the man his offer will not be accepted."

"I'll take your opinion under consideration. I appreciate your stopping by this afternoon. I'm sure Mother would love to say hello."

"I hope you do consider what I've said. Your father would not wish his daughter to end up in such a *mésalliance*." Aunt Ophelia turned, nodded to Joanna, and left the room. Joanna followed her out, afraid to see whether Robert seemed to be considering their aunt's request or had set it aside completely.

CHAPTER FIFTEEN

A collision between two carriages blocked an intersection delaying the arrival of David and his family at a grand home in Mayfair. A long line of carriages waited to draw near and allow their passengers to disembark. David would wager the delay was a plot from a merciless God trying to foil his plans to show Lady Joanna how he felt about her.

"David, if you scowl like that when we get inside, no one will ask me to dance," Hannah complained.

"With the variety of rakes and popinjays who are likely to attend, that would be a blessing," he muttered.

"You could have gone to your club, and no one would have missed your curmudgeonly presence."

Mother waved her lavender-scented handkerchief beneath her nose. "Children, please, do not give me a headache before we arrive. The crush will do that soon enough. Let me have some peace while I can."

Banished to the nursery until he could behave. He was seven-and-twenty, for God's sake. He should be due some leeway in behavior now that he was a man. Allowed to have moods on occasion. It wasn't as if he was always cross. Only when his plans went awry.

Hugh poked his arm. "Shall we divide the ballroom again to find Miss Clawson and Lady Joanna?"

"That would be smart. Reserve whatever dances might still be available."

Mother turned her attention back on David. "You dance often with Lady Joanna."

"She's pleasant company. If I must attend these assemblies, I see no need to be miserable the entire night."

"No one is twisting your ear to make you attend." In the light from the carriage lamps, he thought he detected a small smile on her face.

"You threatened me before the Season began. I thought it was expected of me to accompany Hannah to as many balls as I could."

"That was before Hugh came to Town. He enjoys dancing as much as Hannah does. I suppose if you'd prefer to travel with your horse, I'll excuse you from further obligation."

Now he felt like a heel. He didn't mind watching out for his sisters. Truth be told, he couldn't help but feel protective of them. And now he needed to go to as many assemblies as possible when Lady Joanna was in attendance. "The Season is half over, and we'll be leaving soon for Stephen and Jane's wedding. I won't mind joining you for the short time I'll be in Town."

"Besides, Lady Joanna will be there," Hugh added.

Mother nodded. "Is that important to you? To continue to see her?"

Her piercing gaze probed him. "She makes the evening more pleasant."

Mother smiled and looked out the window. "That's often how it begins. If one is lucky."

His luck hadn't been good on a regular basis of late, so he

would not look for that to be the foundation of his marriage. He shook his head.

Luck.

Marriage.

The word still made him quake. While that was the logical progression of an acquaintance made during the Season, the idea made his heart race. He needed to adjust to the thought before speaking of it aloud.

The carriage lurched forward a few more feet, carrying him closer to Lady Joanna. He pulled back the velvet curtain to see how far they had to go. Still too far to suggest Mother walk the distance with them. She would not be pleased if she were glowing before she crossed the threshold.

Hannah also looked out her window. "Look at all the people. So many are walking up to the house from here."

"They most likely rented hacks," Mother said. "You will look all the more distinguished when you step out of your father's carriage."

Hannah sighed. "But anyone who matters will already be inside, and partnered."

Mother lifted her chin. "Anyone who matters will be waiting for you to arrive before asking the other ladies to dance."

David smiled. His mother played the countess well. It was hard to look at his sister and think she might one day be a countess, or a marchioness. She'd only begun wearing her hair up.

Hugh adjusted his waistcoat and tugged at the sleeves of his coat. "I hope Miss Clawson thinks I matter and saves a dance for me."

When they finally made their way into the ballroom, David spotted Lady Joanna first thing. She was in the center of the floor, gaily bobbing through the dance steps. Her cheeks were flushed most becomingly, her smile bright.

He looked for Lady Ophelia, believing that was where Lady Joanna would return after the dance. Making his way around the room, he took up watch near where the older woman stood. He surveyed the room for familiar faces and realized with whom Lady Joanna danced. Sir Frederick.

Bollocks.

That confirmed his suspicions the fates had it in for him. However, if they danced this early, maybe he hadn't asked to sit with her at supper.

David found out soon enough, when the dance ended and Sir Frederick escorted her back to her aunt's side.

"Thank you," Joanna said, sounding dismissive to David's ears, but apparently not to Sir Frederick's. The man remained with her.

Undaunted, David walked up. Before he could speak, Sir Frederick dismissed him with a little wave of his hand. "Move along, Lumley. The lady has a companion at the moment. You are not needed, or wanted, here."

Lady Joanna gasped. Her eyes popped wide open.

David feigned a stab to his chest. "I'm wounded you aren't delighted to see me, Sir Frederick. That was the sole purpose of my venturing to this corner of the ballroom. I suppose I must continue my turn about the room." He bowed to Lady Joanna. "Would you care to join me?"

Sir Frederick stepped forward, blocking Joanna. "She's with me, as you can plainly see."

"What I see is that your set of dances ended, and you neglected to offer refreshment or see if she'd prefer to step outside where the air is cooler. Neither of which precludes me from doing so." He held out his arm. "My lady?"

Her blink broke her blank stare, then she smiled. "Thank you, sir."

David led her away before Sir Frederick could say more. "Lady Joanna, how is your evening progressing?"

"Very well, now, thank you." She smiled up at him, her eyes sparkling in the light from the chandelier. "I'd begun to think you would not be in attendance this evening."

"I fear we were on the wrong side of a collision and had to wait for the carriages to be moved."

She frowned. "I hope no one was hurt."

"There didn't appear to be any injuries to the occupants, and the drivers were fit enough to right the one that toppled, with the help of some men on the street." He saw her concern increase, and added, "None of the horses were injured, either."

Her breath escaped in a sigh. "I'm glad to hear it."

"I would be glad to hear you have a set open for me. That was my biggest concern while waiting on the street."

"I've the third set free."

"It would be an honor to dance it with you." The room was not so large they could remain away from her aunt—and Sir Frederick— for long, But David walked as slowly as possible. "Which meeting will Patriot enter next? Does your brother tell you his plans?"

"No, he doesn't. Where is Triton entered?"

"To be honest, I've considered taking him north, seeing what the competition is like there."

Her right eyebrow lifted behind the curls on her forehead. "Are you afraid he'll continue to lose to Patriot?"

"I'm not afraid of anything." He let that hang in the air a moment as they completed their circle. "It's purely business. Give him the best record possible."

Lady Joanna nodded. "Ah, yes, to increase his stud fees."

Sir Frederick must have been listening, for he jumped in, his arms folded across his chest. "Really, Lumley, to speak of such things with a lady, and in such a social setting."

"Mr. Lumley and I often speak of our horses. We are both fond of runners."

Shaking his head, Sir Frederick said, "I'm certain North-cotte would not approve. And neither do I. My wife will not discuss horses, or gambling—"

"Then perhaps you're considering the wrong lady for your wife." David forced himself to keep his voice down. "Would not it make more sense to find a woman who already has the qualities you seek, rather than mold one of your choosing into something she isn't?"

Lady Ophelia's friend, Sir Jasper, stepped in. "Is there a problem, gentlemen?"

David gave the man a slight bow of acknowledgement. "None, sir. We're merely discussing runners. You know how passionate we can become over our horses."

"Quite. I'm glad there's nothing to be concerned about." Sir Jasper didn't move from Lady Joanna's side.

The way Sir Frederick remained planted in place, his legs spread slightly, arms still folded, he appeared to be marking his territory. It wasn't jealousy coursing through David at that moment, but a need to protect a friend. Sir Frederick rubbed him the wrong way, beyond his grating manner. There was something pure evil in that man. Why had he singled out Lady Joanna? There were plenty of pretty ladies seeking husbands. Any one of them stood a chance of being the type of wife he claimed to want, many even more so than Joanna. It didn't make sense.

At that moment, a young lad who didn't seem old enough to have chin whiskers approached hesitantly. "Lady Joanna, I believe this next set is mine."

"Yes, it is." She offered her gloved hand to the lad. "If you gentlemen will excuse me?"

David watched her glide away. The moment she disappeared into the crush, he turned on Sir Frederick. "You were out of line. A gentleman would never speak so plainly at a gathering such as this."

"I only spoke the truth. If society cannot stand to hear that, they should pay attention to their own conversations and not mine."

"So you say, but you hoped others would hear so you and she would be forced into the situation you desired." David didn't want to say the word *betrothal* for fear he'd do exactly what he was accusing Sir Frederick of. He needed to end the discussion before it got more heated. He casually moved to Lady Ophelia's side. "You aren't dancing, my lady?"

She waved her fan slowly. "I prefer to watch the younger set perform. Why aren't you dancing? There are plenty of ladies who lack partners."

"Perhaps later." He didn't enjoy dancing the way some did, and he only performed the steps with minimal grace, if their tutor had been correct. Part of him felt guilty letting young wallflowers wilt with each passing set, but he wasn't certain partnering with them, letting them have some hope he was attracted to them, was any kinder.

He didn't have Knightwick's cachet, so being seen on his arm would not draw other men to the wallflowers. And he didn't have Hugh's exuberance in conversation to carry him through a set. Therefore, he stood on the outside and watched Lady Joanna move with joy.

JOANNA COULD BARELY CATCH HER BREATH WHEN THE MUSIC ended and her partner led her back to Aunt Ophelia. Seeing who else stood there made her stop breathing altogether, at least for a moment. Mr. Lumley and Sir Frederick were the bookends to Aunt Ophelia and Sir Jasper, and that bounder, Lord Westbourne had joined them while Joanna danced.

Mr. Lumley appeared nonchalant, but Sir Frederick's eyes shot daggers at him. Lord Westbourne, on the other hand, was as cool and collected as if he believed no man was competition for him. Yet Sir Jasper flexed and opened his fists, practically daring anyone to challenge him.

Good heavens, what a recipe for gossip! Were she and her aunt to be fought over in front of half the ton? The men might as well rip off their shirts and box each other to the floor. A nervous giggle escaped, and she quickly covered her mouth. Perhaps that would not be the best thing, having them disrobe in the ballroom. The matrons might gasp if a fight broke out but would faint dead away seeing half-naked men.

She carefully avoided greeting anyone by name, so she didn't have to acknowledge Lord Westbourne. The man made her shudder. She thanked her partner for the dance, stepped between her aunt and Mr. Lumley, and pulled out her fan.

"You dance so elegantly." Mr. Lumley's voice next to her ear sent shivers down her spine.

"Thank you. Sometimes I feel as though I'm galloping about the floor."

"You're exuberant without losing grace."

Feeling even more heated, she fanned herself hard. "You're being too kind."

"I'm not. I would never beguile you with flattery. There's no need, with such a specimen as you."

"Now you do go too far," she whispered. "Everyone will hear."

"I'm not afraid to let them know I think you're lovely."

She could think of nothing to say in response. His words overwhelmed her. If what he said were the truth, she wished Sir Frederick would hear. She wanted to tell the man *this* was the way to court a lady. She wanted to believe Mr. Lumley was courting her.

Sir Frederick wandered away. Sir Jasper left, too, and

Lord Westbourne took his place beside Aunt Ophelia. He spoke in low tones, but his voice carried to Joanna. "Have you considered my offer?"

"Do not speak of it here," Aunt Ophelia bit out.

"I'm not a patient man."

Aunt Ophelia turned to Joanna. "I saw Lady Jersey earlier. Have you seen her gown? The embroidery at her hem must have taken the seamstress months to complete. I've never seen the like."

"I shall look for her when I'm dancing. I did see the most exquisite hat, though. Large rubies surrounded by white, downy feathers on an emerald turban." Joanna had seen nothing of the sort. *Lady Jersey's gown* was their secret code to launch into a conversation sure to send off whatever obnoxious gentleman had joined them.

"My, it sounds striking. I wonder if I could find the right shade of gold silk for a turban to match the topaz pendant my dear husband left me. What do you think? A matching gown and hat to draw out the amber in the stones."

Joanna grinned. They enjoyed seeing who could design the more outrageous costume. "I wish Mama would allow me to wear red. I would dress in it from head to toe, with ermine at the sleeves and around the train. Do you think I should borrow Mama's rubies or emeralds to wear with it?"

Mr. Lumley coughed beside her. She smiled at him. "What do you think? Should I have a red gown made this Season? Or wait until winter?"

He cleared his throat. "If a red gown would make you feel like a Diamond in the Water, I say you should have it."

She tipped her head and studied his eyes. Was he laughing at her or with her? "Very well. I shall ask Mama to take me to Bond Street tomorrow. Will you come, too, Aunt? You may inquire if they have gold satin in stock."

Just when Joanna was running out of inane conversation,

Lord Westbourne took his leave, promising to call on Aunt Ophelia soon. Joanna turned away and covered her mouth with her hand to contain the laughter bubbling up. Too late, she realized she was practically nuzzling Mr. Lumley's shoulder. The crisp scent of his soap filled her nostrils.

Joanna sobered instantly and lifted her gaze. He looked down at her, his nostrils flaring briefly. She quickly flung open her fan and brought it between them, fluttering away the heat that overtook her. That motion only brought another wave of his fragrance to her. Her shoulder brushed against his firm chest, making her hands itch to explore the muscle there.

What was she thinking? Her thoughts became so wicked when he was around. Another wave of warmth overtook her.

Mr. Lumley's mouth pulled back on one side. "Yes, red becomes you."

The music started up. She straightened her shoulders. "I believe this is your set, sir." She took his arm and followed him to the center of the room. He looked so handsome tonight, although his dark green waistcoat and black jacket were nothing unusual for him. The wave in his hair had been tamed, the chestnut color slightly darker in the light from the multitude of candles and lamps than when they stood in the bright sunshine. His eyes looked more golden than green, burning with some emotion she couldn't name.

That heated glow caressed her, sent ripples through her middle. She had to tear her gaze away for fear of bursting into flames in the middle of the dance floor. Besides, everyone was bound to see the way they held each other during long, passionate looks. She didn't need to be the object of gossip and innuendo. It was bad enough Mr. Lumley and Sir Frederick had been so close to blows in front of everyone. She couldn't let her own behavior be called into question.

Yet her smile must have touched each ear, she was so happy dancing with Mr. Lumley. This was what she'd hoped for from her Season. This was what she wanted in her life.

After their set, they joined Lady Hannah and Hugh for a brief walk outside. The cooler air made Joanna aware of how damp she'd become while dancing. She shivered as a breeze danced across the bare skin of her back above her gown.

"Are you cold? We can go back inside," Mr. Lumley offered.

"The cold is refreshing, actually. I'd prefer we remain out here."

"Then we shall." He led their group to a stone bench and motioned for the ladies to sit.

Lady Hannah tucked a lock of hair into the twist on the back of her head. "You're so lucky your brother doesn't accompany you to these affairs, Lady Joanna."

She laughed. "I should think the guaranteed dance partners would be a boon."

"It's embarrassing to have to dance with one's brothers. Everyone knows who they are, so everyone knows you had no other offers to dance."

"But it allows you to demonstrate your grace, so others might see and wish to stand up with you." Oh, dear, she sounded just like her mother.

"I suppose." Lady Hannah sighed. "By now, the gentlemen should know who I am, and watched me dance at every assembly and ball. I don't understand why I've so few offers."

Hugh piped up. "Perhaps they also saw the scowling watchdog hovering nearby."

Mr. Lumley growled. "I do not hover."

Joanna laughed. "But you do not dispute the growling watchdog claim?"

"I'm an elder brother. I have a duty to watch over my siblings."

"I do not see you observing Hugh's partners between sets. Don't you worry about him?" Joanna didn't feel the need to hide her flirting from his siblings.

Mr. Lumley looked up at his younger, slightly taller, brother. "I worry more for his partners, than about them."

Hugh punched Mr. Lumley in the arm and they all laughed. Joanna enjoyed seeing how they acted with each other. They were so close. And seeing Mr. Lumley's concern for his sister was touching. Did Robert worry about her in that way? He almost never accompanied her in the evening, and when he spoke of her finding a husband, his role in it sounded more like a duty than a concern.

Mr. Lumley truly cared for his sister's safety. He'd never consider an offer from the likes of Sir Frederick.

Joanna realized her friends were preparing to return to the ballroom. She rose and took Mr. Lumley's arm. She wished she could see into the future and know if Mr. Lumley would make an offer for her. She couldn't imagine marrying anyone else.

CHAPTER SIXTEEN

*D*avid arranged for a picnic on the Friday before he was due to leave for Bridgethorpe Manor. Hannah was disappointed to learn she and Hugh would be the only other people invited, but he'd insisted he needed time with Lady Joanna without all the interruptions a larger party provided.

Hannah smiled knowingly. "Oh, I understand."

"Don't read too much into this. I'm still not certain where I stand with her."

"Take a measure of advice from your little sister, then. Your picnic will be much more enjoyable if you *sit* with her."

Waving an arm in a pretense of hitting her, David fought not to laugh. He'd arranged for a meal to be prepared and the basket loaded into his curricle, along with some pillows, and a carpet to sit on. He made certain a nice bottle of wine and stemmed glasses were included.

After handing Lady Joanna into the curricle, David drove to Richmond Park. Hugh and Hannah rode in a second curricle, and their servants traveled in a cart with the supplies. The park was a short distance from London, and the rolling meadows were an escape from the city. He followed a path to one of the ponds and chose a spot under a tree where they could sit. They disembarked, and the servants set up the picnic.

"This is lovely." Lady Joanna spread her arms and spun on her toes, taking in the scenery. "Look, there are deer."

David glanced where she pointed. "It's difficult to imagine we're so close to the noise of the city, isn't it?"

"We should—that is, *I* should come riding here one day. I imagine there are no rules against galloping here." Her cheeks flushed, and he was pleased to hear her slip and let him know she thought of them as a couple.

He looked in the distance, where a pair of horseback riders loped up a gentle rise. "It appears not."

Hannah also looked in that direction. "What fun. It would be like being home at Bridgethorpe."

The carpet, spread under a tree, held the baskets and a pile of pillows. David motioned for Lady Joanna to join him on the carpet. "Are you hungry? My father's cook outdid herself and will be very concerned if we return with any of this food." He unwrapped some cheese and located the knife to cut a piece.

Kneeling nearby, Lady Joanna looked over the tins and bundles. "She must have imagined you invited a much larger party. How are we to eat so much?" She gracefully rolled to sit on one hip, her legs curled close.

"Perhaps we can take a turn around the pond later and work up our appetites for a second meal."

"I should have to dance all night to be that hungry. But it looks delicious, so I'll at least sample everything."

"That should satisfy the cook. Would you care for some lemonade?"

After he poured their drinks, they ate and made small talk. Surprisingly, Hannah and Hugh ate without joining in the conversation. David made a mental note to thank them later.

Birds sang in a stand of trees nearby and the tension in David's muscles melted away. He hadn't realized just how relaxing it was to be outdoors in a quiet setting. He spent so much time in the paddocks at Fernleigh, it was just a natural part of his day. "Are you outdoors with the horses much when you're in Hampshire?"

"As much as I can be. Mother insists I spend a good portion of my day behaving as a lady should. I easily escaped her notice, though, and put Patriot through his paces each day. I often rode one or two of the other colts around the paddocks. If I had my way, I would spend my entire day with the horses."

He nodded. "It doesn't seem fair we must do those other things, like eating and sleeping."

Laughing, she agreed. "It's quite inconvenient, isn't it? Although I imagine the horses need their rest, too."

"I'm lucky my father has Fernleigh." David leaned back on one arm. "I can't imagine what I'd have done if I'd been required to find work. Managing Fernleigh isn't work, it's a joy. Hugh seems to feel that way about his law studies. While I'm happy for him, I just can't imagine spending the day with my nose pressed to a page as I scribbled proceedings."

"No, I can see where that would be dull, although some of the cases must be quite interesting."

Hannah rose from the carpet. "I'm going to walk by the pond." Hugh followed when she walked off.

Lady Joanna nibbled like a mouse at her piece of cheese, and David popped a strawberry covered in cream into his mouth. "Tell me something about you."

Her brow creased. "Like what? Hmm. I love horses."

"No, something I don't know. Something no one else knows."

She peered at him from the corner of her eye, and he wondered if she trusted him with such intimate knowledge. They knew each other so little, yet entire lifetimes had been born of such short acquaintance. She lowered her hand to her lap. A small grin pulled at her lips. "I hate peas."

He burst out laughing. "Now we are getting somewhere. I love peas but hate turnips."

"We are in agreement there. I love the color green and hate red. It's so bold."

"But what of your ermine and red silk gown?" he teased. "Weren't you and your aunt to shop for such a garment?"

"Oh, I'd forgotten. Maybe I'll discover a quiet red."

"I believe that would be pink," he suggested.

"I look horrid in pink. I was thinking more of mauve. I believe I could tolerate mauve."

"The blessings of being a man. I may wear black and navy and never look unfashionable or pretentious."

Lady Joanna nodded. "Robert is much the same in his wardrobe choices. Very safe, unadventurous."

So she thought him safe. That was a promising sign. Or did safe equal dull in her mind? "Safe and unadventurous are not the qualities of a good horse breeder. Perhaps I need a red waistcoat."

She turned to contemplate him. "I cannot imagine you being afraid to take a risk with your stable. You seem to have the ability to know what risks are worth taking."

He smiled and tipped his head. "I thank you for the compliment."

"I didn't mean it as flattery. I've seen the skill in you. A good quality to have in your type of work."

Noticing she'd stopped eating, David rose. "Shall we take a turn about the pond?" He held out his hand to her.

"Thank you." She brushed the wrinkles from her skirt and took his arm.

David kept their pace slow, to keep the distance between them and his siblings. How pleasant it was to stroll beside her like this, an easy, relaxed moment where they had no duty but to enjoy the time together. He inhaled deeply. "Even the air is nicer here."

"Nicer than the paddocks? Why yes, I must agree." She slanted him a playful look, her eyes crinkled in the corner.

"I was comparing it to Town, but you're correct, as always."

"I like that, 'correct as always,'" she echoed. "How good of you to notice."

"I fear with my upbringing, I would never say anything to the contrary, no matter how erroneous a lady might be."

Her lower lip jutted out. "Is that so? And here I thought you so intelligent for recognizing one of my better qualities."

He turned his head and caught her gaze, his laughter fading as his body warmed. The sunlight fell on her face, bathing her porcelain skin with golden light. He swallowed. "You have many good qualities that haven't escaped my notice, my lady."

Her lips parted. David stopped walking, pulling his arm from hers and taking her hand. She hadn't put her gloves back on after eating. "Your fingers are so soft. Long and slender." He stroked her skin there, and her hand trembled. Raising his head, he watched her tongue swipe across her lower lip.

He groaned under his breath and lowered his mouth to hers. She met him partway, kissing him back. She clutched his arms as if to steady herself, and he grabbed her shoulders to pull her body against his.

She tasted of the apple slices she'd eaten, sweet and intoxicating. When her lips parted, he almost let his tongue explore, but feared frightening her. Instead, he kneaded his mouth against hers, taking as much as she offered and treasuring it.

He pulled away, suddenly remembering they weren't alone. "I should not have done that."

"I'm glad you did." Lady Joanna smiled, her cheeks becoming pink, then she turned away and continued to walk along the pond's edge.

David followed, his heart still pounding in his ears. She was so much more than he'd ever imagined her to be. He was grateful he'd come to his senses in time about his foolish obsession with her brother and father.

They caught up to his siblings on the far side of the pond. Hugh skipped stones across the surface while Hannah appeared absorbed in studying something beneath the rocks on the shore. Lady Joanna walked over to Hannah and they began to talk.

Hugh came over to stand by David. "Shall we race the curricles?"

"No, not today."

"Stephen wrote that he'd found a good mare for his breeding program. Bought her off Northcotte."

David was surprised. "I wonder if he discussed it with Knightwick before purchasing."

Lady Joanna perked up at the mention of her brother's name. "You don't think your cousin should have added one of our horses to his stable?"

David noted her use of "our horses." He considered his words carefully before speaking, not wishing to upset her. "I'm simply surprised he didn't use one from Fernleigh."

Hugh explained. "He wanted to introduce new blood, and said Northcotte's Willow came from heavier stock. He's looking for harness horses, not runners."

Lady Joanna nodded. "Willow has some plow horses in

her background. My brother wanted to add some strength to our line. I think her foals would do well under harness."

"I haven't seen Willow," David said. "I'm sure she's a sound horse. Northcotte knows his horseflesh."

Her chin lifted. "He does. It's apparent in how well Patriot is performing."

David couldn't prevent his wry grin. "Yes, he wins too often for my taste."

Lady Joanna's features softened, then a flirtatious gleam appeared in her eyes. "Perhaps you should use Patriot to cover one of your mares. The combination of our lines might prove unbeatable."

His heart raced at the thought of combining their own lines, not their horses'. Something primal awoke in him. He wanted to claim her as the mother of his children, parade their offspring about and proudly display their talents as they grew. He tugged at his cravat, which was suddenly too tight. He cleared his throat after a false start at replying. "Yes, I must speak to Northcotte."

But he would not be discussing horses.

Hannah let the rock in her hands fall into the water. "I can't wait to see Stephen and Jane." She turned to Lady Joanna. "Our cousin is marrying our neighbor and my dearest friend. I wish they could have waited until the Season was over, but Mama and Jane's mother wanted to avoid the heat of summer. We leave first thing tomorrow and will be gone a fortnight. I hate to think what I'll miss while we're away."

Lady Joanna turned to David. "You're all leaving, then?"

"Yes," he said. "I'm uncertain if I'll stay up north for the Chester Race Meeting or return as soon as Stephen is married."

"Oh yes, you mentioned going to some of the northern meetings."

He couldn't decide if she was sad or worried. Could he say something to reassure her? Was it too soon to press his suit? He held out his hand. "Shall we walk back? I find myself growing hungry again."

She gave him her hand but said nothing. In his thoughts, he began and tossed aside sentence after sentence. Finally, he took an indirect route. "Would you have any objection to me requesting an audience with your brother before I leave Town?"

Lady Joanna peered at him around the brim of her bonnet, then quickly looked down. "No objection whatsoever."

"I shall leave my card when I take you home. I don't know if I'm what he would prefer for a husband for you, but perhaps I can persuade him."

"You are what I would prefer, and that's all that matters to me."

His heart swelled and he stood a bit taller at her words. He covered her fingers with his own on his arm. Now all he had to do was find a response for any objection Northcote might have.

CHAPTER EIGHTEEN

hen David and Lady Joanna pulled up in front of her home, David hopped out and signaled to a boy on the street to watch his horses. Handing Lady Joanna down, he led her up the steps and inside. The butler appeared from deep in the house. Lady Joanna asked, "Is Lord Northcotte at home? Mr. Lumley wishes to speak with him."

"I shall enquire, my lady."

As the butler walked away carrying his card, David's hands shook. He'd assumed he could leave his card and work up the nerve to return. His mouth was bone dry. There was no air in the entryway, and his cravat had shrunk even more. He cleared his throat.

"He's my brother, not my father," Lady Joanna said softly. She waited beside him, looking up into his eyes with a trust that hit him hard. She had faith in him, in his ability to provide for her and make her happy for the rest of her life.

David wasn't sure he could live up to her dreams. "He's your guardian, and at the moment, he has the power to destroy my future." He combed his hair back with one hand.

He couldn't recall any situation where another man held his life in the balance. The feeling made him ill.

The butler returned. "His lordship is in his study. This way."

David squeezed Lady Joanna's fingers before following. Northcotte's study was a dark, cool room, not at all welcoming. The air smelled somewhat stale. The curtains were closed, and the only light came from an oil lamp on the large desk.

Northcotte rose. "Lumley. To what do I owe this visit?"

David bowed and remained standing. He decided not to belabor the painfully uncomfortable meeting. "I wish to marry your sister."

Northcotte showed no reaction. After an unbearable pause, he motioned to a chair. "Pardon me. Please, sit." He lowered himself into the chair behind the desk.

David sat, his thighs tense, his hands clenching his knees. The cheese he'd eaten at the park was curdling in his gut. *Just say yes so we can get past this.*

"I'm surprised, I must say. Lady Joanna mentioned you were chaperoning your sister, but she didn't imply there was any stronger attachment between you."

Wishing for a drink to wet his throat, David nodded. "That is how it began. We find we both enjoy the horses quite well." He closed his eyes. There was the weakest excuse for marriage he'd ever heard.

"Yes, of course. That's important to her." The crease between Northcotte's brows softened. Something hidden beneath his rigid posture told David he really cared about his sister.

"She's an enjoyable companion, and she gets on well with my family. My mother, especially, likes her. I haven't spoken to my father yet. I understand there is a concern about Lady Joanna marrying soon, so I came to you straight away."

Northcotte broke eye contact. He reached for the whiskey decanter and poured two glasses. When he replaced the crystal stopper, it rattled against the bottle. He handed a glass to David. "Yes. I've been putting pressure on her."

"Do you approve then? I leave tomorrow for home and will speak to my father. He can have his solicitor meet with yours at your convenience."

Frowning, Northcotte took another drink. "You haven't said anything about your feelings toward her. Do you love her, or is this some scheme your father has cooked up?"

"Bridgethorpe has come to terms with whatever happened between our fathers years ago. He doesn't even know I'm close to your sister, but he wouldn't object to our marriage."

"Are you certain? When Zephyr died Bridgethorpe accused my father of the crime."

Bollocks. David couldn't deny it. "Your father's name did come up in the investigation. They inquired about anyone who might wish Bridgethorpe ill."

The earl's voice rose. "And my name came up last year when more of your horses took ill at a race meeting."

"We were merely trying to help solve the crime. Many names came up. Well, a few. My father doesn't have many enemies."

"Neither did my father. Yet your family continues to defame him two years after he was buried."

"We answered the questions the constable asked, that is all." David tried to keep his voice down, to keep the conversation calm, but it wasn't working. He was torn between wishing he'd never brought up the Northcotte name in the investigation, and defending their natural inclination for doing so.

"And what of the accusation you and Knightwick made to the investigators of my groom's death? Did you honestly assume I was behind that, too? You don't need to answer. The constable grilled me about that incident, too."

"At the time, I believed you could have killed the boy, I won't deny it."

A loud crash came from the hallway. David looked toward the door, but it remained closed. He used the distraction to gather his wits. "I couldn't understand why you would have done so, but in my stubborn way, I needed someone to blame. You were a convenient target. I only know that horses from both Fernleigh and Northcotte were entered in the race meetings where anything untoward has happened. I feel confident that no one from our stables would have killed Zephyr nor made the others unfit to compete. My family has discussed the evidence, and lack thereof, repeatedly, and pushed the constables to find the culprit. And it was all for naught."

David rose, unable to sit with the emotions battling inside, but he kept his voice down. "This battle between our fathers has stolen every ounce of joy from Bridgethorpe. He can't find pleasure in the horses, in his family. He sits and stares out the window, searching for I know not what. I don't know what disagreement they had. Whatever it was, your father is no longer here to resolve the matter." He quickly held up his hand. "I'm not saying he was at fault, only that they cannot mend their differences when only one remains living."

He stopped, pushing his hair off his forehead, and eyed the whiskey on his side of the desk. Giving in, he downed it in three swallows. It burned its way down, but the wetness allowed him to swallow again. Setting down the glass, he sat once more.

Northcotte cleared his throat. "I've a suspicion why they fought, although Father never spoke of it. Bridgethorpe's name was never mentioned in our house. The goal of our trainers was to give Father a horse that would beat anything Fernleigh raced."

David wondered again if that drive had caused the elder Northcotte to do something foolish, something dangerous, to Zephyr. His hands knotted into fists. He hated himself for not being able to let it go. And he began to realize his obsession was no more justified than the elder earl's had been.

Northcotte reached for the decanter and poured a splash in both glasses. He took a swallow and held the glass aloft, his elbow resting on the desk. "However, my father would not allow the use of a whip or a crop in training. He loved those horses. At times when I was a boy, I felt he loved them more than me. When I came home from Cambridge, there were signs my father had slipped into madness. They were subtle at first, but grew more obvious over the next few years."

He paused, swirling the liquid in his glass. "He bought and sold horses, over-bred a few of our mares so that I feared for their health. It wasn't until after he'd taken his own life that I discovered he'd used the services of several money-lenders to pay the stud fees."

David shifted uncomfortably in his chair. He hadn't heard it was suicide. "I'm sorry. I didn't realize."

Northcotte nodded. "It was at our home in Hampshire. The local doctor agreed to call it an accidental shooting, to save Mother and Joanna from disgrace."

Acid burned in David's stomach. Was his father's melancholia a blessing, not a curse? He could just as easily have become rabid in his pursuit of wins. David was grateful for the way his life had gone. "I realize I've no right to ask, and you may disregard the question if you wish. How were you able to pay off the money-lenders without selling everything but the entailed property?"

Northcotte's lips thinned and pulled into a smile on one

side. "There's the irony. Some of those foals Father was so madly breeding proved to be fast runners. By selling some horses, I added to the winnings and was able to forestall some of the creditors, and pay some off completely. There is one, however, who has become impossible to put off any longer."

David waited to see if he would add to the story.

"This man has given me the ultimatum of paying him in full, or allowing him to marry my sister. The debt would be considered her dowry."

Those words wrapped like a fist around David's heart. "Sir Frederick Aldwen?"

"The same."

"Lady Joanna told me he'd spoken to you. Does she know you owe him money?"

"Thus far I've been able to keep my mother and sister unaware of our debt. I told Lady Joanna she must find another suitor if she wished to avoid Sir Frederick, but she only has until the end of the Season."

David offered a slight smile. "She has accomplished that."

"There is still the issue of the debt to Sir Frederick if she marries someone else. He will call in the balance due, and I'm not yet in the position to pay it."

For the first time since he'd come into the room, fear crept into David's thoughts. "I'm not a wealthy man but would gladly give what I have to keep her from marrying him. Regardless of whether you allow her to marry me."

Northcotte shook his head. "I don't want something like that hanging over Lady Joanna when she marries. I can't accept your offer. I've posted notices in Newmarket that I've horses to sell. If worst comes to worst, I can auction some at Tattersall's, and hope I can raise enough in the next few weeks. I've already spoken to the auction house, just to learn if I might raise enough that way so Joanna doesn't have to marry until she is ready."

"And?"

Northcotte shrugged. "There's no way of knowing how much people might bid on the horses. All the good runners are gone, except Patriot. He's the only one with a strong record, but if I sold him, I would have to explain to my sister what Father did to the estate's finances. I've been fighting to preserve my father's memory in the eyes of my sister and mother. Mother hasn't taken his loss well."

"It would kill Lady Joanna to lose that horse. Don't you think she has a right to know the truth about her father? Surely, she suspects he wasn't making completely sound decisions, if the situation grew as serious as you say."

"My father was a proud man. Well-respected by many. I want Joanna to continue to be proud to be his daughter."

David locked eyes with the man across the desk, realizing he could be looking at a reflection of himself. He'd spent the past five years trying to bring back the man his family remembered their father to be. Trying to maintain the pride of his family. In the process, he'd blamed all his problems on a son who'd been doing the same thing. He was no better than the elder earl, whom he'd blamed for his father's misery. "I understand. I won't speak of this to her."

He'd not received an answer to his request for Lady Joanna's hand. "Do you approve of my marrying your sister?"

"You have a lot of nerve. You don't deny you've been trying to ruin Northcotte Stud, and you think I'll turn my sister over to you?"

"I wasn't trying to ruin you. I wanted to find the culprit and see him prosecuted, and was fixated about who that person might be. I admit to being overzealous in that. We had no reason to suspect anyone else."

"You had no reason to suspect me or my father."

"If you'd been in our shoes, you'd have done the same. Tell me our names didn't cross your mind when your groom was found dead."

"His death was ruled accidental."

"Before the ruling. It never crossed your mind someone might have killed him?"

Northcotte took another drink. Setting down the glass, he tapped a fingernail against the rim. "If I thought anyone wished me harm, your family is one of the last I'd name. I had a creditor in mind when I first heard Peter was dead."

David leaned his hands on the edge of the desk. "Sir Frederick? And you're considering letting your sister marry him?"

"No, I'm not considering it. I'm considering letting her marry the man who thought *me* capable of killing. And wondering what kind of fool I am for thinking it. Yet the alternative sends cold chills down my spine."

Holding his breath, David nearly pleaded. "You know I'd never let harm come to her."

"I believe you would work as hard to keep her safe as I've tried to do. Yet I don't know if I'm a big enough man to set aside the slander your family has spewed on mine."

"You can count on me keeping her safe. What will you do about Sir Frederick?" David asked.

"Well, if you marry quickly, there is nothing he can do about it. I can request a special license. If he sends me to the workhouse, at least Joanna and Mother will have a home with you."

"No, that won't do. She'd question the rush, and I don't think she's naïve enough to believe I couldn't bear to wait for the banns to be read."

"We can't wait that long," Northcotte said. "Once Sir Frederick saw the first announcement, he would call in the debt. I don't think I can set up the auction by then."

"What if I buy Patriot?"

"You?"

David spread his arms. "After all this, you can't say you don't wish for any Northcotte horses to race for Fernleigh. You sold a mare to my cousin."

Northcotte smirked. "Actually, I wondered if you wanted to retire Patriot so Triton would have a chance at a win."

Grinning, David nodded, the tension draining slowly from his body. "There were times I might have considered it. I had another use for him in mind. I wish to give him to Lady Joanna as a wedding gift. The Jockey Club won't register her as owner, but she would know he was hers alone."

Her brother stared in silence. David began to sweat, wondering what the problem was at this late stage in their negotiations. Finally, Northcotte reached for a drawer and removed a sheet of paper. He scribbled madly, then slid the paper to David.

David read the sheet. He reached for the pen. "Agreed. I'll have the funds sent to you. But let's not tell Lady Joanna about it just yet. I would prefer to surprise her on our wedding day." He signed the bill of sale transferring owner-ship of Patriot to David at a price only slightly higher than he might have bargained for. It was a small price to pay for Lady Joanna's happiness.

They shook hands, and Northcotte agreed not to discuss their conversation with his sister. As David left the study, he was surprised that Lady Joanna was nowhere in sight.

A servant swept up pieces of broken porcelain opposite the study door. As David walked toward the entry, Starley appeared. David said, "I wish to speak with Lady Joanna before I take my leave."

"She's not at home." Starley held out David's hat and gloves.

David hesitated in confusion, then took his items and went out on the street. The urchin he'd spoken to still stood with his horses, he was relieved to see. Shadows stretched onto the street, telling him just how long he'd been with Northcotte. David tossed the boy a coin.

He didn't understand where Lady Joanna had gone. He'd assumed she would wait for him, as eager as she was to know what Northcotte said. She hadn't mentioned having another engagement, and he couldn't imagine anything more important than their betrothal.

He drove to the mews to stable his horses, then walked the block to his home. He needed to send a letter to Knightwick advising him he'd agreed to purchase Patriot and would explain when he saw his brother. Then he'd send a note to Lady Joanna saying he'd call on her in the morning.

CHAPTER NINETEEN

*J*oanna lay on the chaise in Aunt Ophelia's morning room, cradling her foot while tears poured down her cheeks. Her toes felt broken, but she was reasonably certain they were not. Her heart was another matter.

Mr. Lumley hadn't cared for her one iota. He'd merely been looking for another way to seek revenge against her family name. *Win at all costs* must be the Bridgethorpe motto. To think she came close to marrying a man who thought her brother was capable of murder. Believed her father would harm a horse, no matter who it belonged to.

She'd suddenly lost all desire to marry and have a family. Aunt Ophelia would allow her to stay indefinitely in Bath, regardless of what Robert said on the matter. Her aunt had guests at this late hour, but as soon as the visitor left, Joanna would speak to her. If she could speak around the painful lump threatening to block all air as she tried to breathe.

He must have befriended her with the intention of hurting her brother. With no regard to how much he might hurt her in the process. Not only was she facing the loss of what she thought was the love of her life, she could no longer consider Lady Hannah and Hugh as friends.

They had nothing to do with their brother's scheme, but she couldn't see them and not think of Mr. Lumley. Lady Hannah was such a dear friend, too, one of the few she'd met who shared her love for horses.

She drew in a shaky breath and blotted her handkerchief beneath her eyes again. She could cry later, when she went to bed. For now, she must be strong and tell her aunt what had befallen her. When she placed her feet on the floor, the toes on her right foot ached. She took off her slipper and rubbed them though her stocking. Who would imagine a porcelain vase would cause so much pain? She hadn't meant to kick it when she ran away from what she heard beyond the closed doors of Robert's study. She'd just wanted to escape.

Escape the reach of their voices. Escape the hateful words they flung at each other. Pain stabbed in her chest when she remembered their accusations. Her father a killer? It couldn't be. He loved his horses more than he did any of his family. He lived for those horses. He would never do anything to cause any animal injury or illness.

Bridgethorpe must be mad to have accused her father, to suggest he was responsible for Zephyr's death. Bridgethorpe had instilled in his sons his hatred for her father and now they carried on that vile disease.

How could he have pretended to love her? He'd kissed her…he probably had much practice kissing ladies and making them swoon. She had been naïve enough to believe there was emotion behind the tender touch of his lips. That emotion had probably been nothing more than restrained laughter at her innocence.

She'd believed what she'd seen in his eyes.

But no more. Never again would she trust a man. Any man.

With new resolve, she slipped her tender toes into her shoe and went to see if her aunt was free. The drawing room doors were still closed. As she reached for the latch, she heard voices inside.

A man said, "You will want for nothing, I'll see to it."

Aunt Ophelia's reply was too quiet for Joanna to understand. It must be Sir Jasper with her, and it sounded as if he'd proposed. How wonderful for her aunt. At least she was successful in love.

The man spoke again. "I'm a skilled lover. My demimondes are always grateful for my attentions."

Joanna shuddered and stepped back from the door. She should not be listening to such an intimate exchange. Especially since his words didn't ring of love, or the passion lovers shared. They felt dirty. Degrading.

The man continued to sing his own praises. "As my mistress, you will be the envy of so many women. I've a box at the King's Theatre and you may attend every night as you wish. I'll escort you to any ball, or you may hold parties of your own in Westbourne House. And of course, I'll see to it you are outfitted in the latest fashion."

Westbourne.

He was not proposing, he wanted Aunt Ophelia as his latest demimonde. Joanna shuddered again and began to return to the morning room.

Aunt Ophelia's voice stopped her. "You can offer me nothing that would entice me into your bed. I've refused your offers each time you made them. Why did you bother to come here today? My answer is unchanged. I'll never be your mistress, your lover, or any other position you might offer."

"Foolish woman. You don't know the honor I give you. Many women throw themselves at my feet and beg me to show them some affection."

"Well, perhaps you should offer one of them a hand up,

rather than treading upon them like carpet. Not that they deserve you. No woman should suffer the belittlement you force her to endure. I ask one last time that you leave my home, before I call for my footman to escort you out."

Footsteps drew near the door and Joanna scurried down the hall. She didn't want her aunt to know she'd witnessed this embarrassing scene. Overwhelming doubt filled Joanna as she quietly latched the morning room door behind her. Perhaps her dream of love was truly that, a misty wish with no more substance than a dandelion seed on the wind. No one she knew had attained a lasting love without it ending in misery.

When she heard the entry door open and close, Joanna waited a moment, then stepped into the hallway. "Aunt Ophelia?"

Her aunt stopped at the foot of the staircase. "Joanna, darling. I didn't know you'd stopped by. Did I forget about an invitation for this evening?"

"No. May we speak in private?" The hallway was empty, but the butler probably lurked nearby in case he was needed.

"Of course." Aunt Ophelia motioned toward the morning room as she approached. Closing the door, she asked, "Shall I ring for tea?"

"Not on my account." Joanna debated asking for something stronger, a glass of port, perhaps, to calm all the squeamishness brought on by Mr. Lumley and Westbourne. She sat in the chair near the fire where she usually perched when visiting. "I came to ask a favor. I wish to leave for Bath as soon as we may accomplish it. I can't go home, and I can't remain in London any longer."

"What's happened? Is it Sir Frederick, or something Robert has done?"

"Yes, and more." She went on to detail her picnic with Mr.

Lumley, his proposal, and the heated conversation between him and her brother.

Aunt Ophelia pressed a hand over her mouth for a moment, then clasped her hands in her lap again. "Are you certain you heard them correctly? I can't picture either one of them acting in such a way. Accusing Robert of murder? The very idea your father or Robert would hurt a horse or a man... I don't know Mr. Lumley well, of course, but he doesn't seem the type to throw out accusations blindly. There must be more to the story."

"I don't care what led to it, Robert said he'd heard from the investigator the Lumleys had brought up his name. To think I was falling in love with such a man! Please say we may leave for Bath in the morning."

"Robert would not allow you to leave, I thought. Not until you've accepted a marriage offer."

"I've had two offers, and I can't accept either one. What shall I do, Aunt? I would marry a widower with a nursery full of swaddled babes to avoid either of these men."

"Let's not be rash. Your chances of finding a match in Bath are poor at this time of year. Everyone is here in Town. Attending a race meeting with Robert is questionable. The men there will share your interest in runners, but how many seek a wife? You don't have time to browse the market, so to speak. We must change our strategy. I'll review the invitations we have received. I think it's time we accept some of the less popular assemblies. The gentlemen there will have less cachet than at the ones we've been attending, but so will the ladies. You're the beautiful daughter of an earl, so you will quickly be the most popular lady present."

Joanna sighed, accepting the plan of action. "You make it sound like a military battle. It's difficult to continue to smile and be desirable company the way I feel now. I don't know what Sir Frederick sees in me, why he's singled me out for his attentions, but Mr. Lumley gained my trust while believing such horrid things about Robert. He can't love me. I'll never forgive him."

DAVID WOKE MUCH TOO EARLY AND TOOK NEMO FOR A JAUNT to pass the time until he could call upon Joanna. He couldn't wait to see her and tell her the great news. They had Northcotte's approval, as surprising at it might seem.

The sun seemed brighter, the air clearer that morning. Seeing a girl with a basket full of flowers, David bought a posy of purple and yellow flowers before heading to Eaton Place and Lady Joanna's home. It took all his nerve to keep from urging Nemo into a run, and still he arrived a bit early. He dismounted, holding the reins as he looked up at the town house. How soon could they marry? Would she want to be married from Hampshire, or would she be willing to let his mother hold another gala wedding breakfast at Bridgethorpe Manor? He had no preference, he simply wished for it to happen soon, so they might remove to Fernleigh and set up house as man and wife.

Checking his watch for the third time, he saw it was late enough to pay a call and he handed Nemo's reins to an urchin loitering in hopes of earning a coin or two. David trotted up the steps and rapped with the doorknocker. Starley led him to the drawing room to await Lady Joanna.

Her arrival took longer than David expected, since she'd known he would come. Perhaps she was nervous about her appearance and took extra pains with her toilette. He smiled when she entered, leaving the door open. David handed her the flowers, wanting to speak quickly before her maid arrived. "Your beauty is as bright as the morning sun."

She looked up and he saw the shadows beneath her eyes,

the pink rims of her lids. Her smile appeared false. "Thank you." She moved to a chair and sat.

David followed, standing in front of her. "Is anything amiss? You seem a bit under the weather."

"You just told me my beauty shines like the sun. I'm no longer sure what to believe from you."

His gut tightened. Was this betrothal nerves speaking? "I'm never false with you. You are always beautiful, but something is wrong this morning. I can feel it. Have I done something? Did Northcotte say anything untoward last night? He and I parted on good terms, so I cannot think what might have changed since I saw you last."

"I've had a change of heart, Mr. Lumley. I can't accept your kind offer of marriage. I'm sorry for any pain this causes you, but I'm sure it will be of short duration."

Her words sounded like a child's recitation, well-rehearsed and without passion, and were completely the opposite of what he expected to hear. "What has happened?" With one finger beneath her chin, he lifted her face to meet her gaze. "Is it Northcotte? Sir Frederick? I thought we were in agreement."

"No, neither of those men. I do not wish to discuss it further. Please accept my refusal and go. Spare us any more pain."

"This is it? I don't deserve to know why you refuse me? If there is something that I've said, something I've done, that caused you injury, I beg you for the chance to redeem myself."

"I came to know your true nature, if you must know. There's nothing to be done for that."

"What—how—" He turned away and stalked to the window, staring blindly at the garden beyond the window. The only thing he could think of that might have caused her to reconsider was his pig-headed obsession about

Zephyr. "Is it because of Zephyr? If you will allow me to explain—"

"Allow you to explain what? You accused my brother of killing my friend, Bruce. If you believed that, how could you even consider marrying me? I cannot fathom how you thought we could have a happy life together while you believe Northcotte to be a murderer." Her hands knotted around the handkerchief she clutched in her lap, but her eyes were dry. Red and filled with anger, not tears.

"Or was the plan to cry off, making me look a fool, and ending up unmarriageable? If that was all you wanted, you could have left me to Sir Frederick. Whatever his feelings toward me, at least he doesn't think Robert is capable of killing a man."

David gritted his teeth. She must have overheard their argument. Didn't she hear what Northcotte said about Sir Frederick? Or had she stopped listening when Bruce's death had come up?

Regardless, he couldn't betray his promise to Northcotte not to say anything about her brother's connection with Sir Frederick. Anything he said, in fact, came close to revealing what Northcotte fought so hard to conceal, and would not make David look any better in the end. He chose his words carefully. "After speaking with your brother last night, I learned some things about myself which were rather unpleasant. I believe he understood my reasons for acting, and thinking, as I had. I was in the wrong, I admit it, and Northcotte and I have come to an understanding about the past."

He turned to face her, and slowly crossed to her chair. "I deeply regret anything I've done to cause you sadness. Your happiness has been foremost in my thoughts for some time now."

The urge to beg for forgiveness nearly strangled him, but

he drew in a deep breath and fought it. Groveling wasn't the way to atone for his sins. "I hope one day soon you will be able to look back on our friendship and smile at the fun we had. You're a pleasant companion. I wish you well, and will trespass upon your time no longer. Good day." Performing his sharpest bow, he left the house.

As Nemo trotted beneath him down Eaton Place, David gauged from the position of the sun that Pierce would still be abed. David's family had departed at daybreak for Bridgethorpe Manor, but he had no desire to speak to any of them at this moment. He needed to scream, chop wood or something to burn off the frustration roaring through his veins. She'd turned him down.

He knew from the start befriending Lady Joanna was the wrong thing to do. Yet he'd gone against his good sense and pushed ahead, consumed with the need to please his father. Knightwick had tried to talk him out of it, but he'd done so anyway. Barreled on with no thought of whom he might injure in the process.

No, that was wrong. He had thought about how it might affect Lady Joanna. He'd simply been so narrow-minded, he couldn't convince himself to stop soon enough. Before he'd gained Lady Joanna's friendship.

Before he'd fallen in love.

Now she was likely to end up married to Sir Frederick. Remembering the paper he'd signed at Northcotte's behest, David realized that wasn't true. He drew Nemo to a stop. There was one thing he could do to see to Lady Joanna's happiness. He reined his horse toward the office of his father's man of business. He could arrange for the transfer of funds to Northcotte for the purchase of Patriot. After Stephen's wedding, he would sign the horse over to Lady Joanna as planned. No matter whom she ended up marrying, she'd have the horse she loved to do with as she wished. And Northcotte would have the funds to pay off Sir Frederick.

As much as he'd planned the horse to be a wedding gift, he was grateful to have the means of making up for some of the pain he'd caused her. She might not love him any longer, but she'd know he was a man of his word, and he hadn't been lying when he said her happiness was most important to him.

A small voice of doubt niggled at him. Had she ever loved him? He assumed she had. She'd quickly agreed to let him speak to Northcotte, but she never spoke of her own feelings. Perhaps he was twice the fool, falling for her as he sought his evidence, then believing she'd loved him in return. She needed a husband, any offer to save her from Sir Frederick. David might have simply been the lesser of two evils. The very thought stung him to the core.

Whether she'd loved him or not, she'd never have to see him again, unless she continued to attend race meetings where he was present. Maybe the next time her horse won, she'd think of him kindly as she celebrated.

CHAPTER TWENTY

*B*ridgethorpe Manor buzzed like an apiary with preparations for Stephen and Jane's wedding breakfast. David escaped the bustle by hiding in the stables. He'd arrived late the night before, went to his room without seeing anyone, and slipped away in the morning while the others broke their fast.

There was nothing like shoveling stalls to clear his head. The physical exertion felt good after being in London for so long.

Knightwick peered over the stall door. "I thought I'd find you here. Our valet said you'd arrived last night. Are you hiding from Mother?"

Leaning on the handle of the shovel, David wiped his brow with his rolled-up sleeve. "I didn't want to give her the chance to put me to work. I'm not good company this morning."

"Mother has her list and her quill, and is enlisting the aid of everyone in sight." Knightwick folded his arms across the stall door.

"Well, it's the first wedding in the family."

"And the last for a while, unless Hannah rushes into something."

David turned away, set the shovel to one side, and grabbed the rake. He didn't want to think about weddings.

"You're eager to work today," Knightwick commented. "Frustrated about missing another race meeting?"

"No. I've sent word for Triton to be brought to the Chester meeting."

"Good plan. Perhaps he'll win, since Patriot won't be this far north."

David stopped and pushed his hair back from his face. He needed to inform his brother what had taken place but didn't enjoy the thought of going through it all again.

Knightwick opened the topic for him. "How is the fair Lady Joanna? Did you come to a determination about whether to continue your friendship with her?"

"There is no friendship between us anymore." He pushed the stall door open, forcing Knightwick to step aside, and carried the shovel to the storage room. After putting the tools away, David rolled down his sleeves and pulled on his jacket.

"Has she accepted an offer of marriage from another man? From what I heard, you two were apparently quite enamored at her aunt's card party."

Combing his fingers through his hair, David looked toward the bright light washing through the open stable doors. The pain of her refusal still stabbed at him like a fresh wound. "It's as you and Pierce warned me it would end. She and I had an understanding. I spoke to Northcotte. That didn't begin well. He's fully aware of the accusations we've made since Zephyr died. He wanted to refuse me, but it appears he hates Sir Frederick more than he does me."

Knightwick folded his arms across his chest. "That's not surprising. Has he had dealings with the bounder?"

"His father had." David didn't feel he was betraying Northcotte's confidence, since the elder earl's desire to win had affected the entire Lumley family in some ways.

"So Northcotte accepted your offer for Lady Joanna's hand? This is great news." Knightwick clapped a hand on his back. "I had a feeling things might be headed that way."

"Northcotte accepted me, but Lady Joanna did not."

"What? You said you had an understanding."

David shook his head and swallowed down bile. "She heard us arguing. It wasn't a bloody brawl between Northcotte and me, but his words were heated, and I reacted more strongly than I should have. She must have been listening in the hallway."

"That sounds like something Hannah would do. She didn't allow you to explain your words?"

He shrugged. "I promised Northcotte I would not let her know how badly her father had damaged their finances. I shouldn't even speak of it to you. Northcotte has almost paid off all his father's debts. He wishes for his mother and sister to have nothing but happy memories of him."

Nodding, Knightwick commented, "I imagine I'd have done the same."

"All this time we've been at odds with the son, and he was merely acting as we would in his shoes. He's more like we are than I suspected."

"He and I were friends, once. At Harrow." Knightwick's eyes grew distant. "We ran in a small group and got on well. Somewhere down the road, our fathers had their differences. By the time we got to Cambridge, I guess we found it easier to avoid each other than confront the issue."

"You never mentioned this."

He shrugged. "Never had reason to. It makes no difference. That's in the past. Perhaps if he spoke to Lady Joanna, she might understand why you did what you did."

"What I did was unforgivable. Whether or not she comes to understand me one day, she deserves better than the way I treated her." David noticed a spot of dung on the side of his boot and scraped his foot in the dirt.

"If Lady Joanna doesn't marry you, she must marry Sir Frederick, you've said. Surely you can't be the lesser of the two options."

"At least I was able to resolve that problem. I agreed to buy Patriot for an amount that will allow Northcotte to pay off Sir Frederick."

Knightwick offered him a wry grin. "Well, that resolves one of our problems, too. We can't enter two horses we own against each other, so we can improve Triton's chances of winning."

"No, we can't. I thought to gift Lady Joanna with the horse after our wedding."

"You plan to bribe her to marry you? I don't see how that will improve her feelings toward you."

"No. I'll give her the horse outright. It won't make up for what I put her through, but it's rightfully hers."

Knightwick studied him long enough that David grew uncomfortable and looked away. His brother said, "I can't say anything you've ever done in the past has made me less than proud, but at this moment, I'm quite pleased to call you brother."

Try though he might, David couldn't bring himself to smile. He wasn't proud of finally doing the right thing for Lady Joanna. He wished he'd chosen that path from the start. "I need to tell Father what I've done, even though I used my own funds to pay Northcotte. I'd hate for Father to hear of this through someone else."

Going in search of his father, David found him in his study, not at his desk, but in a chair near the window looking out toward the paddock. David hesitated at the doorway. "May I come in?"

Father didn't shift his gaze from the window. "Of course."

"The household is bustling with preparations for the wedding. Mother has the girls tying posies, and Hugh and Sam carrying vases too large for the maids to handle."

"She should let the footmen do that."

"They're busy with other errands. I believe Mother would move the entire drawing room out under the canvas she has set up, if she could."

Father didn't comment. David sat in a nearby chair and mentally tossed a coin as to how to begin. "I must tell you some news that might upset you. But you've a right to know."

"I'm sure you've done the right thing, son, whatever it is."

"The situation is a bit complicated. I made an offer for Lady Joanna Hurst's hand."

His father blinked, then turned to study him, his expression unreadable. "Northcotte's girl."

"Yes. His son is the earl now, if you'll recall."

"I think your mother mentioned that, once."

David waited, hoping he had more to say. After a minute or two of silence, he pressed on. "In the course of the discussion with Northcotte, I offered to buy Patriot."

"He'll be a fine addition to the stud. I'm surprised Northcotte agreed to part with him. I hope you didn't pay too much."

David shook his head, then realized his father wasn't looking his way. "The price was fair, and my reasons for purchasing him were sound."

"That's fine, then."

"I'm not keeping him, though. I'm giving him to Lady Joanna."

Father shifted in his chair, sitting up straighter, placing

his palms on his knees. "Ah, I see. A wedding gift. Not the usual sort of gift one might think of, but probably fitting."

"She refused my proposal. However, I'm still giving her the horse. I...uh, I've done some things of which I'm not proud, Father. While I was getting to know Lady Joanna, I was also seeking evidence against her brother in the poisonings at the race meetings."

His father's frown said as much as his words could. Before the man could comment, David pushed on. "It was poorly done of me, and I regret it, and I deserved her refusal. Her hatred."

"I can't say I'm surprised to hear you pursued Northcotte, after the way his father and I behaved."

David cleared his throat and wiped his damp palms on his breeches. "Would you care to tell me what happened? You've been cold toward each other for as long as I can remember."

"It goes back before either you or Knightwick were born. We were friendly enough in Cambridge until it came to sports. He had a passion for winning. Well, more of an obsession, I'd say. When a group of us would ride home on holiday, he'd challenge anyone who'd accept. Point out a landmark in the distance and off we'd go. Eventually, we were laying down bets on the winner."

All the starch went out of Father as he sighed. "Obviously, we continued to compete after we left university, and each began filling our stables with quality runners. Yet Northcotte wasn't willing to leave the competitiveness with the horses. When he learned I intended to offer for your mother's hand, he became determined to win her away from me."

"He made an offer to Grandfather?"

Father nodded. "My family and hers were already friends, so I had the edge there, but your grandfather asked your mother whom she preferred."

"Well, thank goodness she chose you."

"Northcotte couldn't stand to lose. He vowed to break me. The only avenue he had left was his horses."

To some little extent, David understood how a man could go mad over his runners, but not to the point of destroying a perfectly good animal. "So, when Zephyr began to win, he had to remove the competition one way or another."

"That's what I assumed." Father said. "But we never found any proof."

David had a sudden thought. "Was there anyone else at that time that was angry with you?"

Father's jaw shifted back and forth briefly before he responded. "There were always losing bettors who might wish for a horse to quit running. And the losing owners, of course. Most of them took the losses good-naturedly, though. They knew their horses would have another chance at Zephyr at the next race meeting."

"What about away from the horses? Anyone with an old grudge? A tenant who might have been forced to remove from the estate?"

"I've never evicted a tenant, and neither did my father. As far as I know, they're all happy to live in Bridgethorpe."

Shaking his head, David tried to think of any other situation that might have angered someone enough to kill Zephyr.

"Why all of these questions about Northcotte and Zephyr? It happened so long ago. There's no point dwelling on it."

"You don't think there's a connection to Venus and Bacchus becoming ill at the meeting last year?"

"I thought they attributed that to moldy hay in the course stables."

"Wouldn't more horses have gotten sick, if that were the case? I can't help but connect the two, especially after one of Northcotte's grooms died at Newmarket."

Father breathed loudly and appeared to sag in his chair. "If you have proof, speak to the constable. If you have suspicions, I question why you wanted to tie yourself with Northcotte's family."

"My suspicions were misdirected. Since I met with Northcotte before leaving Town, I can't imagine him capable of such deeds." David couldn't admit his obsession had been based on the desire to please his father. As he studied the man, he noticed how the left side of his face seemed slightly slack, and his left hand was curled hard into a first. He'd lost weight, judging from the hollows in his cheeks. He looked ten years older than the last time David had seen him.

He couldn't imagine losing a horse could have done this to his father. Bridgethorpe's melancholy might have brought on some other illness. "Are you unwell, Father?"

Shifting in his seat, his father glanced at him, his right eyebrow raised. "My health is unchanged from yesterday."

That didn't answer his question. "You would tell me if there was reason for concern, wouldn't you?"

"There's no reason for you children to worry about an old man."

"You aren't that old. And it's natural for us to worry. We love you, Father."

His father smiled, although his smile was unbalanced. "I love you, too, son."

David forced the worry from his thoughts. "Triton is doing well. He wins as many as he loses, if not more." He didn't add that the only horse he lost to was Northcotte's Patriot. No need to mention that, after admitting he'd bought the horse and was giving him away.

"That's fine. You've done well with your program. I'm happy for you." He didn't look happy. He looked spent.

"You should come to a race meeting. It would cheer you to watch him win. We can go to the Chester Meeting, as it's so close. Or come stay at Fernleigh for the October meeting in Newmarket."

"Perhaps. We shall see how I'm faring when the time comes."

David was defeated. Those words had been spoken so many times over the past five or six years, but his father never fared any better. "I'll look forward to it. I'd better not sit here any longer, or Mother will find me. I'll see you at dinner."

"Thank you for telling me what you've been up to."

"You're welcome, sir." Rising, David left the room. He should have been relieved at having that burden off his chest, yet he felt a full stone heavier than when he'd entered the room. The man he remembered no longer existed. Even though David had admitted he no longer blamed Northcotte or his father for their problems, he felt he'd failed his father by not finding the culprit.

THE MORNING OF STEPHEN'S WEDDING DAWNED GRAY AND gloomy, but brightened by the time the entire clan reached the church in the village. David and Knightwick waited with Stephen for Lady Jane Marwick and her family to arrive. As both families were prominent and well thought of in the area, the pews were filled with their neighbors, the ladies in their gayest bonnets, and children defied their parents' attempt to keep them quiet.

Stephen stood proud in his regimentals. The only sign of nerves showed in the way he clasped his hands in front of him. The visible scars on his face were a faint pink now, so that only the eye patch, and the way he turned his head to one side when listening to others, hinted at how severe the injuries were he'd received in battle the summer before.

The vicar came out the side door to where the three men stood. "Sir Perry's carriage has arrived. Stephen, Knightwick, will you come with me?"

David followed them through the door and joined his family in the front pew. He kept his eyes on his cousin when Jane walked up the aisle, and almost felt sorry for the man. An odd mixture of love and…terror was etched in Stephen's features. David could relate, he realized. The love he had no control over, his entire being overflowing with the desire to give Lady Joanna everything she could ever wish for, whether she wanted it from him or not.

The terror he could only imagine, since she'd turned him down. If she'd accepted his offer, she would have been dependent on him for everything in life. Her happiness, her security. Those would have been up to him to provide. Every decision he made at Fernleigh, every chance he took at a race meeting, reflected on his livelihood and the status his family enjoyed.

He wasn't foolish in the risks he took, and Fernleigh Stud had no financial problems to be concerned about. David knew he could put those concerns aside and trust himself to provide for his family. But Lady Joanna had no interest in starting a family with him.

The knowledge burned a hole in his gut.

The service wound down, the couple hurried outside, and everyone piled into their carriages to return to Bridgethorpe Manor for the wedding breakfast. The outdoor room Mother had created under the canvas tent could compare to the finest dining rooms in all of London. The tables were covered in white damask cloths, with pristine white china and gleaming silver at each place setting. Bowls of pink and yellow flowers were dotted about the space, their perfume subtle.

Jane sat at a table near the back, her parents on one side,

Stephen and the Earl and Countess of Bridgethorpe on the other. David's breath caught when he thought how much his aunt would have enjoyed this day. He said a quick prayer for her and his uncle that they continued to rest in peace.

Making a path through the well-wishers, David reached the happy couple. He bent and embraced Jane, who'd grown up on the adjoining property. They'd all been friends since they were old enough to leave the nursery. "Never was there a more beautiful bride."

"Thank you, cousin. You're all my cousins now; I'm so blessed! I might still be lacking in brothers and sisters, but the differences are merely words, aren't they? I'm so pleased to be part of the Lumley family at last." Her eyes glowed with excitement, shifting to a warmer love when she looked at Stephen.

David tapped his cousin on the shoulder to draw the man's attention from his bride. "Good show, old man. May your blessings be many."

Stephen clasped David's hand in both of his. "Thank you. I can't imagine being more blessed than I am now."

Just eight months ago, Stephen had returned from hospital still adjusting to the loss of vision in one eye and hearing in one ear. He'd discovered his parents had died in a fire just days before, and he'd been certain his life was over.

David remembered the early days of worry, when he feared his cousin might harm himself even more, or accidentally kill himself when drunk, but Stephen had healed quickly, in both spirit and body. No one deserved a happier life that these two, who'd loved each other since childhood.

Their betrothal had also had a rocky beginning, with Stephen being deep in his cups when he professed his undying love. Jane had calmed down eventually and accepted his second proposal.

Was there any hope Joanna might do the same? It wasn't

very likely. Being drunk wasn't even close to the transgressions he'd committed.

Pushing on and letting someone else congratulate the two, David found his seat at his family's table, and sat between the twins, Patience and Madeleine. Patience hugged him, as she was wont to do at random times. "I can't wait until you or Knightwick marries."

He chuckled, tamping down the sorrow those words stirred in him. "Why is that?"

"Weddings are so much fun. You're almost as old as Stephen. Will you marry soon?"

He rubbed the pad of his thumb on her cheek. "We'll see. That requires finding a lady who would have me, you understand."

Madeleine scoffed. "Who wouldn't have you? Hannah writes that all the ladies she has met envy her for her handsome brothers."

"There, you see? They wish they had me for a brother, not a husband. My case is hopeless. I'll never find a woman to love me." He cupped his hand over his heart, mocking the pain that was more real than he'd admit.

Hannah chose that moment to join them. "Perhaps if you opened your eyes, you'd see the one right before you."

He glanced playfully around the table. "All I see are my sisters. As lovely as you all are, I cannot marry any one of you. And no woman could compare to your beauty and grace."

Ten-year-old Lucy Anne waggled her head back and forth. "I know who you'll marry. Patience told me so."

The sister in question gasped. "Hush. I said no such thing."

"You did, too. You said Hannah wrote that David was going to propose to a lady named Joanna, and Joanna would be our sister."

David lifted an eyebrow in the direction of the eldest of his sisters. "Is that true, Hannah? And what other tales have you told them?"

"She said—" Hannah's hand abruptly cut off Lucy Anne's ability to speak.

Hannah smiled and fluttered her lashes. "I've been writing them about the balls, who wore what color gown, and which lady cropped her hair in the latest mode."

He nodded, fighting to keep the stern press to his brows. "I'm certain you would never gossip about what your brothers did. Which ladies they escorted about town, or danced with every night."

Wide-eyed, she replied, "Never. My brothers' lives are their own to live. I would never tell tales on them."

"That's good to know. Because your brothers would never speak of the lord who you attempted to step off the path with in Lady Brackelhurst's garden. Or anything else you might have neglected to include in your letters to your sister."

The twins gasped. "What lord is this?"

"Did he kiss you?"

"Who's Lady Brackelhurst?" asked Lucy Anne with a frown. "Do we know her?"

Grateful at least one of his sisters still retained some innocence, David slipped away from the table. He shook his head, realizing in another five years, Patience and Madeleine would take London by storm. By then, Sam would be old enough to assume the role of scowling watchdog. David planned to be busy filling his own nursery.

If only he could convince the woman he loved to marry him. How could he, when she didn't want to see him? He needed an excuse to talk to her, a way to prove how important she was to him, without angering her further.

CHAPTER TWENTY-ONE

*T*wo nights later, David was startled from a sound sleep by someone pounding on his bedchamber door. "What is it?"

"A rider brought you a message, sir. He claims it's urgent." The butler Hodgson's voice was graveled by sleep.

David pulled on a wrapper and opened the door. Hodgson handed him a sealed letter, which David tore open, then took the candle from the butler's hand. The writing was difficult to make out.

LUMLEY,

My sister has taken ill in suspicious circumstances. I fear it's connected to the incidents we recently discussed, and I beg your assistance in finding who did this to her. We are staying at the White Harte in Windsor until the doctor says she may travel, if she recovers. I've sent for my mother to join us.

Northcotte.

. . .

"Damn." He crumpled the letter and tossed it into the cold fireplace. "Is the messenger still here?"

"Yes, sir. He was ordered to wait for a reply."

"Tell him I'll ride with him to Windsor. Wake Knightwick and tell him he must join me. Take the messenger's horse to the stables and have three mounts readied." David opened his wardrobe and pulled out some clothing.

"Yes, sir."

David didn't bother to pack a bag. He could send for his clothes from London, or buy what he needed in Windsor. They must travel quickly, only resting long enough for fresh horses to be saddled along the way. He'd be unable to sleep until Lady Joanna was well.

Knightwick met him in the hallway, buttoning his waistcoat while their valet, still in his wrapper, scurried behind with a coat and cloak. "What has happened?"

"Lady Joanna is ill. Northcotte suspects it's connected to the poisonings at the other race meetings." He trotted down the stairs.

"Was she not in London? I don't see how the events could be related."

"Northcotte said they're at the White Harte in Windsor, so they were likely at the race meeting at Ascot Heath when she took ill."

In the courtyard off the servant's entrance, a man sat waiting on a horse. One groom stood nearby with a lantern, and another held the reins of two more horses. David and his brother mounted. "We can talk more when we stop to change horses. There's no time to waste."

Daylight had come and gone again by the time they arrived in Windsor. The messenger took their horses to the stables while David and Knightwick entered the White Harte Hotel. Upon enquiring as to the location of Northcotte's room, they were led to a small suite on the second floor. David rapped on the door and barged in when it opened. "How is she?"

Northcotte looked quite pale and disheveled, and fidgeted with the bottom button on his waistcoat, his voice rough when he spoke. "She sleeps, still. The doctor says if she wakes, it will mean she most likely will recover. Until then, we wait."

"May I see her?"

"Of course." Northcotte led David to a closed door. Knightwick took a seat in the main room to wait.

David stepped into the dark, quiet chamber. Lady Joanna's maid sat in a chair near the bed. She rose and crossed to the dressing area and made herself busy there. A lamp burned with a low flame on the table beside the bed, throwing flickering light on Joanna's face. The shadows beneath her eyes had a pink tinge, and her lips were almost as white as the pillow she rested her head upon.

He reached a hand out to brush a stray curl off her face, but caught himself in time, remembering the maid's presence. The fact that Northcotte waited in the outer room spoke volumes about his trust in David. Did he know Joanna had turned down David's offer? Her brother had let her attend the race meeting, so perhaps he thought them engaged.

Or perhaps Northcotte had paid off Sir Frederick, and he no longer felt the desperate need for her to marry. As much as David wanted her for himself, knowing he'd had the power to save her from marrying that man gave him some small relief from the guilt he carried over what he'd put her through. Even stronger than the guilt was the knowledge he was powerless to save her now.

Joanna's brows drew together, and her lips parted. Her head thrashed one way, then the other, and her hand pressed against her stomach as she moaned.

No longer caring that her maid might be watching, he ran his fingertips over her cool cheek. "Shhh," he whispered. "Rest, dearest. You must get well."

He reached for the cloth draped over the edge of a bowl on the table. Dunking the cloth and wringing it, he patted her forehead and the sides of her face. She wasn't feverish, but she seemed to calm under his attentions. If he found out who did this to her, he would kill that man with his own hands. She must recover, so he could beg her forgiveness and plead with her to marry him. He couldn't live without her.

"Come back to me."

She sighed. Her lips moved, but no sound came out. He prayed she heard him.

He turned and left her bedchamber.

Knightwick and Northcotte sat discussing the incident. Northcotte imparted the details of the morning at Ascot Heath. "She was in the stall with Patriot. I've tried to keep her out of the stables, even before Bruce was killed, but she slips away from her maid, or my mother. I cannot keep her safe." He shook his head, wrapping his hand around the back of his neck and looking at the floor.

"She's headstrong," David agreed. "But perhaps that quality will see her through this. How did she become ill?"

"Patriot's groom said she watched him while he brushed Patriot and cleaned his hooves after the race. Outside his stall were some oatcakes wrapped in a cloth that an old woman had given him earlier. Joanna mentioned being hungry, and the groom offered her some."

Northcotte rose and began to pace. "During the night, my sister awoke complaining of stomach pains. She vomited for several hours, and eventually fell back asleep. Her maid tended to her, expecting her to wake in the morning feeling better. But she would not waken."

"Do you suspect there was something in the oatcakes?" David asked.

"The groom took ill that night also, but he recovered the next morning. He only ate one cake, and he believes Joanna had at least two. I've no idea what was in them. The groom didn't know the woman who gave them to him. He just assumed she was a villager with a generous heart."

"If he recovered so quickly, there is a good change she will, too." Knightwick looked at David as he said this, his voice reassuring.

"What does the doctor say?"

Northcotte stopped and looked toward the closed door where his sister lay. "He says she's strong and healthy, and should recover. He doesn't understand why she still sleeps, though. I fear—" He didn't finish the thought.

David nodded. "Someone intended to kill your groom. Why? You have other men who can ride Patriot. Why not kill the horse, if the idea was to keep him from competing?"

"I don't know. I thought Patriot might have been his original target, until I spoke with the groom. As it was, I ordered the stallion be returned to Hampshire immediately, to be safe. If my sister recovers, it would kill her to learn her horse was dead."

His chest tightening, David snapped at his choice of words. "She will recover. We must believe it. We can't do anything to help her at this point. Except find the man who did this."

"And let the magistrate deal with him," Knightwick warned.

David met his brother's glare, returning it with all the anger and frustration burning within. "I can't guarantee what I'll do when I find him."

Knightwick's lips thinned, but he didn't comment. He turned to Northcotte. "Have you attempted to locate the old woman?"

"I've had all my men question everyone they meet, as well as inquiring at the pubs. There are a few women who sell cakes and meat pies on the street. The groom hasn't recognized any of them."

"If Sir Frederick is behind it," David said, "you can wager she has been removed to another shire."

"Why do you assume he did it?" his brother asked.

"I assume you repaid your debt after I bought Patriot." David said to Northcotte. "Within a matter of days, someone attempts to keep your horse from running. I've met Sir Frederick, spoken with him when Joanna was there. I don't think it's money that drives him. He seems to thrive on holding the vowels of men who are above him in society."

"True," said Knightwick. "He's known to prefer loaning money to titled men. One might suggest they have a greater income with which to repay him, but their money is usually entailed. Any funds at their disposal have obviously been depleted by the time they come to him. He knows he cannot claim the title to the encumbered properties, so why does he accept their IOUs at all?"

Northcotte pursed his lips. "He has accepted thoroughbreds as collateral. He frequents the race meetings, and is well known by many of those who have entered runners. Why would he want to loan money against these horses, when he could afford to buy them outright?"

David crossed his arms over his chest. "Would you have sold Patriot, had he asked?"

"Of course not. Aside from finally having a runner who could bring my stud back to profitability, Joanna loves that horse above all the others."

Now David took up pacing to help him think. "Aside

from finding the old woman, how can we prove who is behind this?"

A knock on the door interrupted David's thoughts. Northcotte crossed the room and opened the door. Allowing the man to step inside, he introduced him to the others. "Lord Knightwick, Mr. Lumley, this is Mr. Grimford, who is working with the local magistrate to solve this."

The portly man took off his hat and nodded. "My lords, I bring news rather than answers. This morning a groom was found unconscious in the stables. He'd been hit with a shovel on the back of his head. He'll survive, but he didn't see his attacker."

"Who does the groom work for?"

"Lord Apperly."

Knightwick shook his head. "I don't know the man. How many horses had he entered?"

"Just the one, my lord."

Looking at his brother, Knightwick commented, "And if that horse doesn't run, he has no chance of winning, no chance at the purse." Speaking to the investigator, he said, "Find out if Apperly owes money to Sir Frederick Aldwen. He might try to deny borrowing from a moneylender, but we have reason to think that man is the connection between several 'accidents' at race meetings in recent years."

"Very good, my lord. I'll look into it." Grimford paused as he turned to leave. "How fares Lady Joanna? Is she recovering?"

"It's too soon to tell." Northcotte opened the door for the man. "The doctor believes she has a chance, though."

"I'm pleased to hear it, my lord. She's too bonny a lass to die like this."

David shuddered, then quickly schooled his thoughts to a positive outlook. Joanna would get better. He considered the series of poisonings and injuries at the meetings to distract himself. One thing concerned him about the idea Sir Frederick was behind Zephyr's death. "To your knowledge," he asked his brother, "Did Father ever borrow money?"

"No, he's never needed to. When he took to his rooms and I began helping run the estates, all the books were in order, our finances were what I expected to find."

"Then Sir Frederick had no reason to cause problems for Bridgethorpe or Fernleigh Stud. Why would he want Zephyr dead?" Pacing the length of the carpet, David tried to connect the incidents. "I asked Father if he had any connection with the man, and he said no. What would Sir Frederick have to gain by Zephyr's death?"

Northcotte sat with them again. "We know my father was borrowing from the man at the time Zephyr died. Sir Frederick probably knew he stood no chance of being repaid as long as your horse kept winning."

It didn't make sense to David. "There were plenty of race meetings where Zephyr was not entered. Why didn't your father enter some of those? He had some good runners. He would have won some decent purses. Or he could have challenged for some matches outside the meetings. Bridgethorpe said he did that often when they were young."

"I believe it was personal by then. I don't know why he singled out Bridgethorpe, but my father was obsessed with beating him."

From the doorway to Joanna's room came the maid's voice. "My lord, my lady is awake."

David and Northcotte ran to her bedside. Joanna moved about, turning her head from side to side. She mumbled something unintelligible. Reaching her first, David put a hand on her shoulder. "Shhh, it's all right. Do you hear me?"

Her movements quieted, but her eyes didn't open. "Hurts."

"What hurts? What can I do for you?" David pushed her

hair back off her face, his heart clenching at the shadows beneath her eyes.

"Everything hurts."

David looked at the maid. "Did the doctor leave some powders for her?"

"Yes, sir. They're over here, sir."

"Prepare a glass for her, then." He put his arm around her and helped her sit, her eyelids fluttering as she groaned.

"Mr. Lumley? Why are you here? Robert, what is this about? Why are you both in my room?"

"All is well now, Joanna," Northcotte said. "You've been ill. We've been worried."

The maid returned with the glass and gave it to Joanna, who drank it, her face twisting in distaste. "Oh, that is horrid. What are you giving me?"

David smiled. "Something the doctor left for you. I hope it will ease your pain."

She leaned heavily against David's arm, and he let her rest on the pillow. She sighed and her eyes closed.

"Do you want to sleep?" he asked.

"I'm hungry."

David asked the maid to fetch some soup, or something easy to eat. "I will let the doctor know you've awakened."

Knightwick spoke from the doorway. "I'll see to it."

David nodded in thanks. "May I bring in another chair and keep her company?" he asked Northcotte.

"Joanna, would you like some company for a short spell?"

She licked her lips and offered a small smile. "Yes."

Northcotte returned to the sitting room while David carried in a chair. As soon as he sat near the bed, David took a moment to say a prayer of thanks. "I can't tell you how relieved I am to hear your voice."

"Why are you here? I'm sorry, that sounds ill-mannered

of me. Did you enter Triton in one of the sweepstakes at Ascot Heath?"

He leaned his elbows on his knees, so relieved she was willing to speak with him, he didn't care how rude she might be. "No. Your brother sent word you were ill, and asked our assistance in finding who did this to you. But I would have come without his request."

"Who did what to me? Why do I hurt so? Was I attacked?"

"No. There must have been something put in the oatcakes you and the groom ate, as you both took ill after eating them."

"Is the boy recovered?"

"He's well. He didn't eat as many cakes as you."

She closed her eyes, sinking more deeply into the pillow. "Thank goodness. He's a kind lad, very good with Patriot."

"Do you wish to rest? I don't want to overtire you."

"I wish to eat most of all. I'm starving."

He chuckled. "Something will be brought up soon. This sort of establishment must be used to offering meals at odd hours."

"Mr. Lumley, thank you for coming to see me."

"I should think you might call me David by now."

Her eyes blinked open. "But we—that is, I didn't..."

"I'm aware you did not accept my proposal. We can discuss that when you are well." He cleared his throat. "If you don't wish to renew our acquaintance, I'll respect that. But I'll find who did this to you. His deed won't go unpunished."

She nodded. "Thank you."

CHAPTER TWENTY-TWO

A week later, Joanna and Robert were at home in Eaton Place, their lives seemingly normal again. Robert spent his time in his office, or away from the town house. Joanna sat in her room reading or writing letters to her friends in Hampton. She had no strength, no desire to go out for a walk or a ride. For the first time in her life, resting was the only thing that appealed to her.

Resting, however, gave her too much time to think about how foolish she was to have trusted Mr. Lumley. Her heart continued to ache, and an emptiness had taken up residence inside her where happiness should reside. She loved him, or her affections had begun to turn to love. She might always love him, keeping her from considering another man as husband. Being able to trust again would be difficult, that she knew. How did one tell the difference between true love and a false imitation of it?

On the eighth day, when Starley came to tell her Amelia was calling, she allowed her friend to come in. Not wishing to appear the invalid by remaining in her room, Joanna met her in the morning room. "How happy I am to see you again."

Amelia returned her hug. "I've missed you terribly. There have been so many times in the past two weeks where I've turned to tell you something at an assembly only to remember you aren't there."

"Tell me now. Who is dancing with whom? Have any betrothals been announced? Has Sir Richard made his feelings plain?"

"I believe he is close. He left Town for a few days but said he'd call on me when he returns. I'm so excited, I can't sit still." She suddenly sobered. "What of you? Has your brother said anything more about Sir Frederick?"

"No. I don't know whether he's afraid to start another row with me, or if he believes I've an understanding with Mr. Lumley."

Amelia shook her head. "I still don't understand how you came to turn him down. You were so excited about his attentions."

Joanna couldn't reveal the whole tale, even to her dear friend. She was ashamed on some level, both that her family could have been involved in the scandals Mr. Lumley had accused them of, and that she had fallen in love with a man who would abuse her friendship the way he had. "I couldn't accept him once I learned the kind of man he is. He never loved me."

"I saw how he looked at you. Even Sir Richard doesn't gaze at me that way. My cousin and her husband spent hours staring into each other's eyes like that before she married, and they are happy still, four years later."

"Your cousin's husband didn't gain her affections under false pretenses." Pain still stabbed at her heart when she recalled his words in her brother's study. "Please, can we not discuss it anymore?"

"I'm sorry. I don't want to distress you. What will you do now that the Season is ending?"

"My aunt has agreed to let me stay in Bath. Northcotte hasn't given me permission yet, but I'm still recovering from my illness. The waters there will be good for me."

"My offer still stands for you to visit us."

"Won't you be planning your wedding?"

Amelia shrugged. "If I am, you can help me decide between roses and lilies for my bouquet." Her eyes suddenly widened. "Oh, dear, will that be too difficult for you, with all that has happened? I'm the worst of friends to not think of you."

Joanna patted her hand. "You're my dearest friend. Your happiness makes me happy. Even if I don't visit over the summer, I expect an invitation to your wedding."

Starley cleared his throat from just inside the room. "Lady Hannah Lumley wishes to know if you are receiving callers."

Joy filled Joanna. "Yes, show her in, please."

Lady Hannah and her maid entered with the decorum due the finest of houses, then Lady Hannah rushed forward to grab Joanna's hand. "I was so worried when I heard. Are you quite recovered?"

"I am, thank you. Please join us. I'll send for tea." After doing so, Joanna returned to her seat on the chaise near the fireplace. The days grew warmer, but she couldn't seem to rid herself of the chill that invaded her bones. "When did you return to Town?"

"We came back shortly after Stephen and Jane's wedding. Mother, Hugh and I, that is. I guess you know David and Knightwick went to Ascot Heath, not London. They've been on the road more than home since then."

The footman arrived with a tray, which Joanna had him set on the table in front of her. She poured the tea into the cups. "Traveling to race meetings?"

"I don't believe so. Hugh said something about investigations."

"Into what?" Amelia took the cup and saucer Joanna handed her.

"Into who tried to kill Lady Joanna." Lady Hannah's expression said she thought the answer was obvious.

Amelia gasped. "I thought it was merely tainted food. Someone intended for you to die?"

Joanna shook her head. "No one could have known I would eat those oatcakes. They were given to our groom. Someone wanted him dead."

Lady Hannah accepted her cup and saucer then sat back in her chair. "Hugh said that makes two of your grooms who have been poisoned. Why would anyone do that?"

"I don't know. It seems a severe scheme to ensure Patriot doesn't race, or doesn't win. They could accomplish the same with a burr under his saddle."

Amelia stirred sugar into her tea and took a sip. "Please say you won't attend any more race meetings, Joanna. At least not until they find who is doing this."

"I won't be traveling, other than to Bath with my aunt. I tire so easily." Even sitting with her friends was taking a toll, but she nibbled a biscuit to keep up her strength. Speaking of her illness was also taxing, so she changed the subject, asking Hannah, "How was your cousin's wedding?"

"So lovely. I hope my wedding breakfast is just as beautiful." Hannah went on to describe in great detail the décor and the foods served.

Joanna became increasingly tired as she listened. She didn't want to credit it to the thought of a wedding she would not be having, so she smiled and made what she hoped were appropriate comments.

How had her life become such a mess? When she'd arrived in London this spring, she'd thought the best days were in front of her. But they'd quickly proven themselves to be worse than she could imagine living through. She almost hadn't lived through the last two weeks.

Hannah must have noticed her expression. "Are you truly well? Have we stayed too long? You look peaked."

Joanna smiled. "The doctor says I'll regain my strength soon. Cook has been making me some of her horrid gruel. I believe I shall heal quickly if only to escape eating any more of it."

"Would you care to go riding tomorrow?" Hannah asked, then shook her head. "No, you aren't strong enough for that, are you? I could ask Hugh to take us in the curricle. We could go back to Richmond Park and feed the ducks in the pond."

Memories flooded Joanna of David kissing her and asking if he could speak to Robert. It was more than she could bear. Her eyes welled and spilled over. The pain of her loss overwhelmed her.

"Oh, no, what have I said?" Hannah jumped up and rushed over, taking Joanna's hand.

Amelia came to her other side and wrapped an arm around her. "Please don't cry, Joanna. What can we do for you?"

Taking her handkerchief from her pocket, Joanna blotted her eyes. "I'm sorry to fall apart on you this way. All I've been through is catching up to me."

"Will it help to talk to us?" Hannah brought a small stool next to the chaise and sat by Joanna's knees.

Joanna hesitated. "I feel rather awkward discussing it."

"Because you love my brother," Hannah suggested.

"Yes. I don't want to hurt your feelings."

Hannah laughed. "I'm the first to admit when my brothers have done something foolish, but this time even David agrees with me. If he could find a way to undo his mistakes, he'd have done it weeks ago. There's nothing you could say against him that would hurt my feelings."

"Thank you for that." Joanna smiled, the tears not quite dried yet. "In recent weeks I've wished I never came to Town, but I would not have met you two. I'll be forever grateful for your friendship."

"And we are pleased to know you, aren't we Hannah?" Amelia said. "Maybe in time the bad memories will fade, and the good will rise to the top."

"I hope so." Joanna rested her head on Amelia's shoulder for a moment. "Will you both return for the Little Season? If so, we can attend the balls together and meet a whole new set of gentlemen."

Amelia patted the back of her head. "Well, I hope to be engaged by then, if Sir Richard asks when he comes back to Town. But being engaged doesn't mean I must sit home every evening. My beaux and I will help chaperone you two."

They all laughed at the idea of their parents agreeing to that. Joanna realized the friendship she shared with these two ladies was worth all the painful experiences she'd been through.

Well, all except almost dying. Nothing was worth going through that fearful time.

After Robert came home that evening, Joanna found him in his study. "May I interrupt you for a moment?"

He set down his pen and smiled. "Of course. What is troubling you?"

"Lady Hannah was here this afternoon, and of course, Mr. Lumley was mentioned. You know I overheard you two talking that night, don't you?"

"He said as much, yes."

"Yet, you continue to seek his aid in finding the person behind these poisonings. After he told the constable you were guilty of it."

"That's correct. I don't feel capable of the work needed to investigate all the incidents, while keeping you safe. I'm grateful for his help, and that of Knightwick."

Joanna scratched her fingernail on a spot on her dress, trying to find the right words. "How can you forgive him for believing you capable of murder?"

Robert leaned back in his chair, resting his elbows on the arms and making a steeple of his fingers. "Perhaps if he knew me, if he'd been a friend before making the accusations, it might have hurt more. There is history you're unaware of, however, between our fathers. Bridgethorpe and Father had a rivalry of sorts, and David grew up not trusting our father, and by extension, me."

She pursed her lips. "I don't find it any more comforting he thought father was a murderer."

"For as much as he said so, he didn't truly believe it. He was angry over Zephyr's death and needed someone to blame." Robert's lips thinned and he drew in a deep breath. "I have a confession of my own. I have tried to protect you and Mother from the depths of Father's problems in his final years, but I can see I'm doing you no favors. You need to see what kind of man Father was. He'd let his obsession for owning a winning runner drive him mad. He borrowed money to buy horses, but they didn't win. He couldn't see how he was destroying his own life, and all of ours."

"Father was borrowing money?" Those words sank in, making clear some other questions she'd had. "From...Sir Frederick?"

Robert ducked his head as if unable to meet her gaze. "Yes. And yes, that is why I was unable to turn down his suit for you. I thank God that matter was resolved in time."

"How were you able to pay him off?"

Again, he looked away, reaching for some letters on his desk. "I'm not at liberty to say. The debt is paid, and you're not under any obligation to marry Sir Frederick."

Robert's manner was very odd, but she knew better than to push too far. She tried a vague question. "Is Mr. Lumley responsible for the debt being paid?"

"I cannot discuss the business with you. But let me say this: David Lumley is a good man. Whether or not you intend to marry him, you need to move past this if you want to be happy."

"I don't know if I can." She sighed. "Thank you for speaking with me. I shall see you at supper." She rose and went to the small garden behind their home to consider her thoughts. Of one thing she was certain, she owed Mr. Lumley a great debt if he was responsible for saving her from Sir Frederick. But gratitude wasn't enough to base a marriage on, and she didn't know if she could trust him enough to believe he cared for her. He had pretended affection for her while alleging her brother was a criminal. Could she forgive him that?

STARLEY SHOWED DAVID INTO NORTHCOTTE'S STUDY AND closed the doors as he exited the room. Northcotte rose and motioned for David to sit. "Any news?"

David grunted. "None. The old woman at Ascot Heath might never have existed. You?"

"How can he leave no trace? He must pay the men who work for him quite well, because my man has offered a hefty purse in exchange for information."

"Knightwick has been inquiring at the clubs to see if anyone will admit to borrowing from Sir Frederick. I don't know what good it will do us to speak to them, but if he has threatened any of them, or if they've suffered some suspicious loss, perhaps we can persuade them to inform their magistrate, or Bow Street."

"Have you considered stationing men to watch the stables at each race meeting coming up?"

"My brother has several men lined up for Bibury next week. Will Patriot be entered?"

"I don't feel right entering him since he's now your horse. Besides, I still don't think it's wise to enter Patriot. If anything happens to that horse, it will kill Joanna. I have another horse I can enter." Northcotte licked his lips as if he'd swallowed something bitter. "I hate to risk a good runner to draw the man out, but it has to be done. I'll do as you have said, have someone stay with him at all times. And send my older grooms, whom I trust."

"Very well. It will be a long summer if we must continue like this, keeping watch over our horses 'round the clock."

A knock came at the door and Starley opened it. "Sir Frederick Aldwen is here to see you, my lord."

Northcotte met David's gaze before responding. "Tell him I'm not available."

"Very good, my lord."

When the door latched, David asked, "Don't you want to know why he's here?"

"I've paid my father's debt, so the only business he could have with me is my sister."

"You didn't refuse his offer for her?"

"I did, just as soon as I had his signature on my father's vowels. He didn't accept it as my final answer."

David rose. "What does he expect to do? Persuade Lady Joanna with the charm he doesn't possess? I wish she'd accepted my proposal so I could send him away for good."

"About that…do you plan to renew your suit with Joanna?"

"Would it do any good? She was in tears when she sent me away. I don't wish to hurt her further."

"She's been in tears since she refused you. I believe that hurts more than marrying you could ever do."

Combing a hand through his hair, David glanced at the door. She was probably upstairs. He could ask Starley to inquire if she'd see him. He didn't think he could bear it if she sent him away. "You know I'd give her everything she wanted. I thought, perhaps, in time…She seemed happy to see me in Windsor."

"It meant a lot to her that you were there. I think that told her more about you than any prior act."

"I hope so. Maybe when I return from Bibury I'll call on her. Start anew. Will she still be in London then?"

"She and my mother will leave for Bath that week, with Aunt Ophelia. You'd better speak to her before you leave Town."

David nodded. "I'll do so. I've some calls to make, so I'll take my leave. If you need assistance finding men to keep watch at the race meeting, send word here in Town, or at the Shepherd's Inn in Bibury."

Taking his leave more briskly than was warranted, David sought to reach his curricle before temptation won out and he begged Starley to ask if Lady Joanna would see him. He needed to give her time. He'd forgotten to ask if Northcotte had told her she now owned Patriot. He doubted the man had said anything, more likely leaving it for David to do. That gave him an excuse to call before he left Town.

As he trotted down the front steps to the street, David noticed a curricle parked nearby. He thought nothing of it, until he noticed the furry white side-whiskers of the man at the reins. Sir Frederick. Why hadn't he gone when he was turned away? David hesitated, the simmering heat of pent-up anger threatening to surface, then turned toward his own vehicle.

"Lumley."

He stopped. Slowly turned around. Gritted his teeth and reminded himself he was on a public street in front of his loved-one's home. "Sir Frederick. May I be of assistance?"

"You may keep your distance from Lady Joanna. I highly recommend it."

He could have recommended a wine for supper, his tone was so even. David took a few steps closer. "You don't speak for her. Of that I'm certain."

"She's confused by your flattery and pretty face. She will come to her senses soon."

David's arms began to tremble. He flexed his fingers. "Was she your intended target? You nearly killed her. How will that convince her she wants you?"

Sir Frederick sat up stiffly. "I've no idea what you're speaking of. I would never harm her."

Strolling closer, fighting the need to haul the man out of his curricle and pound him into the street, David kept his voice calm. "No, you told the old woman to give the cakes to Northcotte's groom. Why, because he'd paid his debt to you, and you could no longer lay claim to Lady Joanna's hand? But my lady enjoys sweets, and the groom was more than happy to share."

David gave the man credit, he didn't flinch. Sir Frederick could have been sitting in church on a Sunday morning. "I know not what you're referring to."

"Of course you don't. Listen well. The lady does not want you. You no longer have anything to hold over her brother. Don't trespass on their lives any longer."

"You do not speak for them, Lumley." Sir Frederick's calm

broke, and he shouted now. "You have no business ordering me about. You'd best keep to your own concerns."

The door to Northcotte's town house opened and Starley came down the stairs. "Is anything amiss, Mr. Lumley?"

"No, Starley. Sir Frederick was just leaving."

"Very good, sir." Starley remained where he stood, watching Sir Frederick.

Without a word, Sir Frederick picked up his reins and pulled away. David waited until he reached the end of the block before moving. "You'll inform Northcotte of this?"

"Of course, sir."

AS HE'D TOLD NORTHCOTTE HE WOULD DO, DAVID CALLED ON Joanna before he left for Bibury. She had color in her cheeks, finally, and the shadows beneath her eyes had faded. Her smile seemed genuine when he took her hand and bowed. "Good morning, my lady."

"Good morning. Please take a seat."

Nerves made it difficult to remain in one place, but politeness forced him to control the anxiety. "Thank you. I understand you will remove to Bath for the summer."

"Yes, my aunt has extended an invitation to Mother and me."

"Hannah was disappointed you won't be visiting Bridgethorpe Manor, but I can understand your reluctance. If it's any comfort, I'll be staying at Fernleigh in between race meetings, as I usually do." He told himself he wasn't leading her to talk about her feelings for him.

Her cheeks darkened. "I hope you don't think I was avoiding you."

"I'm not sure what to think. You didn't send me away in

Windsor, but you were so sick I cannot credit anything that was said then."

Her eyes widened. "Did I say something when I was out of my head?"

"No, I'm taking hope in what wasn't said." He held up a hand when she opened her mouth. "I'm not here to press my suit again, unless you wish it. I merely wanted to ask that I may still call you my friend."

"Yes, I would like that."

"I'm glad. Now, there's one more thing I must say before I go. I realize I'm not in the position to give you a gift, but there's something I purchased with you in mind. Northcotte will confirm he has agreed to it. Patriot is now yours."

"He's mine?"

"Yes. Your brother holds the signed papers."

"But how…? I don't understand."

"There is nothing to understand. I had it in my power to give you the one thing I knew you treasure most of all. I hope he brings you joy. And of course, wins."

Her eyes were glassy as she stared at him. "I don't know what to say. Thank you, of course, but those words are too weak to express what I feel."

He rose, wishing to leave before she said something she might regret. He would see her again, perhaps at a race meeting, and he could discover if her feelings for him had changed. But if he didn't escape immediately, he would utter the plea he so desperately needed to make. *Marry me.* "Enjoy your visit to Bath, my lady."

With a brief, formal bow, he left.

CHAPTER TWENTY-THREE

*T*he weather at Bibury, in Gloucestershire, was warm, and the stables were humid, their normal odors overwhelming David as he stood in Triton's stall. He wished they could determine who was poisoning people and animals at the race meetings, so he could once again enjoy the thrill of competition.

He smiled wryly. He hadn't fully enjoyed a race meeting in recent years, not until Triton won. He scratched his horse between the eyes. "You have done us proud, old boy. Let's do it again this afternoon, all right? Make this blasted heat worth bearing."

Pacing once more to the stall door, he looked into the passageway. Men walked back and forth, owners and grooms, judging by their clothes. Some entered stalls empty-handed, or bearing a bridle, others just continued out of the building. No one seemed out of place. He began to turn and pace back when movement caught his eye.

A man of small stature with graying dark hair exited a stall with a bucket in his hand. There was nothing odd about that, but the hairs on the back of David's neck rose inexplicably. The man pulled a paper from his pocket, glanced at it, and shoved it away again. He made his way down the row of stalls, glancing in each, then entered one. A moment later, he stepped out and headed for the building exit.

David coughed loudly to signal the others, and followed.

The tack room door opened and Knightwick came out. Sir Jasper appeared from another stall. David indicated the groom with the bucket, and they all began to run. Just as the man reached the sunlight, David caught his arm and spun him about.

"Stop! What's this?" the man shouted.

"We're wondering the same thing. Come with us." David jerked him back into the barn and dragged the struggling man into the tack room. As he pushed the man into a corner, David realized he was shoving a paper in his mouth. "No, you don't!"

David grabbed the man's jaw, prying his mouth open, and stuck a finger inside. Just as he'd curled it around the wadded paper, the man bit down. "Bollocks!"

Punching the groom with his free hand, David shook his other one.

"Did you get it?" Sir Jasper asked, stepping forward to hold the man by the sleeve.

"I did," David answered. He spread the small sheet and walked to the window. "It's a list of horses. Miss Bashful, Vulture, and Ploughboy. What were you doing to those horses?"

"I ain't did nuttin'," the groom barked, then spat on the ground.

"Where's the bucket you had?" David demanded.

Knightwick turned for the door. "I'll go look."

A short time later, he returned. "There was an extra bucket in Ploughboy's stall. I brought them both to be safe. I instructed Gilroy to replace the buckets in all three stalls, and sent for the constable."

Sir Jasper moved toward the doorway. "Is someone watching that those buckets aren't used by someone else? We need to dispose of the water safely. What is the condition of the three horses?"

Gilroy pointed to the buckets he'd set against the wall. "Here's the water, sir. The horses look well. There wasn't time for them to have drunk much, but they'll probably need watching."

"And should likely be scratched from their races," Knightwick added. "The constable will need to inform their owners."

David was too angry to wait on the constable. If this man was behind Lady Joanna's injury, or worked for the person responsible, he should be forced to drink the brew he'd been spreading. David fisted the front of the man's shirt, hauling him closer. Speaking in a low growl, he demanded, "Who ordered this?"

"Ordered what? I was watering the horses. How do you know it ain't my job?"

"Those horses already had water."

"Maybe they was wantin' more. It's a hot day."

Knightwick placed a hand on David's arm. "Leave it for the constable."

With one last shove, David released the groom. "He has to talk. We need to resolve this. Joanna needs her life back."

"Her life? Or is it yours that's bound in place by this?"

It was true. David couldn't stop worrying about Joanna until he knew why someone was doing this. He couldn't focus on his own life, couldn't relax and enjoy the race meetings, knowing they were all at risk by attending. It was beyond a distraction now. He genuinely feared for his family, the men who worked for him.

Time froze until a man finally called out from the stable entry. "Who called the watch?"

"Here. We're holding the man in here," Knightwick said. He introduced himself, Sir Jasper and his brother.

"I'm Eldred Whitmore. What's he done?"

"We believe he was poisoning several of the horses. We spoke to the magistrate in Gloucester and members of the Jockey Club earlier this week about our connection to the various incidents at other race meetings." Knightwick brought the man up to date.

"You see why we were taking precautions," David added. He held out the paper he'd taken from the groom's mouth. "He tried to destroy this list. These are the buckets from the stalls, plus the extra one."

Whitmore nodded. "We'll dispose of the water in them, I guess. Did any of the horses turn sick?"

"Not that we've seen," Knightwick said. "They'll bear watching. We're concerned with finding out who he works for."

"He's not likely to talk. Whoever hired him probably put the fear in him bigger than any threat we bring."

"Have we mentioned the reward for finding the man who poisoned Lady Joanna Hurst?"

David snapped his gaze on his brother. No reward had been discussed. Checking to be sure the groom had heard, David bit his cheek not to smile. The groom eyed them suspiciously, but interestedly.

"A reward might help," Whitley said, also looking in the direction of their suspect. "But likely this man knows nothing. He doesn't look smart enough to be involved in anything that requires brains."

That would either make him talk, or shut him up for good, David thought. He prayed it was the former.

"What kind of reward are we talkin' 'bout?" the groom asked, his gaze dancing around the room.

"Ten pounds." Knightwick took a few steps toward the groom. "Payable on the conviction of the responsible person. So not only do we need a name, we need proof."

David's pulsed roared in his ears. *Please, tell us who it is.*

The groom stared at Knightwick as if weighing what he knew. Ten pounds could easily equal a year's wages, or more. But if there wasn't enough evidence to convict his master, the groom might find himself out of a job, or worse, the next victim. David highly doubted any thought of loyalty passed through this cretin's mind.

"What kind of proof do you need?"

"Witnesses, as many as possible to any of the crimes." Whitley held up the note in his hand. "If you had any other instructions in writing, it would be most helpful."

The groom shook his head. "He told me to destroy the list. Ain't had but one horse name afore this."

"Who is 'he?'" David demanded.

"How do I know you'll pay?"

"You'll have to take that chance," Knightwick said. "We won't pay until he's convicted."

"Pay me part now, for the name."

"The name, and any evidence you can give us. One quid now, the rest on his conviction."

The groom scowled. "And if I don't have a name?"

Whitley stuck the note in his pocket and straightened. "Then I'll have to take you before the magistrate to be charged with all the crimes yourself."

Hanging his head, the man appeared to consider his chances. "Sir Frederick Aldwen is yer man."

David's hands fisted. "Is he here at the race meeting?"

"I dunno. I only speak to him at 'is London house."

Whitley walked between David and the groom. "I'll take it

from here, Lumley. Leave the investigation to me and my men."

"But we have information about all of the poisonings, and a few suspicious injuries," David argued.

"We'll be contacting you to tell us what you know, of course. And we'll see to the arrest of Sir Frederick if the evidence warrants it." Whitley motioned to a large man who appeared in the doorway, then roughly took the arm of the groom and led him outside.

After the constable left the tack room, all the starch in David's bones left him. He sagged against the wall. "Is it done, then?"

Knightwick raised his hands. "Who can say? They need to gather the proof, make the arrest, then take him before the magistrate. They'll have to contact all the other parishes with what they know and try to connect Sir Frederick to the crimes there. We'll be called to testify for the trials we are involved in."

"We must be on our guard until he's arrested. There's no telling what he might do to shut up the witnesses."

Sir Jasper spoke up. "Right now, we need to find North-cotte and inform him of what happened."

"I want to talk to the three owners of those horses today," David said.

Knightwick threw his arm across the doorway, blocking David's exit. "Whitley will take care of it."

"But I need to know—"

"No, you don't. Whitley will find out why Sir Frederick was doing this. Our part is done."

"But—"

"David, speaking to those men won't cure what's ailing you now."

Tension coursed down David's arms again and he ran his hands through his hair to burn some of the tingling away. "I want to kill him for what he did to Joanna."

"We all do," Sir Jasper said. "You can't challenge him to a duel over this, and anything else you tried would land you in court."

Knightwick withdrew his arm and stepped back so David could leave the tack room. "Why don't you go back to London and let Lady Joanna know they are close to arresting the man who harmed her? I'll stay with Triton and speak to Northcotte."

David met his brother's gaze, then that of Sir Jasper, who nodded. "I'll ride to Town with you. Lady Ophelia is concerned about us all."

"Very well, I'll call on Joanna." He turned on his heels, letting the pent-up frustration out as he strode to the inn where he'd stabled Nemo. Perhaps seeing Joanna, reaffirming she was well, would calm him, finally.

As David mounted Nemo ready to return to London, one of his grooms ran up. "Mr. Lumley, Lord Knightwick says you're to come to the Downs. It's urgent."

Waving for Sir Jasper to follow him, David kicked Nemo's flanks and galloped down the street to the stable at the racing grounds. He jumped off his horse, leading him by the reins as he entered the building. "Knightwick?"

"Here." His voice came from the tack room.

David stood in the doorway. "What news?"

"Sir Frederick was in the village after all. Whitley is escorting him to the magistrate in Gloucester as we speak."

"He was here? Did Whitley question him?"

Knightwick shook his head. "There is little to charge him with unless the three horses take sick. Whitley says they'll hold him and contact the magistrates in the other shires where Lady Joanna became ill and Northcotte's groom died. The coroners who investigated those crimes will probably come here to question him and decide which of them will prosecute first. Most likely they'll try him for the groom's death, although unless the man we caught today had more information, they won't have enough evidence."

David gritted his teeth. "Perhaps I should overtake them on the road and question him myself."

"Don't do anything foolish. I hoped you and Sir Jasper would ride to Gloucester and follow the proceedings. Or at the very least, the questioning."

Northcotte entered the stable and called out to them. "Is my man telling the truth of it? Sir Frederick has been arrested?"

"He has. He's on his way to the house of corrections in Gloucester."

"I hope they are able to prove something. I'll ride there and tell the magistrate what I know about Ascot."

"Good. Sir Jasper and I are going, also." David shook his head, knowing this all might come to naught. "Would it do any good to ask others who've borrowed money from him if they experienced any attempts at blackmail?"

Knightwick stroked his chin. "I say it can't hurt to find as many charges as we can against Sir Frederick, in case the two serious crimes can't be proven. I'll finish what I'm doing here in Bibury, looking for Sir Frederick's hired men, and will contact the gentlemen we know who have had dealings with the man."

David had to chuckle at this. "What happened to 'leave the investigation to Whitley?'"

Knightwick didn't smile in return. "I see nothing wrong with speeding up the investigation. Perhaps the gentleman would speak more freely with a peer than a constable. But as my connection to these crimes is less glaring than yours, I think it's better I be the one to do it."

Leave it to his brother to justify doing exactly what he'd told David not to do. Since he was itching to confront Sir Frederick, David was relieved he could finally do so.

NIGHT HAD FALLEN BY THE TIME DAVID, NORTHCOTTE, AND Sir Jasper arrived in Gloucester and found lodging. They had to wait until the next morning to speak to the magistrate. As they sat in the pub drinking ale and eating cold, sliced meat and bread, Northcotte suddenly grinned.

David swallowed what he was chewing, waiting to see if the lord would speak, then asked, "What has you so merry?"

Northcotte raised his mug. "This. Us. A year ago, I never would have imagined we'd be sharing a table and a tankard without guns pointed at our heads."

David leaned back in his chair. "I was never as rude as that, was I?" He tried to recall any time before recent months that he'd spoken crossly to Northcotte. That he'd spoken to the lord at all.

"Sometimes words aren't needed for a message to come through clearly." Northcotte sobered and took a bite of his bread.

Pride pushed David to defend his actions. Perhaps he'd drunk a tankard too many, but he didn't want the lord thinking he bore any ill will from incidents before they were born. "I explained myself when we spoke in your study. I carried the anger my father instilled in me. Or, that I thought he instilled. As it turns out, he didn't bear your father any anger. I think he felt sorry for the former earl."

Sir Jasper studied his food as if he'd never seen such fine cuisine. Northcotte took a drink, set down the mug and wiped his mouth with the back of his hand. "That is not surprising. Among my father's possessions when he died was a letter to a Lady Katharine."

Mother. David tried to choose his words carefully. "Father mentioned an attachment long ago on the side of one party, but not the other."

"That's putting it delicately. She turned him down, yes. It was never mentioned in my lifetime, and I believed he truly loved my mother."

"I don't fully understand how that came to affect their lives so completely when it came to horses. Their rivalry was enough that I believed my father hated yours. We would be wise to let the rivalry end with us."

"If I couldn't set it aside, I would not have accepted your offer for my sister's hand."

David took a long drink and motioned to the innkeeper for another round. "Well, she has her own reasons for keeping our families separate."

"You've asked her again? I was certain she'd come around." Northcotte stared at him with wide eyes.

"No, I'm giving her time to consider her heart. She wasn't as easily convinced to brush aside my believing you capable of murder."

Sir Jasper coughed into his tankard but recovered quickly and continued to eat in silence.

Northcotte chewed his lip. "I can see her point."

"I never really believed it, you know. You were a convenient target for my frustration. I couldn't let on I was incapable of breeding a winning runner." The words were still difficult to bite out. He'd managed Fernleigh for enough years he should have produced another horse like Zephyr. But none of his foals had the right combination of muscle and stride length to run like that horse.

As if Northcotte heard his thoughts, he said, "Zephyr was

one of a kind. Breeders all across England are kicking themselves that they haven't bred his equal."

It was probably true, but it didn't help ease the dissatisfaction David still carried. Triton had winning qualities and was a fine runner, but he wasn't Zephyr.

"You aren't the man I thought you were," Northcotte added, catching David off guard.

David's gaze jerked up to meet the earl's. "What do you mean by that?" he barked.

"I thought you loved my sister. Otherwise, if it weren't for Sir Frederick's threat, I would never have considered you suitable for Joanna. Yet you're willing to walk away without a fight."

David gripped the edge of the table, leaning forward and fighting to keep his voice down. "Walk away? I'm giving her what she wants. She has her horse, and the freedom to find some other man to marry. She begged me to go. I'm not the man to force her into a marriage she doesn't want. That was Sir Frederick's role."

"She didn't object to seeing you in Windsor. She seemed quite taken with you as she recovered. She never mentioned turning you down."

"Well, she did. And that's the end of it."

"It appears you aren't the man for her."

"I *am* perfect for her. Who else would ask her opinion about a foal's future as a runner? Who else would encourage her to spend time in the stables? As my wife, she would be happy for the rest of her days, and be loved, not displayed for social status, or whatever that bounder wanted her for."

Northcotte's eyes narrowed. "But she won't have the chance because you've given up the fight."

"I told her I'd stay away."

"Before or after she almost died?"

"Before. But you sent for me to come to Windsor, so I wasn't going back on my word by calling on you there."

Sir Jasper cleared his throat. "I believe the ladies are removing to Bath next week."

"That's fine. The waters should help her recover." A whisper of jealousy snaked through David at the thought of her meeting other men, but the number of eligible, interesting men in Bath should be fewer than she'd met in Town. He shouldn't feel that way, but he did. He wanted her for himself.

Northcotte chuckled, shaking his head. "I believe he thought you might recall some business you needed to attend to in Bath."

"Of course. I was simply trying to plan my scheme to run into her there." In truth, he was still trying to convince himself she'd see him as something more than the friend she'd agreed to tolerate. Something much more.

Could she possibly be hoping he'd ask her again? He was afraid to let hope into his heart. The pain of being refused twice by the woman he loved would be unbearable. Although he doubted it could compare to the pain he'd put Lady Joanna through.

He didn't deserve her. But he couldn't go through life without her.

CHAPTER TWENTY-FOUR

The next morning, David paced outside the chamber in the magistrate's office where they'd taken Sir Frederick. He'd been barred access to the questioning and was ready to crawl out of his skin with the need to confront the bounder. After several hours, Lord Clermont, the magistrate, came out of the room alone. David jumped at the chance to obtain some answers. "My lord, did you learn anything?"

"Mr. Lumley, I can only speak of what pertains to your own interests, and frankly, I don't think we'll be questioning him on those incidents. We have no witnesses and no evidence. You'd be better served letting us try him on these recent poisonings. The sentence would be the same, and you'd have your result."

"To be honest, sir, I'm most interested in the Ascot matter. Has he confessed to anything?"

"He's too smart to confess to any act. His groom has supplied us with a number of names of men who could have been involved there, however. If even one of them tells the truth, it will be enough."

The relief washing over David wasn't enough for his smile to be natural, but he did so anyway as he thanked the magistrate. "Lord Northcotte will be pleased to know this." He shook the man's hand and returned to where Sir Jasper and Northcotte waited.

Lady Joanna would also be pleased. And he had his excuse to visit Bath, once the proceedings were through. The case would take time to come to trial, but once the constable and magistrate finished gathering evidence, he could go to Joanna and tell her the news.

Northcotte rose from the bench where they waited. "What did Clermont say?"

"Nothing new. Sir Frederick isn't talking. But they might have enough witnesses to proceed anyway."

"As soon as I've given him my testimony, we can leave, I imagine. There's no point in remaining."

David nodded. "I thought I'd ride to Town to let Joanna know. I should be able to catch her before they leave for Bath."

"I'm relieved to hear it. Give her my best, and to my mother and aunt."

The door to the chamber opened again and Sir Frederick was led out by two burly men. He stopped short when he saw the others. "Northcotte. Lumley. I should have known you were behind this blasphemy."

"If you mean, did we tell the magistrate of our dealings with you, then you are correct," David said evenly.

"What dealings do you speak of, Lumley? We've had no business between us."

Northcotte jumped in. "I believe he referred to the matter between you and my father, and the resulting threats you made to me after his death."

Sir Frederick held his chin high, as if to allow him to look down his nose at all of them, in spite of his being the shortest of the men present. His contempt bled heavily into his voice. "I never threatened you. I offered you an alternative if you were unable to raise the blunt in time, to keep you from losing your stud and horses."

"You blackmailed him with his sister's life in the balance," David roared, taking a step closer to Sir Frederick.

One of the bailiffs answered with a step of his own, putting himself between David and his foe. It didn't keep Sir Frederick from bellowing back. "She was mine, until you interfered. She would have brought me the one thing money couldn't buy—entry into the finest homes in London. That was all I needed to complete my scheme."

The bailiffs each grabbed one of Sir Frederick's arms, jerking him away and ending the discussion. Shaking his head, David looked at Northcotte. "He needed richer clientele. I don't understand what he thought to gain from them. Their properties and money would be entailed."

Sir Jasper tipped his head to one side as he watched Sir Frederick walk away. "But their sons had larger allowances than the average young man, and they would likely borrow larger amounts. With the percentage rate Sir Frederick added on, his profits would be endless."

Realizing how close Lady Joanna had been to marrying the man caused a painful hollow to hit David's gut. He'd been no better than Sir Frederick in using Lady Joanna to gain what he needed. To some extent, many marriages were based on that—a young miss in search of a title, a penniless lord in need of an heiress to support his estate. Somehow, those situations seemed less mercenary than what he'd done. With a heavy sigh, he raked his hair off his face. "Well, shall we see if they're ready to record what you know, Northcotte? I'm eager to be on my way."

Northcotte turned to David. "There's no need for you two to stay. I'll ride home to Hampshire when I'm done. If you leave now, you won't need to take lodging when you change horses."

David was eager to see Joanna, to make certain she was happy as well as in good health. He looked at Sir Jasper. "Shall we be off, then?"

~

JOANNA SAT IN THE DRAWING ROOM OF THE LONDON TOWN house and poured a cup of tea for Amelia, who had just joined Joanna and her aunt. "You look rather peaked, Amelia. Are you not well? Or are you sad to be returning home after such an exciting Season?"

Amelia's fragile smile broke and she fished her handkerchief from her reticule. "I have news—" Her voice cracked. "Oh, Joanna, he's eloped with Lady Elizabeth!"

"Who has? Not Sir Richard? I thought her father refused him and insisted she marry another."

"He did refuse, and next month she was to marry the lord her father chose. Sir Richard was to call on me today, and I was certain he was going to speak to my father. But a letter came in this morning's post, and he apologized most ardently for any injury he might have caused, but he had to act in consideration of his heart, so he was going to marry Lady Elizabeth in spite of her father's wishes."

"How shocking," gasped Aunt Ophelia. "And how dreadful of him to send such a note."

"He claimed he didn't wish for me to read it in the papers. He thought it would be kinder to tell me himself."

Joanna set down her cup and saucer so no one would notice how her hands shook. Imagine both of them suffering heartbreak. "I'm so sorry, Amelia. I know how this must hurt."

"I know you do, and I'm sorry for it. Whatever did we do

to deserve such scandalous attachments? I fear I'll never love again." Amelia dabbed her cheeks.

"You girls did nothing wrong," Aunt Ophelia said, patting Amelia's hand. "You will find a husband, never fear."

"I thought I'd found one." Amelia sniffed and reached for her cup.

Joanna sought something encouraging to say, even though her own case was hopeless. "You mentioned some time back the possibility of returning for the Little Season. Perhaps you'll meet the perfect man then."

They continued to console her until the conversation drifted to recent assemblies Joanna had missed. At last, Amelia rose. "I must go. Mama accepted an invitation for cards this afternoon. I shall smile and be gay and not let anyone intimate I was anything but sparkling in my manner."

"That's the spirit. Perhaps after a few days of doing so, you'll come to believe it yourself." Joanna smiled consolingly as her friend left.

When she heard the front door close moments later, she sighed. "The poor girl."

"I'm afraid the end of the Season always yields a few broken hearts. And some successes." Aunt Ophelia eyed her as if judging whether to say more. "I have news of my own. Sir Jasper and I will be wed at the end of the summer."

Joanna jumped from her chair to hug her aunt. "That's wonderful. I'm so happy for you. He is a good man."

"Yes, he is. But he's not the only one in all of England. You'll find one, too."

Looking away, Joanna said, "I hope so."

"I know it will be so. I can feel it in my heart. Robert hasn't mentioned Sir Frederick again, has he?"

"No. He hasn't said much of anything to me since I returned from Windsor. I don't know if he's afraid to press the matter, or if he believes I have, or will, accept Mr. Lumley's offer."

"You need to speak with Robert, my dear. He needs to know you remain unattached."

Drawing in a deep breath, Joanna nodded. "He's at Bibury this week. I'll speak to him when he returns."

Aunt Ophelia rose. "I should allow you to rest. Are you certain you feel up to attending Lady Derringford's ball tonight? It's likely to be quite a crush, as it's the last of the important ones."

"Yes. I should say farewell to any of my friends who remain in Town. If I grow tired, would it be all right if we left early?"

"Of course. We should plan on it, regardless. You still appear pale, to my eyes."

Joanna smiled. "I feel quite recovered." Most of the time. Until her mind wandered down the wrong lane and encountered Mr. Lumley. Every time she thought of him, pain stabbed her heart. Had she made the right choice in turning him down? She hoped so, because she was going to have to live with that decision.

Later that evening, when she stood in Lady Derringford's home watching the first dance of the evening, she was glad she'd come. The music was lively, and laughter rang out around the room. Her heart lightened, and her mood couldn't remain melancholy.

Then Lady Hannah and Hugh found her. "Lady Joanna, I'm so happy to see you!" She squeezed through the crowd and hugged Joanna.

"As I am to see you." Joanna smiled at Hugh who offered her a slight nod in greeting.

"You look very well," he said, his voice surprisingly husky.

"I'm well, do not worry. I've recovered fully from my illness." They'd not let on to anyone outside the two families that she'd suffered anything more than a severe stomach complaint. "Will you both return to Bridgethorpe now?"

"Yes," Hannah said. "As much fun as I've had, I'm ready to go home. I miss riding every day, and there are friends I would like to see again. I didn't have time when we were there for the wedding."

"I understand." Joanna missed her home, too, but somehow she knew life there would never be the same. She wasn't the same person who'd arrive in Town just a few months ago.

So much had happened to her. The good. The bad. The horrid. None of it even faintly resembled what she'd dreamed her Season would be.

Hugh saw a friend and left them after securing a dance from each lady. Hannah grasped Joanna's hand and met her gaze warmly. "I'll miss you most of all. I was certain we would be sisters."

Joanna patted her friend's hand. "As did I. But we can remain friends, I believe."

"Are you certain? I didn't know if seeing me would bring it all back to you. I would have called on you, if I'd been more assured."

Her friend's presence did bring back the painful memories as well as the good, but she cared too much for Hannah to tell her so. "Your brother and I have agreed we can remain friends, so I couldn't do anything less with you. I would miss you too much."

"I'm glad." Hannah hugged her once more.

Joanna's partner for the next set led her out on the floor and Joanna decided to fling her cares aside and enjoy the dance. It wasn't difficult, with the way she loved music and dancing. Her partner was light on his feet and offered amiable conversation when the dance allowed. After their set ended, Joanna was grateful she'd planned to sit out the next set. She still hadn't fully regained her strength.

Seated beside Aunt Ophelia on a padded bench along the wall, Joanna watched the others mill about, hugging friends they would miss over the summer and sharing news of engagements. She wished Amelia were there to keep her company. Hannah had disappeared and was probably busy dancing and flirting, as one should do at a ball.

On the other side of a potted palm sat a pair of matrons who had obviously not learned the skill of gossiping quietly. Joanna tried to ignore them until one name was mentioned.

"Yes, that's what my husband told me. Sir Frederick Aldwen was arrested in Bibury during the race meeting." The first woman's voice was rich with the glee of knowing something her friend didn't.

"That awful man! He nearly had my son sent to the workhouse. My Harrison had to pay the debt. Whatever did they charge him with?"

"Murder. Can you believe it?"

"I can. It's said he comes down very hard on those who can't repay."

"My dear husband said this was about keeping the borrower from being able to repay."

"No! Can they charge him for that, too?"

"He didn't say."

As they continued to chatter, Joanna's blood ran cold. The man she'd barely escaped having to marry was charged with murder. As uncomfortable as she'd been around him, she never would have imagined him capable of such an act.

Yet she had no difficulty believing he'd done whatever he'd been charged with.

Shivering, then growing uncomfortably warm and nauseous, Joanna touched her aunt's arm. "I'm not feeling well. May we leave?"

"Of course. Would you prefer to lie down here for a spell, or are you able to make your way to the carriage?"

"If I may sit while they bring the carriage 'round, I'll be fine. I must leave now."

"Very well." Aunt Ophelia steadied her as she stood and put her arm around Joanna's shoulder while they walked.

Joanna caught a footman to bear the news of her departure to Lady Hannah and Hugh. The merrymakers in the ballroom became a blur, and she concentrated on putting one foot in front of the other. Aunt Ophelia helped her onto a bench in the entryway where they waited for their cloaks and the carriage to be brought to them. Thoughts spun through Joanna's head, only one landing long enough for clarity.

A murderer.

She's practically been engaged to a murderer. Joanna shuddered again. Her London Season had ended with a shocking surprise.

CHAPTER TWENTY-FIVE

*W*hen they arrived at the house in Eaton Place, Aunt Ophelia stepped down from the carriage to assist Joanna, not waiting for the footman. Joanna took her arm as they proceeded to the door. "I'm capable of walking," she complained.

"You're like a daughter to me. Allow me this one indulgence to make certain you are well."

Starley waited for them at the open door. "Lady Joanna, you have a caller."

"At this late hour?" Aunt Ophelia asked.

"Who is it?" Joanna tucked a loose curl into place.

"Mr. Lumley, my lady. He waits in the drawing room."

Her heart jumped, then raced like a runner. Why had he come so late in the evening? Had something happened to Robert? "Has his lordship returned?"

"No, my lady."

"Thank you." She gave Starley her gloves and cloak, as did Aunt Ophelia, who followed her into the drawing room.

Joanna stumbled when she saw him by the window, looking out over the street. A single lamp glowed on a table nearby, giving her enough light to see his strong features. Absence had improved his looks, which she'd already thought perfect. He smiled and walked to her.

"You look very well, my lady. I'm happy to see it."

"Is my brother all right?"

Mr. Lumley's brows drew together. "Of course. Or he was when I left him." He must have noticed Aunt Ophelia who sat on the settee near the empty fireplace. "Good evening, Lady Ophelia. Sir Jasper and I rode back directly, and Northcotte remained to take care of some business. He will go straight to Hampshire, I believe."

Joanna exhaled in relief. "When Starley said you were here, I feared the worst. I heard some gossip not minutes ago regarding Sir Frederick. Is this why you have come?"

"Yes. I thought you'd want to know they are hopeful they may charge him with attempted murder against you and the groom. And, they might have found witnesses to connect him to Bruce's death."

Her legs became weak, and she grabbed for his arms to steady herself. He caught her and led her to a chair. Tears flowed freely, and Joanna batted at them in embarrassment. "I'm silly, I know, but I'm so relieved to know this."

Mr. Lumley stroked his thumb across her damp cheek. "It's not silly. You've lived through some upsetting times."

His sympathy made it all worse. She'd been so cruel to remain distrustful of him, when he'd proved he was better than his early mistakes. She began to blubber her feelings aloud. "All I wanted was a husband, a kind man who would let me have my horses. I never expected to be fought over by beaux, or to be a pawn in anyone's games. I'll be such a good wife to a good man, why did you both choose me?" She punched weakly at his chest.

He pulled her into his arms, placing her on his lap as he sat. She curled up there and cried on his shoulder, feeling the calming stroke of his hand down her back and arm. Weeks of heartache, of weakness and recovery, of dreams shattered and not yet buried had built up and could no longer be contained. She didn't know how long she cried, but Mr. Lumley continued to say sweet things and calm her with his strong embrace.

David's heart was breaking.

He knew the pain in his chest couldn't compare to what he was certain Joanna had gone through. What nearly killed him was knowing how large his part was in her agony. Nothing he could do would ever erase that memory for her. "For my own part, all I can say is I didn't know you when I considered how your friendship might help me find the answers I needed. And it did, although they weren't the answers I expected. But you taught me much about myself."

Her tears had slowed, so he helped her to sit up, allowing him to look her in the eye. "I was a foolish man with an even more foolish dream. My focus was narrow in seeking someone to blame. I wore blinders, not realizing the true cause of my concerns."

"I don't understand. I thought you sought Zephyr's killer."

"I did, although I know now I may never find him. I believe Sir Frederick might have been involved, seeking to alter someone's financial status by removing a winning horse. But he'll never admit to it, so unless a groom confesses, we'll never know for certain. But Zephyr's loss wasn't the true cause of my father's problems. It might have made them worse; I don't know. His health has been failing since the winter after we lost Zephyr."

"Will he not recover?"

"I don't know. He won't discuss it with me. Mother says

he sees the doctor often, so if there is a treatment, Father is receiving it." David toyed with the curls resting on Joanna's forehead. "Now I make decisions based on what is best for Fernleigh, not how my father will receive them."

"That is how it should be. You've done well with Triton, you should be proud."

"I am. Perhaps next year I shall have two great runners, and more the year after that."

Joanna tilted her head and raised an eyebrow but said nothing.

David wasn't certain what she questioned, but his words were flowing like the Thames and couldn't be stopped. "I realize now I require a partner at Fernleigh. Someone who understands all the qualities a horse needs to compete and can recognize a horse that enjoys running. I also need a wife. In particular, one who will not complain that I spend my days in the stable and return to the house smelling rather ripe."

He pulled a curl straight and let it spring back, afraid to look Joanna in the eye. Afraid she'd turn him down yet again. It mattered more to him than all the winning horses in England. He was approaching the end post; it was time for the final push. "These past months in London I've discovered something I love more than horses, and it gives me more joy than winning a stakes plate."

Drawing in a deep breath, David forced himself to meet her gaze. "Joanna, I will never deserve someone like you as a wife, but if you will have me, I will work every day to try and be worthy. I'm a better man for knowing you. And I love you more than I know how to express. Please, say you'll be my wife."

Joanna's eyes glistened, and David feared she would refuse him. She blinked and a single tear ran down her cheek. He wiped it away, noticing the coolness of the soft skin of her cheek, and prepared for the worst. He opened his mouth to tell her he understood, when her fingers pressed against his lips.

"I've seen the kind of man you are. You aren't perfect, but I would not be happy with a man who was. That man would chastise me for tracking mud—or worse—up the back stairs. He would expect me to have the neighbors in for tea, not make certain the new foal was nursing well. My life might not be what my mother dreamed for me, but I want something else."

David thought his heart would burst, it swelled so as she went on.

"From the start I knew you were my best hope for the life I longed for, although I thought it was your love for your horses that proved it. I was wrong. Your love for me is what makes you perfect. No other man would tolerate me with a smile and encourage me to give a horse his head. You're perfect for me, Mr. Lumley, and I would be proud to be your wife. I love you."

David's breath caught, and he placed his hands on either side of her face, lost in the love he saw in her eyes. She did love him, and it seemed she liked him, too. He pressed his lips to hers, gently at first, then building with the emotion within him that burned for release.

When he lifted his head, he remembered Lady Ophelia was in the room. He jerked his gaze to the settee where she sat, but it was empty. He sighed with relief. He wasn't sure how long they'd been alone, or how quickly Lady Ophelia would return, so he lifted Joanna to her feet. Vacating her chair, he walked a few feet away and straightened his waistcoat and cravat. "I do have a request, however."

"It begins already." Joanna's eyes flirted with him.

"Will you call me David now that we are engaged?"

She laughed. "If that is all you require of me, I will do my best."

Lady Ophelia chose that moment to return. She glanced discreetly their way and resumed her seat. Joanna rushed to her aunt. "Mr. Lumley has asked me to marry him, and I've accepted."

Her aunt grinned and clasped Joanna's hands in hers. "How lovely. I'm very pleased for you. You must tell your mother so we may begin to make our plans."

"She's asleep by now, and I don't wish to waken her. I shall tell her in the morning."

"And send word to Robert. He will be relieved to know it."

David cleared his throat and walked toward them. "He's aware I'm here, and knows I planned to renew my offer. He approves of the match, to my surprise and great relief."

Lady Ophelia took on that worldly, wise manner she often wore. "It's often easier to see the good in a man when one is looking from the outside. I know you'll make Joanna very happy in life."

Giving her a nod, David said, "I intend to do my best. Now, it's time I took my leave. I wish you both a good night."

CHAPTER TWENTY-SIX

September 1810
Near Chester, Cheshire, England

Once again, Bridgethorpe Manor was in an uproar as Lady Bridgethorpe prepared for another wedding. "Two, in one year," she said with a sigh at supper one evening. The weather had yet to cool as fall was still a few weeks away, so she'd ordered the canvas tent be set up in the park near the pond.

Lord Bridgethorpe appeared several years younger than he had at the last wedding, which pleased David. Something he'd done was responsible for putting a small spark of life back into his father's eyes. "The year's not over yet," David said. "Perhaps Knightwick will make it three."

"I don't recommend making a wager on it," his brother grumbled.

Hannah set down her napkin. "If Mama will allow me to

return to Town for the Little Season, maybe I'll find a husband."

Mother smiled in that way she had which said she wasn't even considering whatever one of her children was asking for. "There's no rush for you to leave us. I know your friend Amelia will be in Town, but she's older. You can enjoy a few more Seasons before your father will complain about the expense."

Father chuckled without comment. David wondered if Father was ready for his daughters to leave the nest. With the twins and Lucy Anne still at home, not to mention Sam, there was no chance of the house becoming too quiet any time soon. And, as Joanna's family was about to arrive, David was eager for the ceremony to be done with so he and Joanna could escape on their wedding trip through the Lake District.

Pierce sat on the other side of Hannah, a seating choice David would not have recommended. He still recalled what his friend had said about men noticing his sister's comely shape. He wished he could hear what Pierce was saying that kept sending his sister into giggles. Perhaps after supper he should renew his warning about staying away from any of the Lumley girls.

The Lumley brothers, along with Pierce, took to the billiards table while the ladies set to whatever they had planned. This was David's last night to relax with his brothers before Joanna arrived. In two days, he'd be a married man.

"Nerves bothering you already?" Pierce asked.

"No, why?"

"You've been chalking your cue for three minutes straight."

David looked at his hands and tossed aside the chalk. "I was waiting for you."

"I had my turn already, but if you prefer I shoot again, I'll be happy to oblige you."

Glaring at Sam and Hugh, who snickered from the table where they played cards, David walked around the table to line up his shot.

Knightwick leaned against the wall laughing at their antics. "What about you, Pierce? Any plans to fill your nursery soon?"

Pierce snorted after taking his shot. "I don't know that I'll ever have a nursery. I've no need for one. Any money I haven't spent before dying can go to my cousin. He has a wife and a little girl; he can use the funds."

"Be careful," David warned. "As I recall, I was protesting the idea, myself, not long ago."

"Yes, but you were foolish enough to fall in love. I've no plans of ever doing that."

Hugh looked up from his cards. "How do you stop yourself from falling in love? I believe I fell three times during the Season."

"Guard your heart, my boy," Pierce said. "Find a lightskirt to distract you, or avoid London altogether in the spring."

Chuckling, Knightwick ruffled Hugh's hair. "Do no such thing. I do recommend not acting on your feelings, but you've a kind heart and will find love returned before you know it."

As was his wont, David hid in the stables when the carriages began arriving. As much as he longed to see Joanna, he'd prefer to greet her in private. Once she and her family were settled, he sent word for her to meet him in the garden.

There, they could speak their hearts without interference, but still be within sight of worrisome mamas.

Standing in the shade of a wisteria arbor, he watched her walk the path. Her bonnet hid her eyes, but her cheeks turned rosy when she drew close enough to meet his gaze. David held out a hand to her, pulling her into the shade. "I've missed you."

"And I you. We've been apart now as long as we were together. Well, as long as I knew you before we became engaged."

"It won't happen again. If I could have stayed with you in Bath, I would have."

Joanna's grin couldn't be wider as she gazed up at him. "I had a sad thought as we traveled here. Never again will Triton and Patriot compete against one another for a purse. They will both be considered your horses."

"This troubles you? We will never know which is the better runner, will we?" He ran his fingertips down the bare skin below her sleeve, watching the gooseflesh that followed in its wake. "I could always challenge you on the lane at Fernleigh."

Her lips parted. "What would we race for?"

David leaned still closer. "I'm certain—" He kissed her briefly. "We could—" And pressed his lips to hers again. "Find some stakes—" And once more. "Worth our while."

She rose to meet his kiss, and he let her experiment with her lips, heat building in his blood. She tasted of mint, and he craved more of it. When her lips parted, his tongue dipped between them.

Suddenly remembering they were likely being watched, he gripped her shoulders and set her back. "Tomorrow evening you may continue that."

An attractive flush stole over her neck and up her face. David made himself a promise to learn just how low that warmth spread. But for now, he'd better get her to the safety of her family. "Let us go inside before I lose my resolve."

❦

WAITING AT THE ALTAR HAD TO BE SOME FORM OF PENANCE for the dreams David had the night before his wedding. The small village church was much too warm, and the number of fans waving in the pews told him it wasn't nerves making him so hot. He resisted the urge to tug at his cravat, knowing all eyes were on him to learn how nervous he was, or to determine if he'd walked into this mousetrap willingly or not.

If possible, Mother gleamed even brighter than she had at Stephen's wedding. It was natural, he suspected, given Stephen was her nephew, but Mother had never applied labels to her love. One received all of it or none, and there was always enough to share with new family members.

Father showed the effects of the heat, but pride still brimmed in his eyes. For some reason, that emotion tugged at David harder than his mother's love. He looked away to Lady Northcotte. She was a fragile sort, petite and pale, but she sat tall, a wistful expression on her face. Her sister-in-law, Lady Ophelia—now styled as Lady Johnston in honor of her marriage—sat beside her, and that lady nodded when he met her gaze. Sir Jasper looked as if he'd be happier when they returned to the manor.

Just when David began to wonder if Joanna had changed her mind, she and Northcotte stepped through the door. A gasp rang out in the church, echoing the stammer in his heart. Her beauty was stunning. Her ivory dress was trimmed in mauve ribbons and tiny silk rosebuds, which matched the posy in her hand. A few of the silk rosebuds were tucked into the curls atop her head. The color of the flowers made him laugh in memory. *I look horrid in pink. I believe I could tolerate mauve.* He made a note to ask if she'd chosen that color purposefully.

The future held the promise of laughter, and the shared pleasure of watching their horses run. He couldn't ask for more, or for a more beautiful woman to stand beside him. From this day forward, he would no longer look back on where they began, or how they finally came to be in love. Perhaps all of that had been necessary for him to feel as strongly as he did about Joanna.

The exchange of vows passed in a blur, as did much of the wedding breakfast. David couldn't take his eyes off his bride. His wife. The woman he would cherish all of his days.

As they rode away from his parents' home in their carriage, Joanna tipped her head to one side and studied him. "You've had the silliest grin on your face all day."

"Have I? I must make amends. Is this better?" He puckered his features in a horrid frown.

She burst out laughing. "Not at all. I hope I never give you cause to repeat that look."

Planting a kiss on the end of her nose, he said, "I can't imagine ever being cross with you."

"I will remind you of that when we are old and you spend your days complaining that I've spent too much at the modiste or rode astride while pregnant."

"You will never ride astride while pregnant, my dear. I won't allow you to sit on anything higher than a chair, and even then, I might have to place pillows around you to calm my fears."

She was surprised to be warmed by his words, rather than angered he might treat her like fine porcelain. "I would go mad. You don't treat your mares that way. I will not break easily."

He wrapped his arms around her, nearly crushing her to his chest, before relaxing his hold and stroking her back. "I've come too close to finding out how easily you can be broken. I won't let it happen again."

His heartbeat pounded in her ear, the sound most comforting. "For all you've shared with me, I'm grateful most for your love."

Lifting her head, she found his lips with hers and poured all her emotions into her kiss. She was his to treasure now, and he was hers. For the rest of their lives.

I HOPE YOU ENJOYED THE INCORRIGIBLE MR. LUMLEY. PLEASE read on to enjoy an excerpt of the next book in the Bridgethorpe Brides Series, Charming the Vicar's Daughter.

You'll find Hannah and Laurence Pierce's story in Her Impetuous Rakehell, book four in the series.

EXCERPT: CHARMING
THE VICAR'S DAUGHTER

March 1811
Bridgethorpe Village, Cheshire, England

*N*eil Harrow was ready to cross the final item off his checklist. Once his cousin found him the proper pair of carriage horses, Neil could journey to London. There awaited the curricle he'd ordered with red wheels and leather squabs, thus forming the need for said horses. He was beyond eager to take up residence in the rooms he'd leased in Albany House.

His cousin, David Lumley, had other things on his mind. Neil had never seen him so distracted. After insisting they stop in the village before arriving at Bridgethorpe Manor, David had practically leaped from the carriage as it rolled to a halt in front of the vicar's cottage. "I won't be long," he called out, slamming the carriage door behind him.

Neil shook his head, feeling no better than a servant in the way his cousin neglected to invite him to go along.

Looking out the window at the village, he plucked at the seam of his gloves where the threads had worn thin. Now was as good a time as any to look for a new pair.

He opened the carriage door and stepped out, grateful to be on unmoving ground after three days of travel from Fernleigh Stud in Newmarket. They had slept in inns along the way, but those beds were never as comfortable as his at home. The air in the village was crisp, clear, as if winter hadn't fully given up despite the narcissus bulbs coming into bloom along the vicar's walkway.

Neil walked up the road a short distance, grateful for the recent lack of rain that made for a dry road. The shops were on the main street, not far from the vicar's cottage, and he soon had a new pair of riding gloves as well as some cotton evening gloves the proprietor assured him were all the rage in London. Taking his packaged purchases, along with a sack of peppermint drops for his cousins, he began to walk back toward the carriage. As he strolled, he heard a voice from nearby. A sweet, cajoling, very feminine voice.

"Come, you minx. Be a dear and come into my arms."

Neil paused, his attention fully engaged. He should leave the lovers to themselves, but the voice was like a siren's call. She continued to utter small cooing sounds, each sound causing his imagination to summon the most delightful vision. Curiosity won out over the lovers' need for privacy, and he stepped through a break in the hedgerow to take a closer look.

A ladder leaned against a bare black poplar tree, and the owner of that lovely voice stood high on its rungs, reaching into the branches. The object of her entreaty sat just beyond her reach. A brown tabby, its expression more bored than frightened, yawned and stretched out a single paw.

It wasn't the scene he expected to find, to be sure.

The toes of the young woman's boots were barely

perched on the ladder rung, and her petticoat peeked beneath the hem of her skirts, delicate lace edging and all. "Minxy, come, kitty."

She looked ready to topple the ladder. Neil's gut tightened with each stretch of her arm, certain she would fall. He couldn't stand by and allow that to happen. He approached the ladder. "Might I be of assistance?"

The slender young woman didn't even deign to look his way. "Thank you, no, I'm not in need of help." She reached up higher, fingers wiggling at the cat.

Rather than resting his eyes on her derriere, Neil studied her boots, which were even with his chest. Worn, but well made, they most likely didn't belong to a servant. He looked around but saw no maid chaperoning the young lady. She must live in one of the nearby cottages. Her precarious, leaning perch concerned him. "It's no trouble, I assure you. I can climb up there and bring him down."

She didn't budge. "*Her*. Minx is a she. And she doesn't care for men."

"Ah, forgive me." He glanced at the cat, his lack of sleep making him rather silly at the moment. "My apologies, Miss Minx, for mistaking your sex. If you'll come down, I shall buy you a saucer of cream."

Now the lady pivoted, offering him a look that questioned his sanity. "I thank you for your offered assistance, but I must insist you leave, or my cat will never come down."

No matter how much the young woman insisted, he couldn't walk away from a woman standing on a ladder. Yet the cat looked comfortable enough to remain in place until summer. "Will you allow me to fetch a servant? A maid, perhaps, to climb the tree for you? Or a large footman to catch you when you fall?"

When she glared down at him, her eyes no longer questioned his hold on reality. "Is this some manner of flirtation you employ? Your time is wasted on me. Be on your way."

The boredom he'd sought to relieve melted away. Like the dish of sugarplums Cook kept from his reach when he was a boy, conversation with this young lady became too tempting to resist. "My time is mine to waste. I cannot be on my way until my cousin returns, so I might as well bide the moments here as anywhere."

The girl squinted as she studied him. "Who is your cousin?"

"Mr. Lumley. His family lives nearby."

"Ah, now I see who you are, and I understand. Will you badger me until I relent and let you play the gallant hero?"

Neil tipped his head at that news. Which of his cousins would be annoyingly persistent like that? Sam and Trey were both of an age to flirt with a young lady such as this, who appeared close to Neil's twenty-four years. Did either of them have an affection for her? She was more than pleasant to look upon, even with a frown marring her smooth peach-tinted skin. The brim of her beribboned hat shaded her eyes, but they were darker than the light brown curls framing her face. A beauty, she was. He suddenly needed to know if she was married. "I do not wish to badger you. Say the word and I shall summon your husband to play hero for you."

Her expression went even more bland, if possible. "I do not seek a hero. I only wish to be left to my own devices. Will you kindly be on your way?"

So, she was a worthy adversary, all the better. "I could not bear to later hear a young miss had died of a broken neck because no one had helped her fetch her kitten from a tree."

She continued to gaze on him with no humor.

He grinned, unable to control the lengths to which he would go to relieve boredom. "Have those Lumley boys been a complete nuisance? Which one was it? I'll take him to task.

Knightwick and David are too old for shenanigans, which leaves Trey and Sam. Give me a name and he'll bother you no more."

After a long pause, she said, "Are you quite finished? I would like to retrieve my cat and get on with my day."

Neil held his hands out at his side. "Do not let me delay you, Miss…"

She ignored his implied request for her name and turned on the ladder. She stretched her arm upward again, leaning precariously to the right as she did.

Neil took a step closer to her, lifting his arms at the ready. Whether he thought to catch the cat or the woman, he wasn't certain.

Minx looked at him, then at her owner, and rose, hopping over the woman's outstretched hand, bouncing off a branch, and leaping at Neil's head.

He ducked, but not soon enough to avoid the claws scraping his cheek as the cat flew past. He brought a hand to his cheek, and glanced up again just in time to see the woman lose her balance on the ladder.

Neil dove as she fell, only succeeding in placing himself beneath her before they both landed in the dead grass with a *whump*. His lungs deflated. Her weight, insubstantial as it was, kept him from inhaling.

"Oh, dear," the miss on top of him moaned. As she shifted, she dug an elbow into his ribs.

He groaned with what little air remained inside him.

The lady rose on her arms, peering down at him with a wrinkled brow. "Are you all right? Your face is bleeding." She touched her fingertips to his cheek, then prodded his head in search of lumps.

His skin burned at her touch. Her position, perched as she was now at his side and leaning over him, was suggestive of an exchange far beyond the flirtation he'd planned. Yet she wasn't seducing him. Her concern for his injury seemed to prevent her from realizing just where she was. Where they lay.

A gravelly voice called out to them. "Miss Cookson, you should be ashamed!"

The young lady jerked, her eyes widening and her mouth forming a perfect O.

Neil closed his eyes and bit back a curse.

"Only steps away from the vicarage," added a squeaky voice.

Groaning, Neil rolled away from the lady—Miss Cookson, apparently—and climbed to his feet, dusting off his breeches and sleeves. He held out his hand to assist her.

Miss Cookson jumped up without his aid. "Mrs. Carlyle, Mrs. Benjamin, how lovely to see you. You're mistaken about our actions, however." She motioned toward the ladder. "This gentleman was helping me get Minx from the tree."

The short, round one of the pair shaded her eyes and looked upward. "He did a marvelous job, I see, as Minx is no longer trapped. But I question your display of gratitude."

"You misunderstand," Neil jumped in. "Miss Cookson lost her balance, and I wasn't able to catch her. We both fell to the ground."

"Where is Minx?" The second woman, who was nearly as tall as Neil and half his healthy girth, had her hands on her narrow hips as she glared at the two young people.

Miss Cookson looked around. "I don't know, Mrs. Benjamin. He jumped down and scratched—" She turned to Neil. "I'm sorry, I don't know your name."

Over the gasps of the two old women, Neil introduced himself. "Neil Harrow, at your service. My cousin, David Lumley, wished to have a word with the vicar. I was biding my time while I waited."

At that, the two women lit up, smiles stretching wide.

Mrs. Benjamin spoke first. "You're a nephew of Bridgethorpe's? How lovely. Miss Cookson, you never told us you were courting a member of the earl's family."

"I am not courting anyone, ma'am. You heard me ask the gentleman his name."

Mrs. Carlyle patted Miss Cookson's hand. "Never worry, dear, we shall keep your secret. We love secrets, don't we, Milly?"

A third sharp voice rang out from the direction of the vicarage. "Secrets? Milly, Ursula, what is amiss? You must tell me what I missed."

Miss Cookson bit her lip and closed her eyes as the two women bustled off to greet their friend. With heads bent and voices low, they spoke, occasionally glancing at Neil and the young lady. Then they hurried away.

"This is not going to end well." Miss Cookson sighed and straightened her bonnet. "I had better go see if my father has finished speaking with Mr. Lumley so I might explain the situation before he hears it from the Widow's League."

Neil fell into step beside her, cringing at the realization of who had been discovered practically lying atop him. The vicar's daughter. Neil would have to do some explaining of his own.

ABOUT THE AUTHOR

USA Today Bestselling Author Aileen Fish is an avid quilter and auto racing fan who finds there aren't enough hours in a day/week/lifetime to stay up with her "to-do" list. There is always another quilt or story begging to steal away attention from the others. When she has a spare moment, she enjoys spending time with her two daughters and their families.

She also writes steamy romance under the pen-name Ari Thatcher.

Stay up to date with book releases at her website http://aileenfish.com, or on Facebook, Twitter and Pinterest.

Finally, if you have a bit of time, I hope you'll consider leaving a review. Your opinions can help readers find books that are the right fit for them, and are always very much appreciated.

OTHER BOOKS BY AILEEN FISH

Excerpts and buy links are available at http://aileenfish.com

The Bridgethorpe Brides Series (Regency)

His Impassioned Proposal

The Incorrigible Mr. Lumley

Charming the Vicar's Daughter

Her Impetuous Rakehell

One Last Season

Captivated by the Wallflower

Captain Lumley's Angel

Betting on the Duke

That Matter of Mischief

Miss Harrow's Tenacious Duke

Falling for The American

Regency Romance Novellas

A Bride for Christmas

The Mistletoe Mishap

Once Bitten

A Christmas Promise

Piper's Proposal: Eleventh Day of Christmas

The Viscount's Sweet Temptation

Chasing Lord Mystery

A Marquess for Christmas

His Unsuspecting Heart

No Mistletoe Required

The Duke, The Wallflower, and the Holly Tree

Her Christmas Kiss

A Beau for Christmas

Revenge of the Wallflowers Series

To Captivate the Viscount

To Charm the Marquess

Deceiving Her Duke

My Sweet Scoundrel Series

The Rake Takes a Wife

That Miscreant Marquess

Earl of Basingstoke

Earl of Woodcliffe

Earl of Barrow

Once Upon a Duke Series

Her Secondhand Duke

The Duke Who Loved Her

The Duke's Scandalous Kisses

Regency Tales Series

Masquerading as a Miss

His Elusive Nightingale

Rescuing Lord Ravenscliffe

One True Wish (Only in the Once Upon a Happenstance boxed set)

Anthologies

Charmed at Christmas: A Bride for Christmas. The Mistletoe Mishap, The Viscount's Sweet Temptation, Chasing Lord Mystery,

A Marquess for Christmas, His Unsuspecting Heart, His Heart for Christmas

Once Upon a Happenstance: Masquerading as a Miss, Rescuing Lord Ravenscliffe, His Elusive Nightingale, and bonus short story One True Wish

A Kiss at Christmastide: Piper's Proposal, A Christmas Promise, No Mistletoe Required

The Bridgethorpe Brides Books 1-4

The Bridgethorpe Brides Books 5-7

In The Duke's Embrace: Her Secondhand Duke, The Duke Who Loved Her, The Duke's Scandalous Kisses

Contemporary Romance

The Dream Guy

That Dream Girl

Warming the Cowboy's Heart

Soaring into His Heart

The Cowboy's Christmas Bride

Christmas in White Oak

Rescuing the Cowboy's Heart

Hope

Marni

Cruising into Christmas

Almost Christmas in Connecticut

Young Adult

Cat's Rule (In the anthology Wild at Heart Volume II)

Outcast (Apocalyptia Book One)

Paranormal Romance

The Lives of Jon McCracken

Children's Picture Book

My Cousin has a Broken Heart (all proceeds are donated to the American Heart Association through Reid's Roundup)

Written as Ari Thatcher

(steamy to erotic romance)

Regency Romance

The Duke's Scandalous Christmas Wish

My Lady Rake (Coming April 2023)

Defying the Duke (Coming August 2923)

Paranormal Romance

Immortal Temptress

Renegade Wolf

Bewitched Familiar

Spirit Medicine

Loving Her Alphas

Contemporary Romance

His Wedding Date

The Rock Star's Wedding

Christmas with the Best Man

Honey, I'm Home

Kiss Me Now

Love Me Now

Love Me Forever

Fighting Downforce

Theirs

Death by Sex